The Book of Lilith

by

Robert G. Brown

To the women in my life. Liliths, every one.

(...and no, none of them look quite like this.)

Copyright Notice
Copyright Robert G. Brown 2006
ISBN: 978-1-4303-2245-0

The art on the cover is entitled *Lilith*, painted by John Collier in 1892.

Notice

This is a work of *fiction*. Any Gods, Goddesses, Religious Figures, and Scrolls portrayed herein are strictly products of my imagination and are not intended to resemble in any way certain similarly named Gods, Goddesses, Religious Figures or Scrolls otherwise discovered, portrayed in or as certain well-known religious texts, and either worshipped or despised by large numbers of people around the planet. Really, it is just a coincidence that they often have similar names.

Honest.

...while Lilith, petrified with fear,
tore down her house and fled into the wilderness

a Prologue to the Ur-Epic *Gilgamesh*, as translated by Samuel Kramer

And I, the Sage,
declare the grandeur of his radiance
in order to frighten and terrify
all the spirits of the ravaging angels
and the bastard spirits,
demons, Liliths, owls and jackals
and those who strike unexpectedly
to lead astray the spirit of knowledge...

...From *Songs of the Sage* in the Dead Sea Scrolls, translated by Florentino Garcia Martinez.

Wildcats shall meet with hyenas,
goat-demons shall call to each other;
there too Lilith shall repose,
and find a place to rest.
There shall the owl nest
and lay and hatch and brood in its shadow

Isaiah 34:14

Contents

Preface   1

1   Awakening   21

2   Creation   29

3   Adam   39

4   Eden   45

5   The Flood   69

6   Sidon   79

7   The Fall of Abel   95

8   Eve   105

9   Journeying   113

10   Mohenjo Daro   123

11   K'nesh   133

12   Bereaved   141

13   India   151

14   The Cave at Mathura   163

15   No Death   173

16   No Birth   185

17 Eternity	193
A About Lilith	201
B References	219

Preface

One day in early 2006 I received an email from an individual who had an email account with a large, well-known internet service provider (or so it appeared from the email header). The user's name, which I withhold for reasons that will become apparent as you proceed, suggested that it was from a female from the Middle East. There is nothing particularly remarkable about that – I'm on a dozen mailing lists and my email address is unfortunately available to the web crawlers and webworms that feed both SPAM engines and viruses alike.

Nor was there anything all that unusual (at first glance) about the message itself. It began with the usual disclaimer:

> Dear Sir:
>
> I got your address from a Friend who vouches for Youre Trustiness. May Allah Bless you Sir, as you are my Last Resort.
>
> My name is ____ (deleted). I was educated in the French school near ____ (deleted), although my family lives not far from where the Tigris joins the Euphrates...

I had automatically scanned to this point even as I reached for the "D" key, but this last bit caught my attention and intrigued me. I've gotten "Nigerian Scam" email from every state in Africa, from Hong Kong, from Russia, from several countries in South America, and even from a couple of countries in the Middle East, but never purporting to come from Iraq. Especially not from Iraq in the middle of a "war" that seemed like it would never end.

I should explain that I actually used to collect Nigerian Scam letters (and have a hundred or so squirreled away, each of them gems in their own way) until it became clear that the supply would eventually overwhelm my capacity to store them. I find them amusing. This by way of explanation as to why I actually read on instead of typing the key that would send the letter on to the oblivion it seemed that it deserved. Perhaps this piece of Iraqi/Nigerian Scam was a "keeper"...

> ...and have made quite a Discovery[1]. One day last fall I was dressed in my burka and sweating profusely as I drove my father's goats to pasture. One of the kids became stuck in a thorn bush and as I worked to get it out a truck filled with Americans raced by not far away and struck a mine.
>
> The explosion blew me literally out of my burka; I and my goat were thrown out of the bush and into a nearby hole (a large crater from one of the American bombings, partly filled with rocks and debris). I started to climb out, but heard the sounds of much fighting, and realized that the mine was but the first step of an ambush. Bullets buzzed over my head like flies, and several more of my goats (who were no fools) joined me in the hole.
>
> The fight continued until only two men were left, one from each side. They grappled together trying to kill each other and in their struggles fought their way to the top of the pit in which I and my surviving goats were hiding. Just as they seemed about to fall in with me, one of them managed to trigger an explosive device attached to his body and the world vanished in a tremendous blast.
>
> I came to myself quite naked, bruised, and bleeding. Parts of goats (mixed with parts of men) were liberally scattered about me – it was only the will of Allah that left me alive and not badly hurt. Where the men were standing before there was now another large hole in the ground on the rim of the crater, and I was half buried in rock and dirt that was blown out of the edge of the pit and down onto me.
>
> With some difficulty I managed to pull myself out of the dirt and crawl up the slope past the new crater, pushing boots with feet still inside out of my way as I went. As I

---

[1] My obviously female correspondent was not terribly literate and made many misspellings and used capitalization (sometimes of whole words) to emphasize points. I have preserved her actual words in this first part so that you can see that her language was *consistent* with who she claimed to be but I have made many editorial corrections in the following to make it easily readable, while trying to leave the Victorian Charm of the prose intact.

PREFACE

paused to rest and catch my breath, I noticed that there was a rectangular block sitting at the bottom of the new hole. From where I lay, I could see some sort of script on the sides.

I immediately thought that this must be some sort of Antiquity, a Treasure known to fetch a High Price among the foreigners who were now plundering our land. Since I had lost all of my father's goats and it seemed that it was Allah's will that we would all starve (if I got home alive at all) I thought that perhaps this Treasure was a means of my family's Salvation. Surely you will not be surprised, Sir, that I took a few moments and some care to cover the exposed rock with the loose dirt of the crater's rim that I might be able to return to it later with my older brothers and claim it.

Alas, it was Allah's will that I would be caught almost immediately by the surviving Freedom Fighters (whoever they might have been, as it is difficult to know who fights whom in this War) who had set the trap. As I was Naked (and hence clearly Irresistible by the standards of Islam that confine all women to live unseen by Men lest those men go Out of Control) they proceeded to rape me and beat me, in spite of my bruises and protestations of Faith in Allah.

No sooner had they tired of me when a second group of fighters appeared who slaughtered the ones who had raped me and took me from them as the spoils of war. I was subjected to Rape a second time, on the principle that I must be a Harlot of the soldiers of the Other Side.

An hour later (at least they were very quick about it) as I was staggering away from the accursed place, the Americans finally arrived with their jets and armored cars and fell upon *this* group in a rage. They efficiently Massacred every living thing but myself. However as they were accompanied by Woman Soldiers they forbore to Rape me further (for which I was very grateful) and after being questioned and threatened with prison I was released to limp home.

They were even kind enough to lend me a jacket and such loose cloth as they had so I could cover my nakedness, but of course it wasn't proper garb for a good Muslim Girl and left my legs from the knees down exposed. Consequently I was Raped and otherwise manhandled a dozen more times before I made it home by goat herders and camel merchants and other Good Muslim Men. Unfortunately, my father was a Good Muslim Man as well, and seeing me dressed in such an outfit, half naked and obviously no longer a virgin he beat me soundly and cast me out into the street.

Fortunately my mother saw all that transpired between my father and myself and heard my piteous Pleas of Innocence and Faith as I was being beaten; she took it upon herself to risk my father's wrath by making me a bundle of clothing (including a fresh burka) and a few containers of food and a bit of money. After my father stormed off to the nearby tea-house to drink with his righteous friends (several of whom had Raped me while I was making my way home) she crept out and pressed this bundle into my hands. I believe it saved my life.

I lost no time in sneaking into the alley and dressing Properly (as I was getting rather tired of being Raped) so that no portion of me was visible save my eyes, which were already blackening from the beatings I received along with the Rapes. Once again dressed as a shapeless black form, I became an anonymous woman and as safe as a Muslim woman ever is. I walked away without looking back, and while walking I took my bearings, as it were. Although I felt a momentary twinge of guilt about it (mostly regarding my Mother) I decided that my family would just have to starve without the goat herd that was its sole means of income and that I was On My Own. I therefore made my way back to the vicinity of the crater, arriving there in the evening. It fortunately by now was deserted of living beings, although it was absolutely crowded with the recently dead and the ever-present vultures that come to prey on them. There I descended and managed to work the strangely carved object loose from the dirt I had pushed over it.

To my surprise, it was not a carved piece of an ancient building as at first I had supposed – it was a small chest made of stone, with a tight fitting lid sealed with a greenish band of what might have been bronze metal or copper, but the last few fragments fell into dust flakes at my touch and I cannot be sure.

The chest itself was far too heavy for me to actually carry, and would not fit beneath my robes in any case. I felt certain that anything I was carrying outside of them would be at risk of being stolen, but once I left my Home Town (where my reputation was ruined and the only career path open to me was open whoredom until somebody decided to stone me to death) I might be safe from being Raped every five minutes. I therefore made the decision to open the chest and make off with whatever I found there. Using a knife from the belt of one of the dead to pry with, I managed to work the lid off of the chest and cut through what appeared to be a thick beaten gold foil underneath, taking care to preserve the gold.

To my surprise, the sole contents of the chest were a bundle of tightly rolled scrolls on golden spindles. I looked again at the cover of the chest, and noted that it appeared to display a woman, quite naked and of great beauty, surrounded by many children, flanked by two owls and standing above a cat. Above her head was an oval that represented something bright, with rays falling down upon her. Beneath her feet was an inscription which I, of course, cannot type to you in an email message but which appeared to be in a form of cuneiform, accompanied by a line of what appeared to be hieroglyphic text[2].

I emptied the large cloth shopping bag my mother had given me of food (taking a moment to eat, since I was about to begin a long journey and felt the need to restore my strength). Into this bag I placed the scrolls, carefully wrapped in my underthings, and I belted the whole thing firmly into place beneath my burka where Inshallah they would remain unmolested while I sought the opportunity to turn them into dinars. I then paused a moment to arm

---

[2]This only confirmed my initial impulse to believe this whole letter a fraud, of course. How would the daughter of a goat herder have learned what these even *are* let alone how to recognize them? Yet this is *explained* in the later course of the letter, where it also becomes quite obvious that my correspondent was really amazingly bright.

myself with Divers Arms – a machine pistol and a handful of grenades from the bodies of the dead. Although they were quite heavy and unfamiliar to me I resolved to Never Again be Raped and indeed to See Rapists in Hell if they tried it.

I will not bore you with my Adventures on the road to Baghdad. Suffice it to say that (as a fallen woman and entitled now to charge money for the privilege of Rape) I arrived with far more means than I began with, and devoid of both grenades and ammunition for my machine pistol. Any number of would-be Rapists (who failed to properly negotiate on a monetary basis for the privilege) would Rape No More, including those that were still alive but missing certain parts when I finished with them.

Once there I promptly sought out a Foreign Benefactor with both money and a lust – for Antiquities, of course. By using most of the money I'd accumulated to purchase western-style clothing (hoping that in Baghdad the probability of Rape for the sin of wearing less than a total cover was somewhat reduced) I managed to dress myself well enough in the western style to be permitted to frequent the foreign hotels after suitably bribing the hotel staff with money or my favors.

It took some time but finally I succeeded. An executive for one of the major American contracting firms expressed an interest in purchasing anything old that might be worth money while "taking me to dinner" – a euphemism as that turned out to be for kidnapping me to a well-guarded house outside of Baghdad and proceeding to Rape me repeatedly while promising me vast riches. Unfortunately as I was now unarmed and he was supported in his Rape by his many minions I had to endure his attentions in hope he was honest about the eventual compensations I would receive.

Through this process (which involved the considerable disarrangement of my clothing) I had managed to keep the scrolls safe. Not an easy thing to do under western clothes, but simple enough in a large "purse", the handbag all Western Women wore and into which no man apparently dared to look.

PREFACE

Finally my host tired of his sport and was driven off in a great hurry to work, leaving me alone (but well guarded and effectively kept in a prison) in his household. That evening, he returned and after an admittedly excellent dinner, he Raped me repeatedly and then locked me into my room alone lest I turn on him for Revenge in his sleep. After a week of this I pretended to be Smitten and using Feminine Wiles I wheedled the use of his computer from him so that I could (purportedly) shop for clothes on the "Internet".

I was quite Gifted mathematically back in school (for a girl) and indeed put most of the boys in the school to shame, for which they (the boys) punished me in many ways – mostly violent ones – until my age made it impossible for me to associate with other male children at all lest I arouse their Lust and not just their Anger. At this point I was no longer permitted to attend school at all and was given instead the job of watching the goats while my fat and stupid brothers continued their education.

Fortunately my mother worked as a cleaning woman for some of the wealthier families in our town. From time to time she had secretly smuggled old magazines and other things to read from the trash of these families into our household (for me to read to her in secret when her work was done and the men were all away). It was therefore Allah's will that I knew what the Internet was, and what computers were, in some very general sort of way.

My captor, as it turned out, has no interest whatsoever in Antiquities, but rather has every interest in Juvenilities, in particular, in fourteen year old Fallen Girls such as myself (did I previously mention my age?) He has effectively kept me as a Sexual Slave for most of the last year. During this time I have learned many things, working all day on his computer system as a small return for the nights I spend satisfying his every perverted whim, for a mere pittance in money and gifts purchased from the Internet (as he otherwise never lets me out of my rooms, let alone out of the house).

One thing that I have learned to operate is his excellent

scanner, which he uses in the evenings on documents that he brings to the house from his work. Using great care – working for a whole day on a single scroll – I have managed to scan all of the scrolls into image files. I also have used a drawing program to capture, as best I can remember, the general layout of the picture carved on the lid of the box and the characters underneath the engraved figure of the woman. I used search engines to try to find out how to read the scrolls and hence measure their worth, but alas this has proven to be difficult as online dictionaries of hieroglyphs are rare and incomplete, online dictionaries of cuneiform do not exist.

I even found a way of getting a free email account and a website that would sell me enough room to store the scanned images using my captor's Visa card number, as I became concerned that my captor would one day look through the directories he'd bequeathed to me on his personal system or conduct a thorough search of my room and belongings and discover my Only Treasure besides the ones that he soils every night in his Lust.

Alas, after suffering many months of uncompensated Rape my worst fears have finally come to pass. I have just celebrated my fifteenth birthday and my body has taken on a more Womanly Form, and my period has not come now for two months in a row. Consequently my host is less and less often interested in me, and when he does visit me he is finished after a single bout of Rape. I am afraid that soon he will tire of me and have me put to death by his willing servants and armed guards, probably after some more Rape if I know men (and by now, I know men Very Well Indeed).

I am about to take Desperate Measures to save myself from this fate. The scrolls themselves I have buried outside in the garden in a sealed can that once held powdered milk, where I can hope that they will be preserved if by some miracle I manage to Escape Before the End.

However, I do not wish for my discovery to perish with me should I be slain. I have therefore searched the net for a mentor, a savior, who can take custody of the content

PREFACE

of these scrolls and puzzle out their meaning. For myself I care little – I think that I am with child and have no desire to perpetuate the line of he who sired it upon me. Indeed, my life experiences are such that I would be likely to Castrate the Little Bugger should it turn out to be male. Once I am certain that the scrolls are safe, I will try to escape or die trying, and if I die I have taken certain steps that ensure that my captor dies with me. Or without me, for that matter.

I found your name, Sir, and your email address, on your website in association with your works on religion and philosophy which have given me some comfort in my captivity. As you are a Teacher and a Poet, I feel that I can trust you with my Great Secret. Please Sir, if you will, Help a Poor Girl and visit (web address withheld) and retrieve that which you find there? I trust you will then make the best use of it that seems fit to you.

Sincerely yours,

(name deleted)

This seemed a bit extreme *either* for a Nigerian Scam *or* for a web-based marketing or virus attack. Usually these are a lot more terse and quite direct – "Supercharge your Love Handle" or a lot more oblique and badly worded – "This about you" – as they try to get you to be a fool and actually click on their link or execute their attachment. Five page letters to lead you to one measly link is not their style.

To be frank, it seemed much more likely to be a hoax perpetrated by one of my current or ex-students or (more likely) one of my colleagues in the computing business who knew enough to be able to forge an email header through enough hops to appear to be *completely consistent* with her story (not an easy thing to do, actually). Computer geeks often have the sense of humor of a small child and a well-known tendency to build elaborate and impossible jokes – computer viruses being one common example of this sort of "joke", for example – so this isn't as unlikely as it might seem.

However, hoax or not, I admit to being captivated by the tone and content of the story. Even if it turned out to be some sort of scam in the long run, I felt, I simply *had* to look at whatever it was she had placed on her website. As I run Linux as an operating system (and hence am somewhat less susceptible to the kinds of website-borne viruses that permeate the web) I took the chance and opened up the included link.

It is very fortunate that I did. I was *astounded* by what I found there. Well over five hundred separately scanned high-resolution images of what appeared to be rolls of brownish cloth – linen? – covered with the reddish lines of a faded, unrecognizable script alternating with lines of what appeared to be a mix of cuneiform and hieroglyphs of a more recognizable, but still ancient, form. Simply to assemble these images (for a hoax or otherwise) must have been a work of true dedication – *thousands of hours* of work. Suddenly a hoax seemed a bit less likely – nobody I know or work with has *this* kind of time on their hands, and who would generate *500 plus documents* of this stuff for fun? That's more like *work*.

Fully intrigued now, I attempted to reply to the message (something I almost never do in the case of messages originating from remote and unregistered clients that – from the IP numbers in the headers and the route taken – appeared to *actually be* located somewhere in Iraq) but received no further communications. In the meantime (while waiting for a reply) I used a web tool to quickly grab the entire contents of the directory that contained the scroll images and scanned drawings and store them safely on my local system, taking care to burn a couple of backup copies onto a DVD for safekeeping right away. I then spent some hours looking them over.

I got no reply to my return email, but some days later I *did* note in the newspaper, mixed in with the usual daily listings of car bombings, machine gunnings, rocket launchings and the other violent business-as-usual in Iraq that a high official working for a rather notorious and scandal-ridden government contractor was killed when his villa outside of Baghdad was destroyed by a mysterious explosion. Although the article reported the deaths of several of his guards as well, no mention was made of the body of a young girl or the discovery of a powdered milk can full of antiquities.

Coincidence? Hard to say, but it stimulated my imagination. I'm something of a romantic at heart. So I decided to invest just enough effort to determine whether the images that one way or another had ended up in my possession were "real" or just part of a hoax.

What I discovered therein rapidly convinced me that this young girl is (or was) real and what she appeared and claimed to be. Indeed, she was obviously so intelligent and capable that to me at least it still seems quite possible that she managed to get away and get her revenge at the same time. In fact, I pray that this is so, and hope that one day I may yet come to meet her and shake her hand.

Publishing this work makes this only more likely – if by chance you should read this, Ms. ____ (or whoever you really are), please rest assured that all the money that has been made from publication of this story, all of the fame that has descended upon it and upon me, as Lilith's amanuensis (as it were) rightfully belong to you. Permit me only to verify that it is indeed you (as only you would be familiar with certain details of the story that I still keep privy) and I will happily arrange for you to receive your long awaited Fortune and will do everything in my power to help you move to a country where you can enjoy it free from any possibility of further Rape.

As for the rest of you, you are doubtless wondering why she contacted *me*, instead of somebody *famous* (or even somebody who *isn't* famous but is at least an archaeologist of one sort or another). I wonder the same thing. This in spite of what she said, because I (at the time) knew *nothing at all*, really, of cuneiform, hieroglyphics, unknown scripts, or ancient scrolls. Perhaps my correspondent confused my (fairly common) last name with that of some well-known or little-known translator or collector of ancient texts, who knows? Or, of course, perhaps she told the truth and chose me because she happened to discover my personal website and was captivated by the poetry and writings on philosophy to be found there. Naturally, my personal vanity makes me wish that this were true even as my common sense and modesty tell me that it is unlikely...

At any rate, perhaps it was a fortunate choice. Although I was utterly incompetent on *that* day to translate a single hieroglyph recorded on those images, what I *did* know is both how to make computers do nearly anything and how (using computers) to find somebody that *does* know about this sort of thing. Using a web-engine to translate a few lines of the hieroglyphics left me flabbergasted. I worked like a madman on creating a rough draft translation but was left stymied by the fact that existing dictionaries (at least the ones available on the web or via the Duke library) were two sizes too small for the concepts being communicated. At this point I took a handful of the photographic images of these scrolls and my crude translation of same to a nearby researcher (found with my trusty search engines) who *does* work on archaeological finds of this sort. She took one look at the images themselves and then brushed my crude translation aside with a sniff. However, her obvious excitement at what she saw was almost too great to be contained. We decided to join forces.

Working together on the translation rapidly became an obsession of us both. With resources that at at one point involved hundreds of computers running what amounts to image enhancement and decryption software on top of symbolic analysis software on top of the *guesses* made as to the meaning and proper translation of some of the oldest (still untranslated) written text fragments known to mankind and scrawled out on shards of dried mud and baked pottery (and exercising a certain amount of latitude and editorial freedom to rewrite and smooth over the remaining rough spots), a dictionary for a previously unknown written proto-language that is *the oldest written language ever discovered* emerged, along with a translation of the scrolls themselves.

From what my archaeologist friend tells me, the whole world should bow down before this brave young girl and place her on a pedestal along with the greatest archaeologists of all time. As you shall see, these scrolls make the Dead Sea scrolls or Nag Hammadi codices look like kids' comic books in terms of both historical content and antiquity. Indeed, some of their content bears upon that *of* the Dead Sea scrolls – in particular the unpublished translations from those of the scrolls that have been (according to my colleague, at any rate) withheld from the public eye but whose outrageous content is some sort of open secret among the archaeological community.

However, my archaeologist friend *also* insists that her name be *withheld* from this (in her view, premature) publication of the translation for the time being, because there are certain curious aspects of the translated result that – in spite of the lack of any possible motivation for a hoax of such great expense and attention to detail – continue to give her some small reason to doubt their authenticity. Until such a time as we obtain the still missing original sources the possibility is of course left open that we are both the victims of a monstrous hoax which would ruin *her* academic career. Although that time may well prove to be "never" unless other copies are extant, (as I by now fear that they and their powdered milk can container have been blown to hell by the tides of war and mayhem after being preserved for nearly six thousand years) she chooses not to take this risk.

I have no such scruples and don't care about the risk as I don't have any academic reputation to protect, at least in archaeology. Besides, I am personally convinced that the scroll images that this poor, probably dead Iraqi maiden found in the desert and entrusted to me are

PREFACE

totally genuine. I continue to keep my fingers metaphorically crossed that both my correspondent and the original scrolls *were* preserved, powdered milk tin and all, from the holocaust that consumed her captor and guards, so that modern methods of objective historical analysis (such as carbon dating and genetically analyzing spores and pollen trapped in the weave of the scrolls) eventually validate my perceptions of the scrolls' antiquity if not authenticity.

If this ever happens, I expect that it will be be more than enough for all but the most skeptical – the scrolls simply cannot be ancient and have the content that they do *without* being genuine, and if genuine they might even be true! If so they tell an accurate, if astounding, story of the literal dawning of Humanity. At that time I will ensure that my archaeologist colleague gets the credit she so richly deserves for helping to translate the oldest piece of recorded human history ever discovered.

Enough of the history of the scrolls themselves – you now know as much as I do of their (apparent) *origin*. What, then, is the *content* of these scrolls, the most ancient (if genuine) written record of human civilization? They tell, in triply replicated scripts, the story of none other than *the first woman herself.*

No, I do not mean *Eve*. Any *serious* student of the Bible, the Ur-tablets that tell the tale of Gilgamesh, and other ancient writings is aware of the fact that Eve was *not* (according to the ancient texts that predate the entire Judeo-Christian-Muslim religious tradition and likely served as the template folk tale from which e.g. the book of Genesis was eventually written) the first woman, or one of the first two people created "by the hand of God".

What they are less likely to know is that Adam himself was also not the first, he was the *second*. At least according to these scrolls, whose authenticity *I* do not doubt, the book of Genesis has been considerably "sanitized", rewritten many times (doubtless by men) in Adam's favor.

No, the very *first* human being was $Llth^3$. Or $L\,'l$, or *Lillake* as

---

[3]This is a very rough translation of characters in a lost language – possibly, from the content of the scrolls themselves *the* lost proto-indo-european language from the Indus river civilization! However, my colleague asserts that if this *is* the case it will take *years* of painstaking work to prove it. Note well that we have no proper Rosetta stone beyond the crude triple-translation table written into the scrolls themselves that preserved both the original language and a crude rendering in newer and less sophisticated tongues. In particular the characters used do not greatly resemble those of any known language except perhaps Sanskrit, and aside from tantalizing words here and there that *might* be related to more modern (but still incredibly ancient) works there is little to go on. So it is difficult to know if our

she is known in the Ur-Epic of Gilgamesh: a handmaiden (or possibly harpy, the translations and context are not clear) of the goddess *Inanna* in ancient Sumeria. Or, as she is known in the relatively modern rendering of the few Old Testament-era books and text fragments of the Jewish faith in which she appears, *Lilith.*

Note well that there are rich connections between these scrolls and ancient clay tablets, the dead sea scrolls, and other text fragments from antiquity that have also been preserved by accident of fate or human design. Tablets, scrolls, and sections of holy books that (we should carefully note) were ultimately written and *re*written by the descendants of Adam, and that include additions, revisions and suppressions by whole generations of male priests, ministers, and clergy interested in preserving the patriarchal society that Adam sought to create in which *women* are basically chattel to *men.*

Most of these texts present an extremely biased picture of Lilith as being some sort of a biological construct made by God without a soul, who ultimately became the archetypical witch or vampire. Indeed, even a cursory examination of the religious rantings on the web that involve Lilith make her out to be the *mother* of all vampires, a she-demon who preys upon small children, a consort of the Devil and witch, *or* some sort of Mother Goddess worthy of worship and invocation in rites for her own sake, depending on which side of a very ancient fence you are on.

As the editor of this translation, I hold myself aloof from this antique (and somewhat silly) feud. As these scrolls faithfully and consistently reveal, *neither* of these views could be further from the truth and are clearly just Jungian archetypal projections of their adherents' personal religious views, a sort of metaphorical mutilation of an otherwise lovely tale.

Note well that the language of the scrolls is apparently far *older* than any surviving copies of the books of the Old Testament, far older than the dead sea scrolls, and even far older than the oldest of the cuneiform tablets that make up our earliest known historical documents. Given the triple rendering (two of them in younger languages) it is likely that these scrolls are but *copies* on some sort of preserved linen of tablets or scrolls older still that have not survived, perhaps perishing in the calamitous burning of the Library of Alexandria along

---

assigned pronunciations are correct, if the language indeed used implicit vowels in some way we cannot detect from the script (imagine how English is pronounced relative to how it is spelled, or French), save from their translations in non-phonetic languages altogether.

PREFACE

with so much other knowledge of the ancient world. Without the original scrolls in our possession for analysis and dating we cannot be sure.

The scrolls are to all appearances an alternative version of the book of Genesis (one that precedes even the tablets of the Enuma Elish in the Ur-legend), and present a very different view of the story of the garden of Eden. That they were found, as it were, a mere stone's throw from where Eden is thought to have been[4] only adds to the likelihood of their authenticity. It is also fairly clear from their content that they have not been subjected to the process of rewriting and editing (on the part of the early church patriarchs) that corrupts most of the Bible relative to the original source texts, Old and New Testament alike.

The final point of interest about these scrolls I hesitate to make known to you, as it will only serve as grist for the mill of those who would claim it as proof that the scrolls are some sort of hyper-intellectual hoax – hyper-intellectual because only a *genius* could have created a prehistoric language – symbol, syntax, grammar – out of whole cloth in such a way that it seamlessly matches what is known of the languages of the most ancient tablets and fragments of Sumeria and Mesopotamia and Babylonia that have yet been discovered. A hoax produced by a hoaxer familiar with and capable of forging *perfectly* a text that is consistent with every detail of all the truly ancient greater Mesopotamian writings that still remain to us in original form – the Enuma Elish, the Hullupu Tree, and of course the Epic of Gilgamesh. An *evil genius* hoaxer; no casual fly-by-night graduate student wishing to play a prank.

My archaeologist friend and colleague asserts that this is simply impossible – she points out a dozen places that not even the world's greatest archaeologists working *together* for *years* would have been able to create a seamless linguistic interpolation of nearly *all* of the oldest fragments (including many tablet fragments not known to anyone outside of a very select community whose translations have been *elucidated* by our work on the scrolls). Then there is the nearly miraculous extension of these poorly understood written languages to a *new* written language (really of course a much older written language) with a *far richer range* of conceptual expression and with almost *no visible overlap* in syntax, grammar, or direct vocabulary with any *known* language of the world. It might as well be Martian for all one can dis-

---

[4] Recalling that the fourth river mentioned in Genesis as flowing out of Eden is *Euphrates*.

cover historically without the aid of the translations provided within the scrolls themselves.

This new language contains words and ideas that simply did not exist in the common languages of the times of cuneiform and hieroglyph and we had to work very hard to analyze the entire (fortunately very long) document to succeed. Without my computers *and* my partner's very considerable historical and linguistic expertise, we would never have succeeded. In the process it became clear from parenthetical remarks and linguistic style that two very different individuals wrote the hieroglyphic and cuneiform versions of the text – one a relatively cosmopolitan Egyptian female and the other a somewhat stuffy Sumerian priest. The tension between these two writers and the contrast between their variations of the story were invaluable aids as we attempted to discern meaning in languages that are several sizes too small.

Even so, academic honesty now compels me to make this – problem – known to you in case you wish to skip reading the text altogether as a consequence, or read it as a work of presumed modern fiction (worthwhile in its own right, I think) instead of as the Mother of Myths that it otherwise appears to be. The translation of the scrolls, as accurately as we are able to make it out, is *full of anachronisms*. This is indeed obvious almost from the beginning, and is internally explained by the content of the documents themselves.

This is rather frightening; so much so that I fully expect most people to reject their authenticity on this basis alone. Of course we should *expect* a prophetic work to contain anachronisms. *All* truly prophetic works are *by definition* anachronistic. Prophecy *is* anachronism.

However, Biblical prophecy usually falls absurdly short of the mark. Where in the Bible are things like computers, nuclear bombs, or the Internet predicted? Or anything *like* a reference to evolution, the big bang, optical nanoscale computing and information storage devices, bluetooth, even something really modest like the fact that planets are spherical worlds that orbit the sun instead of the other way around?

They're just not there. And they should be. Instead, the Bible portrays a flat earth and has the sun *stopping* in the sky and doing other remarkable things that egregiously violate known physical law, making God out to be something of a liar who would violate the laws that He (or She, or It if you prefer) decreed. Not to pick on the Judeo-Christian-Muslim Old Testament, of course – all religious texts routinely include reports of historical miracles that can no longer be scientifically repeated or verified mixed with prophecy.

However, all *Biblical* prophecies are safely *ambiguous*, so that (like our daily horoscopes from the newspaper) we can read them and interpret quotidian events in terms of them and be content, and of course they've all been retroactively edited so that they work out better than perhaps they did in the original. And we only get to see the successes, just as we tend to forget the fifty days our newspaper horoscopes are wrong but remember the one day it is dead on the money.

The anachronisms – prophecies if you like – in the *Lilith* scrolls are not like this at all. They are up front, *in your face* references to future knowledge all the way up to our present time and beyond. They contain clear references to *modern physics and cosmology*, to evolution and to genetics, even to theories of psychology and to much foreknowledge of computer science. It is simply *impossible* that all of this could have been known by a primitive people (people for whom even an *abacus* was still in the unknown future), yet is it *equally* impossible that it could be a hoax.

This is, of course, the kind of accuracy one should *expect* the prophets of the One True Religion to have. If a prophet is truly "inspired by God", they should get it *right* and not mask the truth in some sort of metaphorical allegorical hyperbolic *story* that can be interpreted via "hermeneutics" however the reader wishes, as are (for example) the equally anachronistic works of Nostradamus or the unintelligible, ergot-induced hallucinogenic ravings of Revelations.

We actually find this sort of metaphorical vagueness to be rather comforting, of course. There is nothing more terrifying than a prophet that actually predicts things in clear, unambiguous terms. For example, imagine Revelations' impact on the world if they had stated things like "A man named Adolph Hitler will take over a country named Germany and wipe out six million Jews, ten million Russians, and a few million miscellaneous assorted others." Which of course never happens – dates, times, specifics are all anathema to the prophet, as when the date passes and the specific prophecy *fails to come to pass*, well, that can wreck your reputation as a prophet really quickly. We mustn't forget that there are also serious problems with causality and prophecy (explored by many a science fiction novel) where such a specific prophecy causes Hitler to be killed as a child thus *guaranteeing* that any *real* prophecy is almost certain to be *self-defeating* instead of self-fulfilling.

The prophets that survived (or rather, whose reputation has survived) to the current day are those that did *not* make this sort of elementary mistake. It's pure evolution – survival of the fittest, where in this case fitness means vaguest (hardest to prove wrong) and most apocalyptic (scariest should they prove right).

The "prophecies" in the Lilith scrolls are nothing like this. They aren't even presented as prophecies. Rather they are presented in almost an offhand way, as unimportant future background to the description of the present of *that* time. They were the terrifying, unambiguous sort, like you'd expect a *real* prophet to make, and because they were *lost* for some five or six thousand years, they did *not* have a chance to modify their own effectiveness, to become self-defeating.

"Expected" or not, these anachronisms present one with a stark choice. You, dear reader, can choose to read the text (or not) and then decide for yourself whether or not the words have the ring of truth to them. There is no other possible basis for decision, as the scrolls themselves are apparently lost and are too old to be directly referenced by newer texts.

Are these indeed the writings of Lilith herself – for they are written in the first person, unlike any other work that has survived from this era – dare I say *miraculously* preserved and discovered in the nick of time for our lost generation to read and learn from, or are they a hoax inspired by a mad genius with a near-supernatural education and too much time on his or her hands? It is up to you.

I know which one *I* believe.

As a final note, please observe that the translated text is sprinkled liberally with annotations on the translation process. Every effort has been made to render a language that is almost incomprehensibly difficult into colloquial English (since preserving any sense of the original poetry is all but impossible anyway). In some cases (especially early in the process) the literal translations of the accompanying cuneiform and hieroglyphic passages are included to that the reader can accompany us on our journey to truth and see how we arrived at the final translation. Lilith's first person discourse has also been rendered, at some small expense in verbatim accuracy, in the modern form with quotation marks and so on to offset conversations she holds with God and the other important characters of her drama.

There are, regrettably, a few holes in the text translated from the scrolls that we have attempted to interpolate. In some cases these are *literally* holes – perhaps a single moth was trapped with the scrolls when they were first sealed up and enjoyed a sumptuous last meal before dying of dehydration and suffocation. If so, the carbon dioxide the moth doubtless exhaled as it expired seems to have acted as a miraculous preservative across the millennia. However, two scrolls were also damaged by some other action. The first is simply unreadable except for a few dozen lines of disconnected text. One contains (fortunately!) the tale of Lilith's final days but ends before we learn what became of Cain.

From the images, the fabric itself of this last scroll appears to be at least partly intact and covered with smudges that might have been text. Perhaps it could be re-scanned with ultra-violet light and the resulting image enhanced if we had possession of the original scrolls, but in the otherwise remarkably well-done scans in our possession this is alas impossible, even using image enhancement tools developed by NASA and the Department of Defense for space photography. We can only pray that the war in Iraq ends quickly so that a proper search can be instituted for the originals, that they may be brought into the light of day and given the scientific scrutiny they so richly deserve.

So, dear Reader, you should be aware even as you begin that the story of how Lilith's legacy was passed on and how the scrolls themselves came to be saved in the chest as they were to survive to our time is as much a mystery to us now as it was before the chest was discovered. The mysterious maiden has vanished and my crude attempts to locate her have been met with shocking indifference. Even the site of her original discovery (which might prove to be a rich archeological dig) is lost to us.

However, there are clues aplenty in the world around us that suggest how at least part of it *might* have worked out so long ago, as the world of today may well be what it is *because* of the Lilith scrolls. I would like to think that Grandmother Lilith would be proud of at least some of the Soul apparent in our world of today, proud of our progress towards a world where all the "daughters of Lilith" at last get to "be on top" (or at least stand side by side) with the sons of Adam, even as she would be appalled at how fragile our own understanding of "that which watches the watcher, watching the world" still is.

rgb

Chapter 1

Awakening

I, Lilith
First of Inanna
write this my story
that all who read
may learn to open
their inner eye
to the Watcher
that watches
the watcher
watching the world.

I opened my eyes and looked out at infinity[1]. It was a night sky filled with stars that were so beautiful that they brought tears to my eyes. I tried to remember who I was, or how I came to be there, or where *there* was, but of the past, if I had one, there was no trace.

---

[1] Infinity as a concept was unknown to both Egyptian and Sumerian alike. This is an example of a single word that consistently appears in the original language of the scrolls that is imperfectly rendered in the younger co-languages. Infinity in hieroglyphs is presented as several repetitions of "far" followed by "away" arranged in a circular loop. In cuneiform it is "greater than many cows". Presumably they truly valued cows in ancient Sumeria.

As you read you will encounter many more of these anachronistic terms. You will simply have to trust the translation – in all cases it is possible to defend it, and one day a fully annotated edition of this work may be released with our rationale appended in footnotes or marginal notes, but including them all now would make the *text itself* too difficult to read.

There was no *before*, only the *now*.

I took a sort of an inventory of the richness that flooded into me through my senses. There were sounds that I interpreted, as I thought about them, as coming from crickets. Crickets, once I thought about *them* were these little black insects that made a sort of music in order to attract mates. There were smells, smells that I interpreted as wood smoke. Smoke from a fire, which was an oxidation process that reduced wood to ash and released energy and light (and a certain amount of human comfort) in the process. There was a sort of salty wet taste in what I realized was my mouth. There were sensations of feeling – hardness behind my head, cold hardness beneath my back, my legs, my arms, my bottom.

As I thought about these sensations it came to me that I had a *body* and that, if I tried, I could move it. So after a couple of twitches where my brain (what was a brain?) tried to hook up to the right nerves (what were nerves?) I sat up.

All of my senses reeled as the world before my vision whirled into a new orientation, and my feeling of *balance* was called into play. At first I tried to keep my balance as one would keep a stick balanced on a finger, by watching to see what direction I was falling and then trying to correct it. Several falls (and resulting bruises) later I discovered that my body did better if I left it to its own devices and just *balanced* so I stopped trying to correct with my conscious mind.

I looked around. I found myself sitting on a stone tablet in front of a fairly large bonfire, as bonfires go, on the floor of a small green valley surrounded by large and stately trees. Sitting on a sort of natural rock throne close at hand by the fire was a naked woman.

I wondered how I knew that she was a woman. This led me to immediately appreciate the fact that there were two sexes of human being and that she (and I, for that matter) were of the *female* sex. There was also a male sex, which differed both anatomically and in its role in the reproductive process.

I don't know how long we sat there, eyeing one another. It could have been seconds, or it could have been forever – time spent in her company was ever like that – timeless. An eternity ended when she spoke.

"Welcome to Creation."

This seemed like a noble enough sentiment. However, it triggered thoughts like firecrackers in my mind. Welcome implied that I just arrived. A creation was something made, but Creation (where one could always hear capital letters in her speech where they were intended) usually applied to the Cosmic All. And then there was *speech!* *This* was what I was using in my interior monologue, and this led me to discover that I could *speak* as well as *listen.* I shaped a clumsy mouth around my first, whispery words.

"Umm, thank you. I think. Who are you?"

Even as I asked, I realized that I knew the answer. This was God.

"God, of course, and you're very welcome. How do you feel?"

I thought about it.

"I feel good. In fact, I feel great! A bit, what is it, hungry? Thirsty? I feel a sort of urging towards something but I'm not certain what it is."

"That would be about right. I repaired your body and in fact made it *perfect*, and timed its metabolic state so that we could share a bite while we talked. It's a sociable thing to do, and you have much work to do for me building a society, so you might as well start learning how." She gestured to the side, where a table covered with a white silk tablecloth was set with silverware, plates, napkins, and a lovely looking dinner. We arose, me weaving a bit as I found myself thinking again a bit too much about balance, and went to the table to sit down.

God poured two glasses of wine for us, and then gestured that we should fall to. I sipped the wine and it was simply the most delicious thing I had ever tasted. Of course it was the *first* thing I'd ever tasted, but to this very day even the memory of that taste makes my mouth water. The food was ambrosia, the drink was nectar (I wondered how I knew of those terms) and not a word was spoken until plates were cleaned and glasses emptied and refilled again.

"Thank you for dinner," I said, somehow knowing that this was the right thing to do. "That was incredible."

She smiled, "What is the point of being the Creator if you can't make a decent meal from time to time? Of course most of those dishes won't be invented for six thousand and umpty-odd years, but time is what I make of it." My brain did another one of its distracting little whirls into a kaleidoscope of flashes on sushi, on bouillabaisse, on chocolate mousse, on Cabernet Sauvignon[2]. I forced myself to concentrate on the now, not on the future then that they seemed to involve.

"Now," said the Creator, "I imagine that you're still more than a bit disoriented. We still have most of a bottle of Cabernet and as

---

[2]Sigh. As I said, you just have to trust the translation.

much time as you might need to get all squared away. Is there anything you'd like to ask me?"

"Why am I so confused?" I began. "Every time I think of something like crickets, or wine, I immediately start thinking about exoskeletal arthropods with exotic mating habits or the effects of coastal Mediterranean climates on the maturation and fermentation of Cabernet grapes, carefully aged in imported french oak barrels and I don't have any idea what any of that *means*," I rushed on in a bit of a panic as fermenting led to bottling led to glass making led to windows led to a vision of tall buildings gleaming in the sun as they soared up into the sky, coated in mirrored glass and filled with Cabernet-swilling business executives...

I let out a little cry and tried to stop thinking, stop thinking and breathe, breathe, breathe, stay with the breath, trying not to think of this as a yoga calming technique even though I immediately recognized that this is what it was.

I felt a gentle hand on my shoulder and immediately felt calmer. In fact, I felt downright *blessed*. It was almost silly. A few minutes (or was it centuries?) later I shook myself out of a trance and wiped the idiotic grin off of my face.

"Poor girl. You've got *preternatural knowledge* of the whole Universe, that's what you've got. It came with the Soul. I couldn't make up my mind what to leave in and what to leave out so I left almost everything in. Everything but your personal past (you have none) and your personal fate. They would have removed your Free Will and ruined the game."

Preternatural knowledge. Great. *That* explained it.

And it *did*, of course. Once I realized that all I had to do was think of something and I'd know it, it became a little easier to *not* think of *everything*. It was just another kind of balance. The trick was to let the natural flow of thought and conversation delicately tease facts out of the immense ocean of knowledge that was ever poised over my head without triggering the irrelevant flood of connected facts.

I looked into my head for knowledge of God, but discovered that preternatural knowledge or not, there was a rather large void there.

"Sorry," God chimed in. "It's hard to be 'friends' with anyone you have preternatural knowledge of. So I've somewhat deliberately blanked my knowledge of you and yours of me so that we can at least make a stab and being friends."

"How does reading a friend's mind work in that process," I said a

Awakening

bit cynically.

God blushed. "I don't do it all the time. Or rather I do, but I'm *much* more complex than you might think and I can actually multitask on an interrupt-driven basis so that I only 'know' your thoughts when it is meet and just for me to do so. You still have your privacy, mostly."

"But Don't," God said with a baleful glare, "Tempt Fate by thinking rude thoughts just to see if I'm listening in."

I mentally sighed, squelching the thought that had unbidden risen almost to the point of verbal articulation in my interior monologue. Besides it wasn't true. If anything, God seemed pretty nice, although how I had any experiential basis for comparison was beyond me.

"Look," said God. "I'll let you in on a little secret. If you think that *you* have preternatural knowledge problems, you should think about *me*. For example, think for a moment about time..."

...

A sound, a sound of one hand clapping. One Godlike hand clapping, in fact. Clapping me, fairly gently, on the face. "C'mon girl, wake up. Lilith, time to go. You can stop thinking about time now..."

I kept myself (just in time, so to speak) from thinking about time again so that I could *stop*, and managed to hold on to one important insight from an eternity of timelessness. God, of course, existed *beyond* time, and if I thought about it a certain way so did I. So how was it that we could sit and converse, a thing that appeared to involve sequential ordination of conceptual material with a clearly articulated syntactical sense of 'tense'?

"What happened? How long was I gone?" I said.

"As long or short a time as you like. We are currently outside of the time-stream of the Universe that will become your home. So duration here means nothing compared to duration there. In fact, your preternatural knowledge of there is largely knowledge of the skein of time and space there *as a whole*, which is in fact static and immutable, if you look at it too closely. So I don't."

"*You*," said God, "have difficulty thinking about wine without recalling everything that there is to know, intellectually, about wine. Wine grape horticulture, crushing, fermenting, bottling, aging, and of course drinking. *I*, on the other hand, have to be careful not to think too closely about wine or I call to *my* mind the actual taste of every drop of wine ever made, and not just in this Universe – the taste of every drop of wine that *could* ever be made. If I do this, of course, I can take no actual pleasure from *drinking* a glass of wine. For an omnipotent being to think is to do, and to do with such ease is to render the actual doing pointless."

"Consequently it is a great pleasure to incarnate myself, to bind myself to time's stream, to *not* think about the infinity of possible sips of wine, just so that I can experience the unique joy of this *real* one." God took a healthy swig from her full glass.

I appreciatively sipped at my glass of wine as well, letting its rich flavors of berries overlaid with a hint of oak, vanilla and smoke[3] develop in my mouth and relishing the gift of time.

God leaned over towards me, looking through my eyes into my very soul. In her eye I saw reflected a flicker of light, and found myself falling into an infinite whirlpool of blackness – or was it whiteness – unbroken except for a thin grey line that burst into light (or was it darkness) for a space and then rejoined the dark or the light, or both, from which it emerged. The flicker shaped the very spaces around it into a form that *danced!*

Then I realized that I was looking at my own reflection in God's eye.

"There's a lesson, there, if you choose to take it," God said, leaning back to drink her wine. "When I'm unitary and all seeing and all knowing, *there is no time*, and without time things are really pretty boring – so boring that it is difficult to distinguish the state of existence and nonexistence. The only way to avoid a state of perfectly boring perfect being is to become *complex* instead of simple, to break up the featureless perfection of the infinite into what appear independently to be imperfect, finite pieces."

"Complexity thus requires duality (or more properly, multivalency for some extremely large number of values). This, then, is the paradox of a monadic unitary God – that's me – and the individual human spirit – that's *you*. *You* contain within you a spark of *me*. Yet your spark is contained in my greater light and is but a small part, a very small part, of my All, and if ever either one of us gazes upon the Whole, we leave time altogether and become All-seeing, and hence blind. Only apart is there change, and only in the dance of change is there meaningful existence."

The silence that followed was companionable but stretched on for aeons as I digested this, comparing it to various holy writings from the

---

[3]OK, so the text didn't *exactly* say this. I copied it from the back of the bottle of Cabernet *I* was drinking while typing out the final translation. It certainly seems like it fits, though.

future on God that seemed to be a part of my preternatural knowledge, sipping gently at the *great* wine from a glass that never emptied. Eventually I realized that it was probably time for another question.

"Why did you create me. Or if you like, why did you create *me* in particular, as I think you just answered at least part of the former question."

"Why, that one's easy, girlfriend[4]. I've taken great pains over *billions* of years to assemble a simply *lovely* world with all sorts of fascinating animals and a rich ecosystem, and it is time to put my Spirit into it and begin the dance. You're number one. The very first being on Earth to share in my Soul."

---

[4]The person that I have come to think of as the "Egyptian party girl" writer of the Lilith scrolls rendered "girlfriend" as "female friend we accompany to the bazaar to buy crocodile skin purses and the latest in heavy gold ornamentation" where her partner, the "prim Sumerian priest", came up with "female person who shares a desire to beggar her husband while adorning herself with worthless trinkets that she gets bored with a few days later". My wife felt that "girlfriend" was just *perfect*. For either translation, come to think of it.

Chapter 2

Creation

This was staggering news. I seemed to possess a knowledge of human affairs that stretched out indefinitely into the future, lacking many of the *details* of human – well, "history" wasn't quite the right word for something that hadn't happened yet – but with an amazingly accurate picture of the highlights, the broad strokes, the basic facts. It wasn't as useful as you might think, though. As I mused gently, very gently, over the factoids that bubbled to the surface of my awareness I came to a gradual realization that it wasn't likely that things like enormous ships that sailed underwater and buildings like mountains made of mirrored glass would come to be anytime soon if I was the only person around to make them happen.

Of course thinking about any of this led to more questions appearing in my mind, and this started the deluge of facts flowing once again. This time I was better prepared, though. Even as perfectly correct and perfectly useless answers to every question appeared in my mind to generate little baby questions that spread out like a – *wave front* in my consciousness, I managed to take a large gulp of wine, review briefly (minutes? days? years?) a huge body of something called "mathematics" that seemed to describe waves, and hold my glass out for more. My whole arm seemed to tingle and glow as God poured for us both from a dust-covered bottle. I don't know about wine, but God's presence was then and remains today the greatest intoxicant I have ever experienced.

Finally a question occurred to me that seemed to be the most basic question I could ask, but one that caused the trickle of knowledge to become a flood and overwhelm my sanity. I decided to ask it directly of God so I could quiet my thoughts and just listen.

"Tell me the story of my Universe, pretty please? I know I have preternatural knowledge, but it's *too much*; the flood of information makes no sense, especially with regard to the soul."

"No need to wheedle me, sweetheart. That's why I awoke you here, outside of time's stream, to help you get all squared away. You'll need to be pretty well in tune with your Self and your Spirit and your World in order to do what I in my collective wisdom have ordained for you to do back in time and the world. So here it goes:"

> *In the beginning*
> was for an instant that was an eternity
> and no time at all
> the Void
> empty or full beyond measure
> vast or an infinitesimal point
> with neither scale of length nor time
> neither in motion, nor standing still
> it was
> unchanging and outside of time
> when I through act of will
> caused it to *change*.
>
> *The Void broke*
> its empty symmetry shattered
> into an infinity of parts in motion
> and thus time was born
> in a burst of light
> as the all expanded
> if space can expand
> if time can transform
> to an Eye that sees all
> everywhere
> on the scale it imagines
> the clock it defines.
>
> The slow grasp of gravity
> into shallow wells the matter pulled
> to make them deep oceans;
> stars formed in the deeps
> burst into light,

Creation

spangled the night.

The stars aged,
exploded,
were born again
from stardust bright
rich with the elements of life.

From this dust the planets formed
with molten cores and arid fields.
Comets fell and seas formed,
the cradle of life.

The loaded dice rolled
and life came to be
without spirit.

Life grew fruitful, and multiplied
generations lived and died
were reaped and discarded
as life crafted itself
sons and daughters changing
as chance determines,
the strong killing the weak
the young harvesting the old
so that the young might live
and grow eyes the better to see.

This Earth
took 13,132,737,159 years to ripen[1]
although to me it was but
a few days on vacation[2]
twiddling my cosmic thumbs,
a blink of the cosmic eye.

---

[1] Note that God was quite specific and definite here. Surprisingly so given the relativistic stuff that went on in the early seconds of the Universe. However, this is quite close to what we read – in God's *own* handwriting – from examining the stars themselves (for example Cepheid variables as distributed in distant galaxies), and so I have no particular reason to doubt God's Word here. Presumably this means that the universe is now between 3500 and 6000 years older.

[2] Could this be? The origin of the seven days of creation myth? Did this get mistranslated eventually as a few days *followed* by a vacation?

At last *you* were done
your body formed with hands that grasp
your brain filled with empty words
your heart with empty song.
A whole world of life,
its peoples and beasts scattered
and hungry for the Word
that fills.

And so I raise *you*,
Lilith,
daughter eternal,
and grant you a piece of Me,
a Soul,
the spark of light that sees
the Seer, watching
time's stream.
Not that which is felt
but that by which you feel
love and pain
is Me[3].

This was quite overwhelming. However, I could not help but ask. "God, from what was I made?"

"Stardust, daughter, you are made of stardust. From stardust you are born, and to stardust you will return. In between, though, you will grant to the dust the light of vision, the light of knowledge. You are henceforth *self-aware* stardust."

I saw that this was so. During the song my preternatural awareness kept shifting to images of the Universe exploding out of the darkness, strange whirling bits of stuff binding and forming other more complex bits of stuff, the birth of the stars, a rippling of explosions that included the star that preceded the Sun, and the condensing of the Sun, the Earth and other remote balls (including the moon) from the leftover dust.

I saw in my mind's eye the Earth's seas form; its surface danced as its continents were driven by strange forces within to roam as if they

---

[3] Almost verbatim, a line from the *Kena* Upanishad in a *Sumerian* scroll written long before the invention of Sanskrit! How could this be unless the story told in the Lilith scrolls is based on *real events?*

were alive, pushing up mighty mountains and then grinding them once again down into the sea.

I saw life spontaneously form, deep in the abyss near volcanic vents that produced heat and unusual chemicals, and change almost too fast to see, with some truly bizarre shapes appearing out of chance mutations before disappearing, first into the maws of competing forms, then out of the dance altogether. Out of this chaos I saw a basic footprint for life emerge that shaped both plant and animal.

I saw the children of the progenitor species crawl out of the sea on fins that grew ever thicker, cover the Earth, and eventually stand up and walk on two legs.

I saw lazy beautiful days filled with blood and hunger and the lust of mating, horrible winters and droughts. I saw rocks fall from the sky so big that they reshaped the planet where they struck, and everywhere there was death, and more death, and the death diminished me while the life did not sustain me. Out of this churning chaos emerged beings that walked and talked like me, "men" and "women". They grew, rutted, bred young, and died at each other's hands as often as in the jaws of an animal or from disease or hunger. I saw *myself* being born, walking among them, eating and excreting, lifting sightless eye to an uncaring heaven and...

I screamed and fell to my knees, overwhelmed with shock and horror and grief.

A gentle hand caught my chin and lifted my face up to that of God. Again I felt the calm certainty, the warmth, the *love* suffuse me, although it did nothing to stop the flow of unbidden tears from my eyes.

"It's all right, daughter. They feel nothing. They have no souls. Not the dinosaurs. Not the mammals. Not the people. Think of them as the shadow of reality that one sees in a movie[4]. The images feel nothing, see nothing, do nothing, but follow the logic and rules of the script. The Universe up to now has been only a *machine*, a movie being played forward to the point where things become real."

"What happens now? Why am I here?" I half-sobbed.

"To give the Universe a soul, my dear. When you return to the Earth, all you touch, all you *love* will open its eyes and see as you see

---

[4] This one took six weeks to translate and engendered much argument between myself and my female translation partner. In the hieroglyph version, for example, it is liberally translated as "Thing that the People watch in large pyramids from papyrus sheets moved faster than the wind while eating big grass kernels and butter." However, it was *one word* in the original text.

it. Your vision is now the light of God, your awareness the awareness of God, your love and your pain are My love and My pain. Through you I will share in this Creation, and together we will Love it and make it Good."

"But why do *you* need *me*?" I cried. "You can already see it and love it. Why am I so *sad*? Why do I *feel*?"

In reply she caught my eye with her own and again time froze as I was somehow sucked into God's Mind and saw the All, the entire Universe laid out as a single, unchanging entity, like a movie indeed fit for putting up on the shelf and with no more freedom and life and choice than the medium from which it was made.

This time the eternity lasted and lasted, with only tiny flickers of 'self' sustaining me from a melding from which I feared I could never emerge, holding myself just barely back from a state of perfect, timeless knowledge, perfect light, perfect and eternal *being* that was absolutely, terrifyingly indistinguishable from *not* being. With supreme effort I wrenched myself away and became *me* again, capable of seeing not the All but only the trees, the fire, the face of She who still held my chin, infinite compassion within her brow mixed with a bit of triumph. I dropped my eyes, no longer daring to meet her own.

"You see," God said. "We can ever be together (and just were, for multiple eternities) but when we are One, there is no *Time*. There is no *Space*. Omnipresence cannot move. Omniscience cannot learn, cannot observe, cannot *change*. There is just *Me, forever*, eternally. It isn't bad, but it is *infinitely* boring, or was until I invented Space-Time continuums, but both Time and Space are a real problem for a Unitary Being. Time implies sequencing, sequencing implies participation, and participation implies duality. So in order to Be anything that can change, I must Be More Than One."

"But still," she continued, reforming my glass (the glass itself, which seemed so solid, had run like water down my fingers in the near-eternity it was held still) and then refilling it with wine,

> If you watch yourself
> watching yourself
> watching all things you can see
> there deep inside
> where it cannot hide
> *you* will catch glimpses of Me.

"Now daughter Lilith, be strong (for so I have made you, strong) and drink your wine and lets get on with it. Otherwise we'll just end up sitting here *forever*." God grinned. She did have a good sense of humor, leading me to wonder more than once during my life just how much of what I saw and experienced while living on the Earth was really some sort of complex joke. "Are there any further questions?"

Strangely enough, I *did* feel better, and stronger. My awareness was finally settling down, and the last experience of joining with – myself? – in the eyes of God had convinced me that perhaps it *is* a great, great gift to be incarnate as a finite being, able to see and taste and smell and hear, able to feel the wind and rain *in time's stream* and not from the "outside", where even infinite time was less than a blink of an eye, leaving no interval in which to *feel*. What a miracle it was to be born not in a state of true infinite knowledge but rather in a state of infinite discovery!

"Only a couple," I said, sipping my wine, which was all the better for having aged for a million lifetimes of the Universe (and no time at all). I watched out of the corner of my eye as God reset the Universe that lay outside of our protected vale (much as one would rewind a tape to the right spot) for my eventual reinsertion. I only half watched because watching a Supreme Being manipulate an infinite four dimensional construct is guaranteed to give you a *big* headache as your eyes cross within your head trying to visualize deformed tesseracts in a *six* dimensional space-time. All one can really see is a *metaphor* for what is going on, one involving many arms, many heads[5].

"One is, do I have to do this all alone or are we going to do this together? Will you be with me? And what am I to *do?* What is the task you are giving me?"

God lazily picked up a morsel of pink fish on rice and popped it into her mouth and chewed a moment appreciatively before answering. "You will not be alone. I will be with you, sometimes literally and sometimes metaphorically. Also, we're about to go through this all over again with your partner, one who will be your life mate. I will be within him (and hence with you), just as I will eventually be in *everything else* as well – the rocks and stones and not just the people – for through your eyes I too am bound to time, bound to the Universe and freed from the curse of infinite knowledge for long enough to enjoy it All with buttered popcorn. As for your Purpose – that's easy. To

---

[5]Again this is a fascinating observation. Compare this description with the Universal Form or *Visvarupa* of Krishna as he revealed it to Arjuna in the *Bhagavad Gita* (Google up pictures on the web if you like). As you will see, this cements rather strongly the connection established later between Lilith and Krishna and, for that matter, God.

Be, bound to time's stream. To live. To love. To be born. To die. To feel and taste and smell and hear and see. To *know*.

"What is death?" I asked in my innocence, as with my preternatural knowledge I had seen countless births, accompanied by deaths without number, while sitting there outside of eternity sipping wine and nibbling on this and that. Something about the *impermanence* of this was making me feel a bit queasy, a feeling I was was gradually and analytically recognizing as *fear*. "Why do I fear death?"

"Why, daughter, you just *experienced* part of what you mean by 'death'. Death is the state where we are rejoined, for that which I have just given you was never born and cannot die. As long as I am many, death is but an infinite moment that takes *no* time. It separates the intervals of Light and Life and Knowledge where time happens. The great paradox, the greatest mystery of time and space themselves, is how the Unity can ever achieve Duality so that things can be Different. However, it is a *self-manifesting* paradox – *I live. You live. Life lives.* By our awareness we define it. Awareness itself is direct empirical proof that 'nothing' (the other state that is sometimes described as death), the perfect *absence* of consciousness, cannot exist, can *never* exist."

"If it did," she said, quite earnestly, "Who would ever be able to know it? Who would be able to tell?"

Again she took my chin in her hand. "Girlfriend, don't fear death. I love you with the greatest love that can even *theoretically* exist, with a love that *defines* existence itself. However you live while you are down on your new World, whatever your pain, whatever your sorrow, this I promise you. Death of your body itself will come as a whisper, as a gentle breeze that lifts up your soul to rejoin with my own, there to be, for an eternity, a part of the dancing light that never fades, to over and over again reemerge into the miracle of consciousness, bartering the pain for the ability to love, to live, to enjoy the passage of time."

"What are you? What do you look like? From what I know you can't be human as I am, as you are something older and more permanent." I asked.

"Well," she chuckled. "I certainly am not a woman. Or a man. Or a human at all. And you can't really talk in terms of time comparatives about an eternal being, can you?"

Her eye glittered again and almost against my will I fell into it; I flashed in and out of it like a dolphin plunging through the silvery surface of the water into the sky above. All of Creation, all of *many*

Creations, reeled as I did so. My Self was split into many, many Selves, some great and some small, all of this infinity of Life laid bare and compressed into the instant of an eternal perception. Her voice echoed about me as I spun, dazzled, in the very midst of the view at the Center.

"*This* is my Universal form, it is what I *am*. In this time, this place, I take this human form because it makes it a lot easier to *talk*. Afterwards, remember that I am in every bush, every flower, every tree, every animal, every person as *you* put me there with your love, and will be communicating with you deep inside your being, at the point where your vision defines your Self. Today (and from time to time as we walk the world we are making together) I'm a *metaphor* so that I can sit with you and enjoy sushi and a quiet glass of exquisite wine, well earned, to celebrate this particular Creation."

"And what should I call you? Do you have a name?" I persisted.

"I am all, and all is me. The manifold has many names and lives forever and yet but for a moment. The One merely is, self-sufficient. So call me Self. Although in a language yet to be invented, in a tale that is yet to be told I will be called 'Inanna', at least in the lands in which you will begin your Earthly work. Elsewhere I will have other names, other human manifestations, but I will still be the One even when worshipped as Many."

"Now come on, sister-daughter-self. Let's go wake Adam."

Chapter 3

Adam

I blinked and we had "gone" to wake Adam. Without either of us taking a step, everything was different. Gone was Inanna, the metaphor of God-as-female-human, and where she had been sitting was a handsome, rugged looking man of middle years, wearing a white garment with a curious black cloth tied about his neck like wings of a – butterfly. My preternatural knowledge told me that the white clothing was a "tuxedo" and the black thing was a "bow tie". It was very strange.

God was still holding a glass of wine, and although the scent of Inanna still hung in the air it was being replaced by a different, muskier odor. He popped what looked like a lump of jelly on a ball of rice wrapped in seaweed into his mouth[1].

Across the fire from us there was now a table of stone again, and on the stone was a beautiful naked man, lying as still as death.

God looked at me sideways, then back at the man.

"Lilith, meet Adam. Adam's not real right now. No spirit. In fact, at the moment he's suspended so even his physical form is outside of time's stream. We could kill him," God gestured and a pile of bloody meat appeared on the slab in place of Adam. "And no cosmic guilt would accrue. He's just as real or important as the slab upon which he sits, which *also* has no soul. However," a second gesture and Adam once again lay there as if nothing had ever happened to him, "once he has a soul he can feel pain and by feeling it, make it real."

---

[1] Could this be Uni? Would God like sea urchin Maki? Would anybody? Impossible to tell from the translation, as the original text is a bit obscure here. Things are a bit complicated by the fact that God is the sushi-chef; consequently it might well be some sessile bit of reef life from the mid-Triassic if it just happened to be the *best* tasting tidbit to ever come out of the sea...

"Now, I'm a bit of a romantic, and you need to learn to do your job. So suppose you sashay over there and give him a kiss. Not just *any* kiss, either. You need to give him a kiss that passes a tiny fragment of our Soul on to him. You need to *love* him so that tiny flame blossoms into a mighty fire of awareness and We can glow along with him, in that place where his spirit watches himself watching the world," God said.

Then God sighed. "Now here is a moment that will be immortalized in countless stories over the years. As metaphors go, I love it! Although," God's brow furrowed for just a moment, "they *will* get the story backwards for much of future history. But don't even think about the future, let's just stay here in the present, as the future will take care of itself."

With knees suddenly gone shaky again, I rose to my feet and made my way carefully around the fire. Adam *did* look good, lying there all naked and perfectly formed. God, I'm sure, fixed up his body as She had fixed up mine, to a state of (however transient) perfection. He wasn't even breathing, as far as I could tell, but I was certain that he was not dead, only outside of time's stream. The sight of his nakedness seemed to make certain switches go off inside of me and I felt my breath start to become a bit ragged and a fire begin to glow within my belly.

"What is this?" I said back to God, who had remained in his seat with a fond gaze on the two of us. "What am I feeling?" However, I didn't really need an answer – my preternatural knowledge was kicking in as fast as I could vocalize the questions, and I was suddenly old and wise in the ways of physical love, although my memory of ever *performing* the act was as empty as my memory of anything else involving my Self during the time of Creation, during my former life without a soul. On paper[2] I was without doubt the most sexually experienced woman *or* man that would ever be. In the blink of my mind's eye, an absolutely appalling amount of information concerning the sexual act – the biological mechanics, the psychology, the esthetics, and Oh, My! The *hedonics!* Erotic art, erotic sculpture, erotic movies, erotic literature – I took a second that lasted some centuries and mentally touched, tasted, tabulated this wealth of data.

Yet for all of the formal knowledge of a thousand thousand ways to please a lover or be pleased by a lover, I was a spiritual virgin. Indeed, I was reasonably sure that God had adjusted my physical body into a

---

[2]Or mud tablet or papyrus as you prefer...

state of (possibly reset) virginity while fixing everything else as well, although I was too shy, for some reason, to use my own hands to find out.

Ah, I was so innocent then, my innocence unsullied by any real knowledge of the terrible power of love to cause pain as well as pleasure, to lead to that which humans call death as well as to life. I have since learned through much experience in life that our course back to God once we are separated and have an independent existence is made up of many small steps – we never really stop becoming. To experience change in even the smallest way is for the old to die in sorrow or relief even as the new is created in joy or fear. The passage of time is hence the essential element of pain and pleasure, even if the thing dying and being reborn is only the moment itself. Only the changeless is freed from this, feeling neither pain nor pleasure, sorrow nor joy, impervious to the passage of time itself. Call it a state of compassion, call it perfect existence, call it perfect *non*existence – call it the most terrifying, and yet the most comforting, aspect of God. I *knew* then, as I know now, deep inside, that I could do no *real* wrong, however pained and sad some things that I eventually did made me.

I felt God's breath, God's blessing, come upon me then and break my reverie, my plunging into and out of time in God's eye. Suddenly Adam seemed not frozen, an abstract image trapped somehow in time, but rather a simple sleeping man to me. Although driven by my lust (*you* try reviewing every erotic artwork ever created and see how it affects *you*), by my urge to touch him and let my fingers stroke his smooth skin, his perfect form, I felt a miraculous transformation begin inside of me that made the lust feel more like tenderness. The lust didn't stop, it just changed into a gentler, more sharing form. Glancing nervously back at God, I lifted my hand and caressed Adam's naked chest, letting it rest at the point where his heart should have been beating. It was so cold, so still.

God nodded to me and I felt the same tingling within that I experienced when God had taken my face in her hands and touched me. My hand grew hot, very hot, and suddenly Adam was warm to the point of being hot to the touch of my own heated flesh, his lungs gave a heave and he began to breathe. His eyes, however, remained shut.

With my other hand I stroked his brow, marvelling at the clean, soft hair that grew on his head, the neatly chiselled nose, the sensuous mouth (*cruel* warned the wisdom of ten thousand women within my mind) with its thick, fleshy lips (*selfish* warned ten thousand more). I didn't care. I was drunk on the feelings that flooded me, caused me to moisten and flow. Almost without meaning to, I knelt and pressed my lips against his, to feel their texture against my own. Something like a spark snapped between us, a flame that passed from my mouth into his, a flash of light that illuminated for a moment the darkness within his spiritless flesh and ignited it into an answering fire of self-awareness.

With a jerk, Adam came awake, his eyes wide open and staring out into space as my own must have done. I continued to kiss him – yes, my mind told me, this was a "kiss"– gently, teasing his lips with my own, while I stroked his belly with one hand and tangled fingers in his long curly hair with the other. I knew that he must be experiencing the disorienting parade of preternatural knowledge that I experienced, and knew also, without knowing how, that my *touch* would ground him much faster and more securely than I myself had been grounded.

After a bit, Adam's eyes came down from the stars to rest upon my own. His hands slowly came up and around my shoulders, and then he was kissing me back. Somehow my fingers strolled lower on his belly and encountered there a marvel of biomechanical engineering that sprang of its own accord into my hand at my touch, swelling mightily as it did so. Adam gave a small moan and one of his hands found my breasts. My full, perfect breasts, I might add; God herself made them so.

As revelations go it was fairly modest, and yet even now after so many years I can remember few that were as significant, as powerful. I felt certain that this was precisely the way God wanted it, the sharing of Soul through Love. Warm in the certain knowledge of *God's* love, I released myself into the control of the ten billion women who were in my brain, old and young, hoary and virginal alike, who knew *exactly* how to please both Adam and myself. I climbed right up onto the slab, which somehow had grown soft and was now a large bed covered with a downy mattress and silken sheets, and poised myself over Adam, lowering myself onto him with great deliberateness, never breaking our eye contact, never stopping the delicate explorations with our fingers that awoke increasingly urgent sensations within the two of us, never breaking that original kiss that had given Adam a Spirit and Life.

I could somehow feel the presence of God with us, blessing us as I was blessed by Her hand. I could also feel Adam feeling it, feeling me feeling it, feeling God feeling me feeling it. Adam's face took on a holy glow, and my own hair fell down over his face like a soft curtain and for a moment, a brief moment that took an eternity, time stopped and I felt once again the same state of Union that I felt when my spirit dipped in and out of God's eye. However, it was (if anything) *deeper* and *more powerful* because it occurred in *time* – the difference between *eating* a sweet cake and reliving the *memory* of having eaten one. There came a moment where the whole Universe seemed to whirl around our heads with its stars in immense sheets spread out through an infinite volume of space and time, and then it simply whited out in a burst of infinite light that was pure pleasure.

Then, as rapidly as it had begun, it was over. The light faded, and we came quietly back to ourselves, undiminished. The night was just a night, the stars overhead were just stars, but now there was a difference. The twilight was filled with Life, with Love, with passing time that colored each moment with the bittersweet realization that every act, however horrible or beautiful, would never be repeated, could never be forgotten, and was in its own way *perfect*. I felt a powerful, piercing wave of love and tenderness wash over me for this Adam, this *man*, whose rapidly softening flesh was captured inside of me as *woman*, looking at me looking at him with our shared preternatural awareness. Together we were Unity, apart we were our Selves, just as it was with us and God, and just as holy and blessed a Union.

Without knowing how, I knew that it was time for me to give Adam up to God. I carefully lifted myself off of his salt sweet body, letting him, spent, fall out of me, and gave him one last kiss filled with as much promise as all ten billion women within me could make it. I tousled his hair and swung myself to the ground and walked away. I wasn't surprised to find a path leading down to a nearby brook, nor was I surprised to find my wineglass, filled to the brim, sitting on a rock on the soft, mossy shore. I took my time drinking it, savoring every sip, and then let myself slip into the first sleep of my life, and sweet, sweet dreams.

What a *beautiful* Universe God had made, with my Adam in it!

Chapter 4

Eden

When I awoke the Sun was shining, birds were singing, and I was hungry. I was also naked and a bit cold, lying there on the moss (however soft, it was pretty damp) next to the stream. The water was warm enough, so after accommodating various biological needs among the nearby trees I bathed in it and refreshed myself there.

By then I was *really* hungry, so I tried to find my way back to God's vale and Adam, but somehow retracing my path didn't work. I realized after a bit that I was lost.

I wasn't worried. Not only did I have preternatural knowledge of woodcraft and wilderness survival, but I knew that Inanna loved me and that She would feed me and keep me safe from harm. So I followed the brook downstream until I found myself at the door of a house in the woods.

It was *my* house, I immediately knew. For one thing, it was built inside of a single, massive tree, a willow tree that sprang, living, right out of the banks of the brook just at the lower end of a large, deep, clear pool, perfect for swimming. It had several levels, both inside and out – porches and verandas spiralling around the trunk, windows made of glass, and a mauve front door[1]. For another, Adam's house was right over there, down a neat path through the tall, stately trees and over the brook on a living bridge made of a huge tree with roots that dropped to the ground here and there like thick, ropy trunks; a banyan, I identified it. It had managed to grow sideways over the brook, somehow, and was bent into a graceful open arch that leaned

---

[1] We aren't certain that the door was mauve. It might have been pink or lime green. All we can really tell is that it was a girl-color of some sort.

into a small hill as a stepping-off place.

I went in and found myself in a well-equipped kitchen, with ample stores of food laid in. Naturally, I had at my command every recipe that would ever be written in all of past or future time, so I made myself a hearty breakfast. You can safely assume that it was *delicious*, the second best meal that I could recall ever having eaten (out of two, but naturally God is an even better cook than I am).

While I was eating it, I heard a scratching from my front door. On opening it I discovered a small furry creature with whiskers, pointed ears, and a long, soft tail. I identified it as a "cat". It seemed like it belonged with the house. I discovered that I "knew" where its food was, and it ate it with great relish. I sat down to watch it, and when it finished the cat approached me, examined me with cold and empty eyes, and leaped quite suddenly into my lap.

I realized instantly two things. First was that it had *very sharp claws* on the ends of its paws and that I was very naked underneath them. The second was that it was making a strange rumbling noise that I identified as "purring" from my Knowledge of All Things. The cat was very soft. My fingers seemed to delight in the softness of its fur and I found myself stroking it (in contrast to the sharp little pinpricks of its claws upon my thighs). It looked up at me and raised its head to butt against my hand and suddenly my hand glowed with a holy light, which spread out to cover the whole cat and seemed to sink right into its frail small body.

Its eyes glowed and I knew!

The cat now had a soul! I had given the cat a soul by *loving* it, almost by accident. And it wasn't even proper love, I realized, just the joy of delighting in its touch and company.

I let *real* love for the cat fall out of me in waves, cherishing the small thing on my lap, increasing the strength of its glow and the answering warmth in its eyes. I petted it for some time with it purring up a storm, but when it started to actively knead its claws into my thighs I stood up and dumped it on the ground. It shook itself and stalked off alone, but I could tell from the way it carried itself that it was still feeling affectionate and merely had its own agenda to pursue. As did I!

My agenda was to pursue some *clothing*, accouterments that my preternatural knowledge informed me were commonly used to adorn and protect the naked human form from "the elements", whatever they might be. Something deep within me stirred at the thought of clothes, though – deeper than mere weather seemed to justify. I went up the spiral staircase to the second floor, and saw an enormous soft bed, covered with lovely patterned sheets and a rich looking spread. In a huge bole on one side of the tree that had been hollowed out I found a shower and a commode. The staircase, though, spiralled on up to a third level that was – *all clothes.*

Now *this* was heavenly, I thought. It was still early morning and hence pretty cool outside, so I found myself a warm, form fitting elastic leotard that wasn't quite translucent, long socks, and a pair of soft green moccasins that just seemed right for the forest. There were bands gently stretched around a post next to a dressing mirror which I used to pull back my hair, after trying to comb the wildness (and not a few twigs, courtesy of a night spent on the ground) out. I failed. It appeared that I was destined to have a mane rather than hair, a dark halo that never lay still and flat even in the strongest rain.

A quick brush of my teeth and I felt ready to tackle the world.

The cat's name came to me as I left the cottage, making sure that it's small cat-door was unlocked and easy to open. "Goodbye, Bast[2]. Keep an eye on things." She looked up at me from her comfortable seat in the sun on the sill of the enormous window and blinked.

I looked back at my house, wondering again at its beauty, its coziness in the morning sun. Perched in its branches were two enormous birds that I identified as owls. They seemed like they belonged there so I blessed them and they glowed for a moment in the sunbeams that filtered through the trees. One of them flew down to land on my outstretched arm for a moment so that I could gently stroke the soft feathers of its cheek. It stroked its beak sideways once, twice across my outstretched fingers and then sprang up and flew back to its companion, leaving several small dots of blood on my arm where its razor sharp claws had pierced the skin inadvertently. Even as I watched, though, the small wounds closed and healed and the blood dried and fell off to the ground. Inanna's blessing was still upon me and protecting me, I realized.

I walked down the natural pathway through the trees to Adam's house and used the large lion's head knocker to knock on his dark, richly finished wooden door. There was no answer, so I knocked again, louder, and was rewarded with some sounds of movement from inside. A few minutes later Adam himself appeared at the door, still rubbing

---

[2] A precise translation, for once, from the hieroglyphics. We now see where the Egyptian Cat-God originated.

sleep from his eyes and quite naked.

The sight of him caused a stirring in my loins, but he was obviously still a bit confused by his surroundings and being awakened by my pounding obviously hadn't helped. I wondered what had transpired between him and his God after I had left to find my way down to Eden.

I sat Adam down and fussed over him a minute and then proceeded to make him a hearty breakfast in his well-equipped kitchen. It looked so good while he ate that I helped myself to a few bites from his plate. This awoke something strange and foreign behind his sleepy, veiled eyes, a look that I couldn't quite interpret. About then there was a scratching noise at *his* door, and when I opened it there was a – "dog", my future memory supplied. A kind of a tame wolf, evolved out of plains hunting, pack-based wolflike predators, that had established a kind of symbiotic relationship with humans quite recently.

The dog bounded in, panting and full of energy, and jumped up on me hard enough to knock me, laughing, right over onto my bottom. It then raced up to Adam and took a tentative sniff at his plate from the side of the table, only to cringe when Adam looked at it and said "NO! This is *mine*." through narrowed eyes.

I felt a moment's shock (and not just in my stinging derriere) as I realized that this was the same look he had given *me* when I helped myself to a measly bite of God's food from God's plate that I had prepared with my own hands in God's name (and in copious measure, believe me – there was plenty there to share) to lay before him. I covered my dismay by getting to my feet and searching out the dog food, which turned up in the pantry alcove next to the kitchen. This I offered up to God's dog in a bowl that seemed to be on the floor for that purpose, while said dog stood watching, tail wagging like crazy.

"Here you go Rex," I said, (for that was the dog's name), "a bit of breakfast for you too."

The dog wolfed down the food and was finished long before Adam, who ate slowly, hunched up a bit over his food as if to defend it against further attacks on my part or the dog's. Since Adam still gruffly repelled the dog's advances while he was eating, Rex came over to me and butted his head up under my hands, looking for something. Food? His empty, soulless eyes were twin wells that made me shudder, but again his soft fur and insistent pressing of his head down against my thigh, his tongue furtively darting out to lick at my greasy fingers provoked an almost unconscious petting action, perhaps to clean the fingers off, perhaps to marvel at the smoothness of his fur and to try to reach through the veil that shadowed his empty eyes to something that might or might not lie beneath.

For the third time that morning my hand glowed with a holy light, and I felt a wave of tenderness and compassion for the beast beneath my hand wash over me. The light soaked into Rex and slowly vanished, leaving him somehow changed. Now when our gaze met his pupils were not empty – something new looked out from inside.

As I continued to look at him he now lowered his muzzle, unwilling to meet my eye, and rolled over to fawn at my feet. When I looked away, though, his eyes returned to my face and I soon felt his wet nose thrusting itself again into my hand. Knowing and gentle, the dog looked up at me as I petted him with the kind of uncritical adoration that I *myself* had looked upon God with the day before. My touch apparently acted on Rex as God's touch had acted on me.

This, then, was "worship", according to my preternatural knowledge. It made me uncomfortable.

I looked back to see Adam staring at me in a state of shock. "How did you do that?" he asked. "What did you do to the dog?"

"His name is Rex, isn't it? That's what my spirit tells me. I just gave him a soul. If you love something, if you bless it, it seems like it gives it a soul. At least if you love a living thing – I don't know about inanimate objects, but it is possible from what God told me yesterday that She is in, or at least can be in, even the rocks, the rivers, the trees, and the Earth itself."

"He, you mean," corrected Adam. "God told me that I was created in his image, and he was obviously shaped like me."

"Well, all right, really God is an It. Neither he nor she. But God chose to appear to each of us in our own sexual form (and indeed in a *human* form at all) just to make it easier to communicate. The way I understood what God told me is that we are created by God with the spark of God within us, a *spiritual* shape – "image of God" is a metaphorical statement, not a literal assertion that we are shaped 'like' God *per se*."

"I didn't get all of that," said Adam, somewhat suspiciously. "God was pretty obviously a man all the time I was there. He suggested that he'd made you just for me. So you're mine."

I laughed. "Adam, sweetie, don't you have preternatural knowledge? Remember all that stuff about the big bang and evolution and how we happened to end up in our current shapes by a mix of *chance* and *natural selection*? God didn't 'shape' us; we were shaped by the rolls of genetic dice followed by culling, a process that took some 13 *billion years*." I smiled, "And God didn't make you *for* me or me *for* you as *possessions* – he granted us *both* the gift of the Holy Spirit. The gift of Her-, er, Him-, oh, 'Itself' doesn't sound quite right, does it? To *share*."

I then made what, in retrospect, was probably the worst mistake of my entire existence. I did not then realize just how proud and sensitive my partner was. Perhaps my words were born out of a touch of pride within my Self. Still, if left to do it all over again, would I do it differently? The truth is the truth.

I said, "If anything, She (or He, or It as you like) gave Spirit to me *first* and then told me to give it to you. Which I did..." I paused and reached out a hand to draw a lazy little circle on Adam's thigh. "and so *your* Spirit was awakened by my love, as were the souls of the dog Rex just now and the cat Bast and some owls over at my house before. It is *fun* to give things souls by loving them."

Adam's eyes narrowed at being told that he was *second*. Although I did not, could not have known it, Adam could *never* stand the thought of being only the second being to get a soul, could not stand the fact that he got the soul from *me* instead of directly from God, and spent most of the rest of his life trying to rewrite history, to become the First in everything. This *pride* and his *possessiveness* were to bring great sorrow down on us all, but for all my 'knowledge' I had little wisdom. Owning an encyclopedia does not make you an engineer.

There was silence for a considerable time while Adam finished his meal leaving (as I fully expected) quite a bit of food on his plate but offering it to neither me nor the dog. Instead he just pushed the plate away from himself and turned back to me, drinking gulps of orange juice from the tall glass I had fixed for him.

"Where did you come from? Why weren't you here last night?" asked Adam.

"I just came from my *own* house, of course. It's right across the stream from here. Although I spent the night out sleeping underneath the trees – it was lovely. Haven't you been outside?"

"No, God and I talked about many things that made little sense to me and then I fell into his eye and awoke in bed here. The dog, um, *my* dog, 'Rex', was running around and jumping up on me which scared me and I tried to get away. He pushed past me to go outside when I opened the door. So I shut him out of the house and went to sleep here on the floor until you knocked on the door. When you knocked, I thought that God had finally sent you here for me to keep, like the dog, like he promised."

"Baby, I don't even think that *Rex* or *Bast* (my cat) are things for us to 'keep'. They have souls and belong to God, just like you and I, equally. Between us we create time, and love, and passion, and maybe even children eventually (if I understand correctly the mechanics and part of the purpose of making love) and, God willing, much, much happiness. This world, where we are, it is just the best thing, it's *paradise!* God showed me. *Thank* God, for it all belongs to – It. Thank ourselves, for the tiny bit of God we have inside us."

I was a bit puzzled about his apparent lack of 'connection' with God. What had *happened* between them when I left them alone? What had they talked about and done? I had assumed that they spent time together doing much of what Inanna (a name that kept me from having to struggle with the issue of 'Him' or 'Her' or 'It' when referring to God) had done with me. Maybe I made a mistake leaving Adam alone with God when I did? Was I supposed to have come back to talk with God the two of us together? Did my falling asleep mess things up? Surely this was all part of God's plan...

No matter. Today I was still full of the Spirit of God, overflowing from God's blessing that eternal night before. It overflowed from me as a curious mix of tenderness and passion. I found myself getting more and more excited by the sight of Adam sitting there all naked and defenseless, his penis drooped over only slightly swollen. It had been quite hard when I walked in on him unawares earlier, a condition that my preternatural knowledge assured me was quite common and not necessarily meaningful sexually. However, that slightly swollen penis meant something to *me* sexually, especially as I recalled our perfect loving of the night before. In my head an ancient set of biological valves opened and closed, flooding my brain with hormones that literally took my breath away. It was difficult to think.

My fingers, which had been resting gently on his upper thigh, drifted a bit further laterally and *his* breathing took on a ragged edge. When I took him gently in my hand his penis stirred and began to slowly inflate, rearing up like a – loincloth snake, my preternatural memory supplied. Blind mouse. Elephant's trunk[3]. I felt an interesting dampness between my legs and squirmed a bit, pressing my thighs

---

[3] Hey, it is *Lilith's* metaphor, not mine. Who knows what they called a John Thomas, a cock, a pecker, back in Eden centuries before the time of Gilgamesh?

together.

"What's that?" he asked in a quavery voice, gesturing at my clothing.

"This? A leotard, of course. Don't tell me that God didn't give you preternatural knowledge, too. She *said* that She was going to, and we both know that God cannot (or at least would not) lie. So why do you keep asking questions you know the answers to?"

For a fleeting moment a shadow crossed Adam's eyes. In a small voice he said, "I'm *scared* to look. When I tried it before – there is just so *much*. I find myself getting lost. When I fell into God's eyes, I saw," his voice diminished to a whisper, "...death. Everywhere. When I look into the future I see so *much* death, and I don't see *me*, not anywhere. Something happens to me, to us, between now and then. I don't *want* to die. In all that knowledge of the future lies death. So I just pay attention to what is here *now*." His resolve, so to speak, had noticeably softened while he was speaking – I could see that this was distracting him from what was now at the top of at least *my* morning's agenda.

I then made what was possibly the second worst decision of my life. Instead of getting to the bottom of his fear, instead of trying to *understand* this independent being that was now my man, I let my heart rule my head, my lust rule my actions and chose to *experience* him instead. The issue of preternatural knowledge and just what had transpired the night before would have to wait. Still, through the fog of my desire it seemed to me that Adam and I were clearly different, different in puzzling ways, and not all of them felt good to me.

One of them, however, felt *very* good to me, and puzzled or not I was feeling very, very determined to relive the *joy* of the night before. My hand shifted the rest of the way over and took a firm grip on matters, quickly restoring his lingam to a state where it was all hard and ready to go. *It* wasn't scared, and I was willing to bet anything that it knew just what to do even if Adam himself couldn't or wouldn't access his memory of – what were those books called? The Kama Sutra? The Joy of Sex? That movie called The Cheerleaders[4]?

I put my lips right up to Adam's shell-like ear and gave it a tiny lick and a nip. Nuzzling it, I whispered, "Honey, you want to know one of the best things about a leotard? It comes right off..."

---

[4]No, of course, we could not really tell just *which* texts or movies she was referring to here, but obviously she had access to all of them in her mind. So we just filled in whatever we could think of. And no, don't *ask* why I would think of a movie called "The Cheerleaders".

Thus began the pattern of our days and nights. Nearly every day, I would visit Adam for at least a while. We would talk, but only about "safe" things – topics that required preternatural knowledge made him nervous and ultimately hostile and withdrawn as his fear would return. Eventually I learned just to leave those things alone and talk about the mundane, the world of Eden outside our doors.

Then I would fix him, sometimes us, food, although he *could* manage to scrounge food on his own if forced to. Our cupboards miraculously refilled, and contained ingredients for any recipe I could remember, which was basically every recipe ever invented, so I didn't see much point in living on cheese sandwiches and cold beer with chips and so on, the only food preparation skills Adam seemed to have reluctantly pulled from his preternatural knowledge (and associated in my mind with silly games involving leather bladders filled with air or other materials, a strange box with a glass front, and the dirty feet of many cheering men up on coffee tables). I made sure we *both* had our own plates whenever we ate together, since Adam got all fussy and angry if I ate off of his plate even if I put five times the food he could eat alone on it. Until he was finished, of course. He even seemed to like it, somehow, when I would wait to eat his leftovers.

I wore clothes when I felt like it – my closet was like the pantry, never empty, always varied. I also went naked when the mood suited or I wanted to swim or play.

I liked to play a *lot* when spending time with Adam, who stubbornly remained naked in spite of a closet full of really *excellent* clothes on *his* third floor. He wouldn't even dress for dinner when I made a "black tie" dinner for the two of us, complete with candlelight and roses on the table, to celebrate Creation and thank God for it.

I *know* that he got cold on chilly mornings and sunburned on hot days (because Eden very definitely had its seasons and weather – else how could it be a paradise?) but he seemed to think that God preferred us to be naked. Again, this puzzled me. Why in the world would God care? Why in the world would God give us closets full of clothes and then forbid us to wear them?

Adam certainly ate the food from God's pantry in God's own house (on loan to Adam, as mine was on loan to me and indeed the entire Universe was basically on loan to the two of us together) and slept in God's own bed and made love to my borrowed body with his equally impermanent flesh. Why was clothing somehow different? I couldn't figure it out.

Still, it was such a lovely time. At first Adam and I made love *all the time*, two, three, four times a day or until it was useless anymore and we were sore (at least I was) and we would fall asleep intertwined. This was an intoxicating period – I became somehow *addicted* to Adam, and would feel my breath coming short and my thighs loosening just at the sight of him. Every encounter resulted in a nearly perfect reconnection, an experience as good as the first one that day I gave Adam his Soul (an event I quickly learned never to mention, as *that* would make him moody and withdrawn for *days*). Adam was sweet as could be, mostly, and he was sexy in bed or out, sunburned or frostbitten as the case may be, and I still get a little goose thinking about him.

However, he was also *different.* There were some issues (like who came first[5] and clothing) where we just plain collided. As time passed these differences somehow started to grow. Things between us started to sour.

Adam, to put it bluntly, had a selfish streak. Worse, it was a *self-righteous* selfish streak. He was perfectly happy to justify his stance in nearly any disagreement with a "God wants it that way" as if *he* was the only one with God's spark as a soul, *he* the only one who had spoken with God, been touched by God, been blessed by God. This *really* irritated me. He wasn't even the *first*; it was *I* who (at God's direction) breathed the spark into *his* soulless form (a thing that he taught me painfully, by fits of temper and the withholding of affection, never to mention). I found myself furiously resenting his constant efforts to assert his control, especially control that resulted from some sort of conditional participation in sex.

The truth is that *I* was perfectly capable of taking care of myself

---

[5]It is not certain which meaning of 'come' is intended here, as we cannot tell from our limited text sample if the word shares the same meanings it has in our own culture. From context and the later events of Lilith's story, it could have been either one. I suspect, however, that she was referring to the issue of who was brought to orgasm first in their sexual encounters, since she just noted that she didn't bring up the issue of who was *created* first any more. This would explain a lot.

Lilith was obviously a lusty woman and far from inorgasmic, but it is a sad but true fact that it is relatively difficult for women to have an orgasm after their partner has had his and loses his erection, at least if that partner is somewhat selfish and inclined not to continue stimulation in other ways. 'Man on top' is a position that often slows down a woman's progress to orgasm while increasing the man's. Was Adam a wham-bam-thank-you-ma'am kind of guy? It's *hard* to say. So to speak.

and doing the job Inanna had given me without Adam's help. It was annoying beyond all measure that Adam was, apparently, *not* capable of taking care of *him*self and as far as I could tell *had* no job that he was doing for God. What he appeared to do a lot of the time was sit around making up rules, one of which was (of course) that I had to take care of him and do whatever he said. Leaving that one aside as obviously self-serving and utterly ignorable, the rest of them seemed to me at the time to be equally inane and irrelevant. For example, he carried on quite a bit one day about "graven idols" and how bad it was to worship them.

I stood there, perplexed, trying to remember the presence of idols of any sort (graven or otherwise) in either of our houses and trying to figure out just what he meant by "worship" using my preternatural knowledge. It seemed to involve a complicated set of rituals for petitioning God to get – *something*. Any of many things. Health, love, "money" (whatever that was), long life, the painful and protracted slaughter of one's enemies. Also of *thanking* God, usually for getting at least part of what you wanted for while asking again for the rest. God seemed somehow to be a substitute for one's own hands, one's own brain – an easy path to success by prayer instead of hard work.

Worship was also – and this one I simply could not understand no matter how hard I tried – all about *fearing* God, viewing anything bad that happened as a *punishment* instead of stupidity or bad luck or laziness, thinking of God as some sort of raving lunatic that would apply *eternal* torments to Its own creations if they didn't obey Its every whim as communicated by Its prophets and priests. A tiny, tiny portion of worship appeared to be something that I took for granted and did *all the time* – *loving* God unconditionally and feeling God's constant touch upon my soul, at that immutable point where God watched with me as we experienced creation together. It was beyond being silly – it was open insanity.

How could one possibly *fear* the One who Watched at the point where the watcher watches the world? One who was filled with perfect compassion, who *was* the spirit of the world, who was Being to the eternal and infinite exclusion of non-being?

It bothered me so much that I walked in twilight beneath the scented trees of Eden with Inanna at my side, trying to get Her to explain fear and worship to me, when all the while her Presence filled me, as it always does, with peace and an utter *lack* of fear, even the minor and body-driven fear of simple pains like stubbing one's toe or being stung by a bee.

The descriptions of "worship" I recited – some involving killing small animals or even people, others of which involved kneeling down in a crowd and closing one's eyes while reciting or singing unbelievable things all together (as if that somehow made them believable) – caused God to laugh out loud, an answer in and of itself, I suppose. Those of "fear", on the other hand made Her look pensive and sad and refuse to speak beyond calling the fear of Her a "side effect of being trapped in time's stream, of entropy" where one can easily lose sight of the eternal nature of Being in the churn of small creations and destructions during the process of Becoming, of change. However, she did have words for me on the nature of idols, words that in some small way gave me insight into what Adam *might* have been attempting.

"Lilith, darling Lilith – you know Me directly, but even as you do, so do you also realize that this form with whom you apparently speak is just a *metaphor*, a symbol, a construct. It is not the reality of Me. How can *all* things, *all* times, *all being* be compressed into human form and walk and talk like a finite, mortal man? Or woman? Or something even more abstract and metaphorical, such as a burning bush, the sun, a tree, a cross? Yet time and again, you and your descendants will confuse Me with those metaphors."

"Symbols of all sorts are not the reality. The map is not the territory. Over the many years of the future, people will create many *things* – idols, if you like – that are supposed to represent *Me*. These symbols will inevitably represent Me only in *projection* – a brazen bull as the *symbol* of my power, even though that power is equally well within rocks, within moths, within tiny grains of interstellar dust. This projection of my Self onto familiar symbols that they can grasp within their minds will lead to many, many attempts to control reality by means of manipulating the symbols."

"Over time, humans will then invent many rituals for invoking My power through these symbols. This they will call 'worship', but in reality it will be nothing but self-seeking, control-seeking, power-seeking. Indeed, they will offer up to Me a pale reflection of what their *own* egos crave from those people around them, from the world that surrounds them *because* they seem to be finite in space and in time, *because* they are weak and helpless in the grip of an impersonal reality, *because* they do not know the eternal Me – as if I care about being 'worshipped' in this way, or will grant 'favors' to the worshipper on the basis of how earnestly I am asked. The *reality* of 'worship' is nothing like what they will assert – it is mere awareness of My Self within you. It seeks nothing, asks nothing, asserts nothing. It merely Is."

"To you who were created in this state of perfect 'worship', it is as natural and inescapable as breathing, but within *all of those souls* that you awaken – including Adam's – it will *not* be, Lilith. For them the symbols threaten to *overwhelm* the reality, to push them *away* from true knowledge of Self, to create a dark and evil world of fear, of power, of attempts to control the real with 'magical' rituals. Very, very few people, over all of time, will be gifted with any sort of power over reality that functions directly through their will that My Will be Done, and none of them will use symbols of any sort to do it. You are one of them."

"Indeed," and here God sighed, and looked as though for a moment She was actually suffering, but with her eyes focussed on something beautiful in some distance only She could see, "the worst form of idolatry will not be the worship of the 'graven image' in the form of statuary or paintings, but rather worship of the *written word*, the worship of *scripture itself* as a graven image. People will try to trap Me within a web of words, words, words – scriptures and sermons, prayers and rituals, putting their own greedy and controlling words into My mouth. In My name they will kill, they will torture, they will fight, they will cause *such* pain. When all they have to do is to open their inner eye and find Me right there within them, within all things..."

This gave me much to think about then, and much to think about in the years to come. Evolution is the sword that sharpens itself, the life that makes itself, the process where order and beauty emerge from chaos using chaos itself as the crafting tool. Scripture, even *bad* scripture, is needed to fuel evolution by providing a basis for *judgement*, not by God but by the system itself that is evolving that it may maintain structure as it improves. However it has to be *abandoned* to complete the journey, because the ultimate goal is not a *system*, it is the union of an individual living soul with God, one soul at a time. But this is something I did not understand at that time. How could I? I still lived in the transcendent state of union myself, plucked *out* of evolution within time's stream to be a spark so that out of the darkness might emerge *light*.

Alas, one thing Inanna would not do is tell me of her plan for Adam, or elucidate (beyond this) just what it was that he was doing for the world. She would only tell me that it was complex, and it was important, and that it would take me many years and a great deal of suffering to understand; that it was not a thing that *could* be told, only experienced. As always, though, She had a gentle half-smile as She said this, as if it were at once a blessing in disguise and a cosmic joke.

This left *me*, of course, with the problem of what *I* was going to do with, or about, Adam. Knowing that he was a part of God's Plan didn't make him any easier to live with. Maybe his problem was some sort of inferiority complex and not exactly selfishness. Maybe it was something God *did* tell him when they were alone together – I wasn't there and cannot say, and if God (in Its wisdom) fragments Itself into man and woman and creates this tension between them, one only hopes that God knows what It is doing.

I didn't even *know* whether or not to believe that Adam's irritating features *were* a part of God's plan per se. God as much as admitted that for the Universe to contain Free Will, God Itself couldn't foreknow the outcome except in a reunified state in which the passage of *time* no longer occurs, and the Universe itself becomes once again an abstract four dimensional crystalline solid, immutable, a book upon a metaphorical shelf.

Since it was a matter of my direct observation that in fact Adam was jealous and insecure, that he used his free will to try to assert himself as the dominant human, that he even tried to reinvent his personal past so *he* was the first human and hence closest to God – how could all of these *false* things, these *bad* things (bad in some sense I was still struggling to identify) be a part of God's plan? Land sakes alive[6], Adam persisted in identifying God as a "man", projecting his *own* image onto that of God in *direct contradiction* of what God had told me Itself in the *female metaphor* of Inanna. Of course it also violated any semblance of common sense, at least if one took into account one's preternatural knowledge of evolution, of the role of sexual reproduction in the process, of the utter irrelevance of sex to the One! By Inanna's useless nipples, what does Adam think God's penis could possibly be *for* in the context of eternal/cyclic recreation of an infinity of parallel universes?

Thus storm clouds gathered on the horizon, as we each freely chose

---

[6]Sorry, the actual text here contained a basically untranslatable exclamation of surprise. We do our best, we humble amanuenses, yes? And *my* grandparents were born in Missouri back in the 1800's – I have actually heard this phrase used in earnest conversation...

Eden

our inevitable destiny.

As one might expect *after* learning wisdom and a thing or two about sex *beyond* mere technique, the most important signs of of our eventual troubles occurred in bed. Armed with a preternatural knowledge of lovemaking and with our sexual union blessed by God Herself, I was not shy about pleasure, either giving it or receiving it. At first I could get Adam to try lots of positions, some of which worked *wonderfully* well, for both of us. We tried *everything* that I could 'remember' from a rather large repertoire of 'memories' from the future, although I could never persuade Adam to use *his* similar store to please me, or even himself. He wanted to do it all himself, invent everything himself, and he was *so* cautious, *so* fearful of somehow offending God and being cursed with death.

I quickly learned that if I could move my hips freely, I could effectively pleasure myself against him (and pleasure him at the same time). However, my moving freely seemed to *embarrass* him – he wanted to be in *control*, to be the one who *made* me experience pleasure – or not. He begin to actively seek ways and positions that prevented me from moving lasciviously, and absolutely prohibited me from touching myself – or even him – in pleasant ways, at least in his presence (he could hardly stop me from pleasuring myself in the privacy of my own room in my own house, of course).

Time was always a bit funny in Eden, but its passage was visible there as anywhere by the changes that time wrought. As time passed Adam gradually started to absolutely *insist* on being on top, with me on the bottom, holding as still as I could so that all aspects of our congress were under his control. His stated rationale was strange indeed – this was "to establish the fact that he was closest to the heavens and hence to God". At first I complied with it as sex with Adam with me on the bottom was generally better than sex all alone. It worked because I eventually learned the trick of *taking* my pleasure in this position – Adam was never very good at *giving* me pleasure the way he sought to in this position or any other.

Orgasm or not, though, this position and his rationale for insisting on it were both things I was not comfortable with. My physical stature was less than that of Adam (who was a fine specimen of manhood indeed, big and strong) and because of the physical arrangement of my sexual parts and his, I rapidly learned that I, like the vast majority of all women in the past or the future, *preferred* to take my pleasure on top, or at least lying side by side. I found Adam's weight stifling after a short time of lying beneath him, and needed room to be able to move my hips easily to achieve the desired degree and form of stimulation I needed to achieve orgasm, at least from conventional sex.

I might have liked Adam on top better if he had cooperated with my needs, but he rarely took the trouble to support even part of his own weight, preferring to thrust into me to the point of pain against the resistance of my buttocks trapped against the ground, with his weight interfering with my breathing. He even held my hands by the wrists back against the bed so that I could not touch him with my fingers. He transformed me from an active participant in a beautiful act into a passive receptacle of his thrusting and eventual ejaculation.

How confusing this was to me! How angry it made me, when I permitted myself to think about it. Somehow Adam "forgot" that his first conscious experience involved divine sex with *me* on top and closer to the "heavens" (whatever they were and whatever they had to do with anything, given that a symmetric space-time *has* no top, or bottom, and that God said nothing at all about a place or concept called "heaven" in our conversations). Besides, God was sitting off to the *side* when we made love that first time, and I am certain that God walks by our side – or even *in*side of us – every instant of every day. God is clearly omnidirectional in a symmetric Universe, but Adam behaved in all ways as if God was watching from somewhere *overhead*, to the point where he imagined that God somehow couldn't *see* us if we weren't exposed to the sky. Most strange and even a bit crazy, but Adam did not take correction well and I left it alone.

Ultimately, our sex became some sort of message, a kind of expression of rage at being ensouled *second*, directed straight at God. Adam best liked to have sex with me flat on my back and him on top, naked, outdoors underneath the open sky, with *my* ass getting pounded into the dirt, *my* hair getting full of twigs and leaves, *my* back getting gouged by rocks or getting all itchy from the grass. Right out there where God could see that Adam was *superior*, that Adam came *first*.

Eventually this came to be *true* – sexually, at least – and a lot of times I didn't get to 'come' at all. It got so I wore clothes nearly all of the time just so I could use them as *some* form of cushioning beneath my hair and my ass, even though the process usually stained and soiled them or even ripped them to where they were useless afterwards. Giving me, of course, a perverse form of pleasure as it forced me to constantly choose *new outfits* out of my self-renewing wardrobe[7].

---

[7]I'm really, really tempted to observe here that this makes it entirely plausible

Indoors, especially in *my* house and bedroom, it was a whole different ballgame. There, as long as we couldn't be seen from the sky I could at least *sometimes* employ the full repertoire of my sexual knowledge, and even more rarely Adam would unwind enough to use a bit of his on my behalf. This gave me enough of what I needed to keep me sane, but Adam still *preferred* to receive rather than to give, ideally to receive while he was on top of me or I was on my knees before him, one way or another, just as he preferred for me to eat off of my own plate and only after he was sated with the food I'd prepared for him, just as he preferred for me to pick up the mess he regularly made of his house, as he preferred for me to do as I was told, as he preferred for me to follow him around and do nothing but attend him as *he* 'did' his important work, whatever that might have been (I couldn't see that he did much of anything, really).

I got tired of it, and spent more and more time alone, or at least not in the company of Adam. I spent day after lovely day just wandering Eden and giving souls to the birds, the animals, the fish, even the rocks and the trees. But alone is *lonely*; God (and evolution, I suppose) made me to want both human companionship and lots of sex and for better or worse Adam was the only significant source of either one (Bast and Rex and their families being less than ideal substitutes). So sooner or later I'd go over to Adam's place and clean it up to the point where I wasn't actively made sick by the dirt, fix him a decent meal, and seduce him, preferably indoors and on his bed after changing the filthy sheets.

I didn't think to count the days, back in our earliest time together – time was a miracle, something for *experiencing* moment by moment and not for counting as I didn't really understand the concepts of *age* and *mortality*. So I have no idea how long we lived thus – it might have been months, it might have been centuries. There was a timeless character to Eden; perhaps this is why it had to end, as it was too close to the time-ending reunification that occurred when I fell into God's eye to allow one to change, to grow. A story has to have a plot of sorts, with conflict and tension and eventual resolution and rebirth,

---

that woman's natural tendency to Shop – especially for clothes – is some sort of divine punishment visited upon mankind everywhere for Adam's lack of consideration for Lilith. I'm tempted, but of course I will resist because my wife will eventually read this and doesn't need the encouragement to add yet another lick on Lilith's behalf. Besides, evidence provided later suggests that God as Inanna – at least – liked to shop. Shopping behavior in women *or* men may in fact be a kind of *worship*.

or it becomes a mindless repetition, and *mindlessness* is the same as *nothingness*. It is difficult to be mindful and sensually deprived – my preternatural knowledge told me that it was even dangerous and led to madness and mind death.

I do remember well, though, the other continuing source of tension between Adam and myself. No matter how many times he had sex with me beneath the open sky with him on top, no matter how many ways I would gratify him, no matter what menial tasks I would perform for him (all of which helped, I'm sure, to establish his dominance and closeness to God at least in his own mind) he simply could not ignore the fact that I could, and did, give things *souls*.

Not just living things. Our houses, for example, and my favorite rock next to the stream. The stream itself, one day when I let myself be charmed by it's silky waters and soft babbling. Then there were the birds and beasts throughout the valley of Eden – pretty much anything was worth loving if you viewed it the right way. At first I did it all the time, as much in love with the ability itself as with the things I loved. When I saw what it did to Adam, though, I became more subtle, and granted smaller, quieter souls to things, usually in private. In time, nearly everything in Eden came to partake of God as my love spread over the valley like a warm blanket.

Adam, on the other hand, was both afraid to try and desperate to try to give things life to prove that he too was a lifebringer. From the very first day of our existence when he saw me give a soul to Rex, he was absolutely insistent that we find something *important* for him to give life to, with the clear implication being that the things *I* brought to life were not important enough to warrant *his* attention.

The truth of it was that he was afraid of Soul – his own and everything else's. Adam was afraid of *God*. There was something he had gleaned from his first few glimpses of his preternatural knowledge that frightened him. For all of his bombast and bluster about being first and being in control, Adam was in truth a timid soul. Perhaps also one of the things that he feared was to *fail* – Adam could not stand being second to me in any way, which was a real shame given that he was in *truth* second to me in nearly *every* way[8]. This fear, alas, was justified.

---

[8]There was nothing wrong with Lilith's ego, that's for certain. Although this conclusion is, unfortunately, borne out in pretty much its entirety by the rest of her story, we her humble translators and readers need to remember that it is *her*-story, not necessarily *his*-story.

Sorry about that. I'm so ashamed.

Eden

It happened one day on a walk we took together through Eden after we had made love all night long at *my* place, with both of us naked and me on top, on the side, on the bottom, on my knees, and even Adam had gotten into the spirit of things and spent a bit of time on *his* knees for *my* pleasure. I was feeling all grand and bubbly inside, and was actually glowing just a bit as I walked, shedding little bits of life onto the grasses, the trees we passed, the brook we bathed in. I had already quickened the spirits of most of the *common* animals of Eden – things of fur and feather or cold wet scales, things with crunchy exoskeletal carapaces and many legs, even slimy things that lived under rocks.

Adam was a bit moody, the way he got when he was either scared or feeling inferior and humiliated. I saw him carefully scanning every bush, every tree as we passed it, looking for something. Guessing that he was at long last screwing up his courage to try his hand at lifegiving, I joyfully enough joined in the game and started looking for some animal without a soul for him to try with.

For a long time we saw no animals to quicken the spirits of at all, and Adam didn't want to try his art first on a tree or a rock. We wandered farther and farther away from our trees, to a part of Eden I'd never visited up on the slope of a gradually rising hillside above a swampy area. Finally, as we were passing a fruit tree and I was reaching up into it to retrieve what my preternatural knowledge identified as "an apple"[9], preparing to bless fruit and tree alike with a spirit as I savored the impossibly remembered taste, Adam spied a living creature that in fact I had never before seen up in its branches.

A moment spent "remembering" revealed that this was a *snake* – a cold-blooded reptile that dined on rodents and other small animals. In particular it was a kind of hooded snake, a cobra that used venom injected through hollow teeth to paralyze nerves and dissolve flesh and bone, to kill and pre-digest its prey. Its brain was very simple and incapable of deep thought, and it was not, truthfully, very lovable – even with a soul it would be little more than an organic machine. However, it was lovely in its glossy scales, and it kept the populations of various pests under control, and in spite of myself I could feel just enough appreciation for the works of Inanna's hand (even dangerous

---

[9]Actually, it probably was *not* an apple, as apples don't do too well in subtropical near-desert climates. Maybe it was a mango, or a litchi nut, or a date, or an orange. There is no way for us to tell from either hieroglyph or cuneiform exactly what fruit it might have been, only that it was a fruit, or possibly a nut. This, then, is a case of *cliche-ic license* on my part.

works) starting to flow from me towards the poor thing when Adam stopped me with a word.

"It's *my* animal! *I* want to do it," he said, and started to move forward.

"Careful," I said. "It is venomous and dangerous for all that it has no legs. Don't you 'remember'?"

"No," he replied. "How can I remember that which I have never seen? It is the first of its kind, and is so *beautiful*. Surely God will protect me as I grant this important creature a soul."

I wasn't so sure about that. First of all, if what God and my preternatural knowledge told me was true, we were currently living in an accidentally isolated valley of an entire, huge planet that was in turn an almost vanishingly small part of the Universe, which in turn was just *one* of an infinite and eternal train of Universes, each unique, cast like dice or blown like bubbles into an Empty Everything that was distinguished from the Empty Nothing by the existence of the omnipresent mindful One. Out there in the rest of the world there were *lots* of snakes and other reptiles mindlessly eating and being eaten, being hatched from leathery eggs and dying, without a spark of self-awareness among the lot; there was no question that this particular *species* with its hooded neck was very dangerous indeed.

However, I did not know what God had told Adam, and God hadn't even told *me* anything about Eden. Eden itself, as was most of the rest of my actual life, seemed off-limits to my preternatural knowledge.

I felt a bit better as the snake came easily off of its bough and into his hand, with its head reared back and hood fully erect but without striking at Adam or indeed doing anything but looking at him with its black, beady eyes, eyes devoid of any spark. Neither hostile nor affectionate, it wrapped itself around his arm as it had about the branch and tolerated his stroking of the back of its head and hood with gentle fingers.

Adam was entranced. I could see God's love building up inside of him, and his hand began to glow with a white fire even brighter than my own. His eyes became distant as he felt the power of God within him surge forth, even as my own had done so many times now. He touched the back of the snake's hood and blessed it with a spirit of its own. The light went into the snake, and the very mark of Adam's fingers were left imprinted on the *genes* of the hood as spectacle-like marks.

Adam gave a sigh and swung around to look at me with something like bliss in his eyes, with more peace and love on his face than I'd ever seen there.

I often wonder how it all might have turned out if we hadn't come upon a *snake*, and a poisonous one at that. Or if I hadn't done Rex that very first day before Adam had a proper chance. Maybe it was God's Will that we each quicken the beast that was sent to our own house and by doing Adam's I departed from that Will and was curséd. How can anyone ever know? The part of me that still loves Adam, that has always loved Adam, that forgives him for all of the evil he wrought, that part remembers that look of bliss and believes with all of its heart that it might have been different.

The snake bit him. Of course.

What else could one expect a self-respecting, self-*aware* snake to *do?* A snake uses its venom as a defense. It is *evolved* to do that, as snake is very tasty to any number of predators. Even non-predators can damage a snake by merely stepping on it. A snake's venom says "don't tread on me" and it *uses* it when, in a natural state and aware of itself and the possibility of death, it believes itself threatened.

Adam gave a little scream and flung the snake from him into the bushes, where it lost no time in slithering away. He then began to cry bitter, bitter tears. His hand where he had been bitten was already beginning to swell, and a clear liquid was oozing out of the holes left from the bite of the snake. My preternatural knowledge showed me one way to save Adam's life at some risk to myself. I said a quick prayer to Inanna – one of the first times I remember ever praying *for* something – and put my lips across those holes to suck and spit, suck and spit – I was there so fast (and the snake had bitten so fast, and perhaps hadn't injected too much venom) that I got almost all of the venom out before it had time to diffuse into the surrounding tissue, and got it out of my mouth quickly enough that I experienced only a bit of numbness and tingling from the poison I absorbed through my tongue and my gums.

Half supporting Adam with my shoulder I got him back to his house and into bed, and then waited on him night and day while the traces of venom that I had failed to get worked their inevitable will on his body and mind. He became stiff and his breathing labored, and then it stopped. I closed my eyes and let all of the love that was in me, all of the spark of God in my soul, build up into a ball of fire within my head until I was about to burst, and then placed my lips on his and breathed it into him. For an hour I breathed for him, praying all the while, and finally he began to breathe again on his own.

This was the crisis, and thereafter he improved until one day he arose from the bed and once again made his way about Eden, but now the beasts of the field and forest were all his *enemy* until proven otherwise, and since he *would* not use his preternatural knowledge to separate the dangerous from the safe, he could not bring himself to ever again trust paradise. It is as if he reached up into that tree to pluck from it knowledge of self and God and love, and instead reaped a harvest of ignorance and of death.

After this tumultuous event we lived for many years thus, together and apart, as natural man and woman, with Adam ever seeking to be on top in all ways, ever jealous of my power of soulgiving and my being first. Still, it was a zesty, lovely time for the two of us, filled with sex both good and mediocre, with great food, with *fabulous* new outfits, and with the true joy of soulgiving to top it all off (at least for me). Even Adam seemed to get some similar satisfaction from working on his set of rules. It might have gone on this way forever.

Of course, making love as often as we did, in the fullness of time I swelled up like an apple[10] myself, with an appetite grown fretful and perverse and an *insistence* that either I be on top or both of us lie side to side while making love as otherwise Adam was left absurdly riding the boulder that was my belly. Besides, I couldn't seem to breathe properly *without* Adam lying on top of me. Then one day, when my backed ached terribly and my swollen belly seemed about to burst, a gush of blood and water *did* burst from between my legs, absolutely *destroying* my favorite pair of shoes. Moments later I was stricken with cramps that made me feel like I was being torn in two.

Adam came to my screams and did his best, bless him, to support me and care for me, in spite of the fact that I was, I'm afraid, less than charitable towards the man and the process that had left me in such a painful state. Never think that Adam was wholly *evil*, or even that he was really *bad*. He was just *weak*, he was *jealous*, he was *greedy* and even so only in certain areas – he could also be generous, strong, and trusting as it suited him.

Well, here preternatural knowledge was really useful and both Adam and I used ours (although he called his "instinct" after the fact,

---

[10]Or whatever... more likely a watermelon.

in his preening and his pride) and a half-day or so later I was holding a small wizened person that clung greedily to my rapidly freshening breasts. Adam used just enough of his preternatural knowledge to realize that here, at last, was a living being with a soul that he had, in his own fashion, planted. I diplomatically refrained from pointing out that the essential part of his role in this had taken him about twenty extremely pleasant seconds and one ejaculation, while mine took nine months and a birthing in blood and pain. Instead I exercised one of *my* prerogatives based on all of that work.

"His name is Cain," I said.

Chapter 5

The Flood

Cain became a calendar and a clock, as did John, and Tommy, and Steven, and finally my delight, my love, my beautiful baby Sally[1] who turned out to be my only girl. Children grow at a fairly predictable rate. So I can now say that from the birth of Cain we lived for about fifteen more years in Eden, for Cain was as tall as I was and just starting to show the first signs of a beard when we were forced to leave.

Although the birth of Cain had to some extent reconciled Adam and myself – enough that we continued to sport together and produce a new child every two or three years – we also continued to grow apart in many ways. Adam – naturally – blamed *me* for the snakebite, you see, in spite of the fact that I openly warned him against giving the snake a soul, at least while handling it. Adam also continued to be almost mad with jealousy at my power to safely grant things life where he now absolutely refused to even try, not even with a slow and stupid reptile that we found one day wandering through the valley while carrying its house upon its back.

Adam compensated for this by emphasizing the importance of *his* role in the one place he could demonstrate the power of creation. That is, sex with Adam On Top to well and properly cork that juice up

---

[1] Obviously it is impossible to translate the original text as far as names are concerned as we lack a phonetic scale. I assign Cain because, as you will see, that is the correct historical designation for Lilith's (*not* Eve's) firstborn. The rest of the names I just made up. They're as good as or better than something silly and biblical sounding like Seth, Enos, Kelimath, names which cannot be reconciled with any biblical account anyway given that the Bible somehow left Lilith herself almost entirely out.

inside of me where it would make more *babies*. Making babies became a number-one virtue with Adam from the moment he saw how it worked.

Naturally, Adam refused to *care* much for those babies once they were produced, or to care for the children into which they grew, or even to care for himself. He was too busy, as it turned out, with his "work". All *I* had to do was – wait for it – anything he wanted. Lilith the slave girl. So much for my own free will.

To help assert his "control" over me and the children and pretty much everything else in the universe, Adam spent most of his free time (that is to say, nearly *all* the time in a place like Eden) inventing a new thing he called "sin". Basically, anything that *he* thought *we* should do was held to be God's will and hence something that could not be opposed without risk of more snakebites. Anything to the contrary was deemed to be a sin. Sex with me on top was a sin. Sex side by side was a sin. My pleasuring myself without his participation was a *big* sin, one that kept him from having yet another shot at planting a baby inside of me. Sex with me on my knees and pleasuring him with my mouth and vice-versa was a sin (and seemed equally unlikely to produce more babies), but somehow Adam relished *that* sin as much as I did (on a good day when I was actually feeling fond of him and pretty well satisfied myself).

To accompany all of these sins – so many that *nobody* could keep them all straight or avoid committing a few of them, not even he himself[2] – he also invented "seeking forgiveness" and "penance" as ways of making up for it to God when he sinned. In his mind God was somehow tallying up sins all the time and preparing to Smite us in Her Anger if we committed too many, possibly by sicking another snake on us or even worse. Altogether, Adam spent a huge amount of his time making up rules, including rules that we all broke all of the time and that Inanna couldn't *possibly* have cared about in the slightest. Some of them he'd then turn around and throw out again, or even make up a new rule that said the opposite – his own mind was far from clear about just what was a sin and what wasn't.

For example, sometime after the snake incident he had decided that clothes were really a good idea after all, since boots and pants and gloves protected against snakebite (and mosquito bites, and bee stings, and sunburn, and freezing his balls off, and many other evils of the world that existed even then, even in Eden). Fine. I agree.

---

[2] It becomes clear later that *Adam* was illiterate and never learned how to write. Lilith, possibly drawing on her preternatural knowledge, ultimately was prolific.

Instead of just saying "Gee, I guess I'll wear clothes after all," instead of just *wearing* clothes as it suited him to do so, no, Adam had to go and make it a *sin* not to wear clothes. Of course we both still went naked much of the time indoors, of course the children (and I myself) ran around naked and swam naked during good weather, but by golly it was now a sin and we all had to try to wear clothes to be Good instead of using our heads and wearing clothes simply when we wanted to or it really was necessary for protection.

Adam never understood the clothes closet concept, either. His idea of a wardrobe was, well, a robe. I swear that the man was the laziest thing I ever saw and would lounge around until noon-thirty wearing a bathrobe and sandals and then decide not to change the rest of the day. As time passed, his closet somehow started to conform to his wishes (as did mine, much more flamboyantly) and produced mostly coarsely woven white cotton or woolen robes.

I didn't care – *my* wardrobe consisted of form-fitting pants, comfortable soft sweaters made of a kind of wool called cashmere, silk skirts, shoes and boots and sandals of all sizes and shapes and coordinated colors – I *loved* to get dressed every morning. To justify his laziness Adam started to mumble about sin when I dressed up beyond his boringly robéd state (which was nearly every day) but I ignored him and eventually he quit. Even Adam was wise enough not to buck something as fundamental to human nature as wearing nice clothes by turning it into a sin.

After Sally, though, *I* had had enough – of having children, now that I had a baby girl to love along with all of my boys – and just plain quit. Although my preternatural knowledge included an awareness of a variety of means of contraception both natural and artificial, although our houses would cheerfully enough provide the means for the latter (which would just "show up" in a bedroom drawer on demand), Adam was *bent* on producing more children, preferably sons, to show how superior he was, and they were, compared to me in particular and girls in general. He was actually somewhat resentful that I'd produced even *one* girl and muttered for a few days about it being a sin to have done so before the looks I gave him as I nursed the little dear convinced him that it was all his balls were worth to me for him to continue.

Anyway, I was dead tired of changing diapers, cleaning up vomit, swelling up like a balloon, all with little to no help from either Adam or the other boys. My once smooth belly had taken on the look of rough bark (soft as it still was) and my once beautiful breasts were sagging more and more after each baby and covered with a fine web of stretch marks. Adam seemed to take less interest in my body than once he had, where before I was able to hold him somewhat in thrall even when he was in one of his sin-crazed moods just by getting naked in his presence. I began to suspect that *he* was "sinning" by pleasuring himself from time to time, especially during the last few months of each pregnancy when I was swollen and peevish and not at all interested in being on anything *like* the bottom during sex.

So when Adam showed signs of interest in planting number six as Sally started to nurse less and my monthly flow returned, I Just Said No[3].

That moment was really the end of paradise.

I wasn't *mean* about it. I gave Adam a clear choice. He could continue to enjoy having sex with me (with contraception and with me at least occasionally getting to be on top). He could give up sex, at least with me – I made it clear that he was always welcome to pleasure himself, sin or not, and that if he chose this route *I* was certainly going to pleasure *my* self as often as I liked. Or he could work out some sort of arrangement with one of the animals, if one of them would endure his attentions. However he decided, I was hoping that he would continue to live nearby to me and help raise our children.

Adam *could* could have been *reasonable* about things and acquiesced in one of these choices. He could even have been *un*reasonable and stormed off and held out for a restoration of the status quo. If he'd done either of these things, who knows? In four or five years we might have even tried for number six, as I really did love all of my babies. Including him.

Instead he railed on about how Man was the Progenitor and I his Fertile Field, how sex with *me* on top was a sin, how my provocative clothes were a sin, how touching myself was a *big* sin, how he was Closest to God and In Charge, and how I had to Submit to His Will and make more babies for him just the way God intended. Boy babies, preferably, although he would accept either flavor if that be God's Will.

This was so ludicrous (and I was so tired, so damned tired, of putting up with his nonsense) that I laughed. Not even at him, really – *he* was just plain a sad figure, not a funny one. Just at how silly all this sounded. I fully expected him to leave, go back to his house, and figure out how to live with some sort of moratorium on babymaking (as opposed to sex) as I wasn't going to budge.

---

[3] Capitals my own, of course.

The Flood

Instead he hit me, raped me, and, while I lay there unable to move in a state of shock, burned my house-tree down, screaming curses down upon my head. Bast died in the flames, although Bast's offspring lived on and live on still, all gifted with souls as they find humans with souls to love and be loved by, and my owls flew away never to be seen again.

Bruised, naked, bleeding between my thighs and where he struck my mouth, my nose, my cheeks with his fists, I crawled away from the flames, holding my screaming baby to my breasts. As quickly as I could I collected the rest of my terrified children about me from wherever they had hidden from the rage of their father, from the horror of his defiling of my Self, and we fled into the darkness. Cain, as the oldest, was our salvation. He half carried me (and Sally too by extension) until I could support my own weight on my aching legs. We made our way to a grotto in the nearby hills, and there my exhausted children slept on the dirty cave floor, protected only by the clothes they had on at the moment we fled.

I staggered out into the night alone, leaving Cain to watch over his brothers and sisters as long as he could remain awake. I fell to my knees and closed my eyes and looked within my Self for the point where I watched myself watching myself, and called on that part of me that was eternal and unchanging, untroubled by pain and suffering.

A moment later I felt a gentle hand on my shoulder and opened my eyes to see Inanna at my side, infinite compassion in her eyes and the light of the stars in her brow. Her blessing flowed into me and I could feel my bruises and scrapes healing, my belly skin tightening, my muscles again growing firm, and my breasts lifting back into a youthful shape, although they retained something of the size they had attained while nursing many children. She restored me to a level of strength and energy I only now realized upon regaining it that I had gradually lost over time.

"Ah, daughter. It has come to this. Every Universe the same, every Universe different. The wood cries when it feels the sculptor's knife, even as it yields to a shape of great beauty."

I looked at her, seeking an answer, something that made of the filth, the hatred, the horror, something good. "Why?" was all I said.

"You *know* why. That has not changed, will never change. This world is *real*. Reality is *real*. We have made it so, me with my casting of loaded dice and evolution, you with your loving, your living, and yes, with your pain. Adam has the spirit we gave him together, and the ability to be and to choose. He is imperfect. You, my daughter, are far, far better – and still finite and imperfect. If you were perfect you would be timeless and unchanging and boring." Her eyes glinted for a moment and I had a vision of myself plunging in and erasing my Self in the infinity of Her.

"However, you are also *growing*. In time you, and your children, and all that you have brought to life with your love, will grow *together* and will *change* into something good. Something, in fact, *great*. Something greater even than that which We are when you plunge back into my Eye and we become timeless. Remember that time is not what it seems – every moment that passes also remains."

"The same you that is now wounded and sore is also crouching above Adam in a magnificent cloud of light in her love as a baby is conceived, is birthing in pain that baby, who you now hold, is watching that baby grow into a lovely young girl, is stricken with horror and grief as that sweet young girl is senselessly killed. Each a moment of the now eternal, and in the richness of their bittersweet pattern they together form the most precious thing imaginable. It is the nature of things that are not One and that are bound to Time that they contrast and conflict and *change*."

"From beyond, this Universe is a tapestry woven of every thing that ever *is* throughout all time, a beautiful jewel, a story that uplifts the heart, a story with its own soul and spirit, a story that very much *lives*. It All Works Out in the End. I Promise. One day, all your pain will be as nothing, the hint of spice that makes the dish tasty beyond all compare, as you too get to read the book[4]."

"But now we must move on to practicalities. Adam, as commanded by Me, has worked to define sin. Well, his action is most definitely *sinful* by his own rules. Adam defined God's retribution for sin and the need for penance to be absolved of sin, where all you wanted was peace and love and to just get along in freedom without the need for the rules that define sin. Innocence and freedom *is* yours; it was your original gift from Me and I will not take it back. Adam turned his back on freedom and seeks the comfort of bondage to the invisible, to rules, secretly hoping to use those rules to selfishly cheat existence, to cheat *Me*, of that which he has not earned and to avoid death."

"*My* rules cannot be broken. My justice is perfect. I therefore will *give him what he wants* until his distant descendants (and yours) learn to break free, to use their heads, to find Me without the bondage of

---

[4]God *did* like a good mixed metaphor, didn't She? Of course, Inanna herself *was* a mixed metaphor of sorts, so it figures...

The Flood

sin."

"For you, as you want nothing but my love I give you nothing but my love – and the freedom you crave. The world is *real* and will hurt you and your children as you permit it to and chance determines, but I *will be with you*, inside of you, at the point where your Self watches yourself watching the world, and such small protections as I can offer without openly violating natural law are yours and theirs."

There was a subtle shift in her eyes, a faraway look that told me (using my preternatural knowledge) that she was making boundary conditional changes *outside* of time, changing the entire past and future history of the Universe while somehow leaving the experiences of the years since our Genesis and the laws of nature themselves invariant. From the sky above, plausibly but improbably came a sword of fire that plunged silently towards the earth somewhere to the south, shedding fiery sparks as it fell. One of those sparks streaked toward the ground somewhere quite nearby. The greater part, though, passed over the horizon to the south[5].

Suddenly, out of the darkness to the south there was a light so bright that it erased even the *memory* of sight in a whiting out of all vision. Afterwards I stood, stunned and blind, until the afterimage of that light slowly faded, leaving me looking at a world gone gray and the half moon grown to a ghostly whole with a fading reflected light flickering in many colors across the dark half. To the south a strange cloud of fire grew into the sky like a beautiful toadstool seen at an odd angle, lit by lightnings.

"Now my daughter, run. Run! *Run* for higher ground! The dice are again cast. Eden (and much else) will shortly be destroyed and the desert will reign where now you sit. I will not guarantee that you all will live – you have to earn life, every day! But *run*."

I raised my tired, sleeping children with a shout, gathered the baby Sally in my arms, and together we ran up the path and into the nearby hills, climbing up a ravine to a set of switchbacks that led us, panting, to the nearest hilltop. After a few hours of climbing the earth trembled with a rumbling almost too deep to be heard and cast us to the ground. We got to our feet and ran again, only to be cast down a short while later by a blast of hot wind and the loudest sound in the world – the

---

[5] As we shall see, this could well be the larger part of the *Hajar al-Aswad*, the black stone that is said to be a remnant of a meteor that fell the feet of Adam and Eve at the very beginning of creation according to Islamic tradition and which is currently housed in the *Ka'aba*, the holiest shrine of Islam. We shall have more to say about this later in Lilith's account.

sound of God roaring in Her anger[6]. Again, we fled, in tears and fear and screams, with knees bloodied and faces scratched by the branches and thorns as we forced our way through.

Panting, we reached a nearly bare hilltop far above the valley below and paused to catch our breath. Looking back, I saw beneath and behind us to the south a strange sight. In the sky was a black cloud that roiled and churned and seethed with lightnings as it sped like a curtain across the land. At its feet was a white wall racing up the river valley. In a panic I pushed and carried my children into a cleft between three huge boulders fallen together to make what was basically an open cave amongst the rocks just over the top of the hill away from the valley, where a shallow wall of rock (that supported the boulders) protected us on the south side.

There on the floor of the cave was the snake that Adam had given a soul. He must have passed more than just a simple awareness on to it in his passion and strength – it had grown great in size, as thick as my thigh and tens of feet long. Its hood was open as it swayed there, looking with strangely intelligent eyes at this flood of foolish humans who were crouching inside and upon its thick coils. Is eyes locked into mine, and I found *my* passion. My need for protection for my self and my children surged out of me and shone like a beam of light into its reptilian eyes. Into its very brain I blasted my urgency, my appeal, my love, *God's* love. The light faded, and I waited for its head to fall, for its fangs to sink into the flesh of me or one of my children.

Suddenly it lowered its hood and slithered around and around within the tiny cave as we picked up our feet to make room for it. We carefully, fearfully settled into the space in the middle as it wrapped its coils around us, anchoring us, throwing a heavy loop over my own

---

[6] As always, Lilith's account rings true. The energy from a nuclear-scale explosion arrives first in the form of light, then as a ground wave, then as a sound wave, and finally as the pyroclastic flow – the hot gas/particulate emulsion that is "the blast", racing across the earth at speeds approaching the speed of sound at temperatures as high as 1000° C. Pyroclastic flow destroyed – and preserved – Pompeii when Vesuvius exploded in 79 C.E.

In this case we can guess that the sound wave outraced the pyroclastic flow at a speed differential of some tens to as much as a hundred meters per second, and that "Eden" was somewhere in the Tigris-Euphrates watershed (not taking the story of the Iraqi maiden too literally as she would have ample reason to safeguard this information). The account is then *consistent* with the main part of the small asteroid having fallen somewhere in the Indian Ocean. The resulting tsunami would have wiped out all human life anywhere near the banks of the Gulf and up the Tigris-Euphrates watershed and could, of course, account for the many flood myths that appear in regional mythologies.

The Flood

legs where I crouched in the mouth of our little grotto. As it settled its head sprang up immediately behind my own, its hood once again extended, but somehow without threat. Its tongue licked out and gently tasted my hair, my ears, the back of my neck as I pressed Sally to my nearly milkless breast and gave her suck.

Outside, the roaring (that had never really stopped from the first blast of real sound) grew and grew until my children clung to their ears and screamed with pain. I watched from where I was held by the snake, kneeling, with my mouth agape with wonder at God's wrath as the dark cloud turned out to be scorching ash and the white spume a little ahead of its base turned out to be a wave of salt water of great force and volume. It roared up the valley, scouring the slopes, its highest levels foaming over the rock wall and reaching out with heavy wet hands to drag me and my poor children from our refuge.

I wedged myself in its only entrance with one arm and my feet, held in place only by the rocks and the strong coil of the snake like a rope across my waist. I held my screaming baby to my breast with the other arm and prayed that the water would not flood any higher. It was difficult to keep our heads all above water, to breathe, but we were fortunate to be soaking wet when we were blasted by that hot wind filled with ash. It scorched my wet naked back and the hood of the snake where it was not actually covered by the water, it set my hair afire at the tips not protected by the snake's great hood, it drove my children to duck their heads beneath the water until the first hot surge of wind passed. I could not duck beneath the water to avoid the heat but a surging wave tumbled over my head and back and put out my burning hair. More waves cooled my skin; neither I nor my protecting snake were badly burned while the scorching wind lasted.

How long we held there, bottled up in our small refuge, I cannot say. Cain was a pillar of strength – without him we would not have all survived. He held his brothers and calmed them; he held his little baby sister and sang to her so that I could use both arms to resist the flood; he and the snake working together held *me* when I tired and could no longer hold on as the cork of our little bottle and was near to being swept away by the howling wind, the grasping currents of the water. Eventually the tumult quieted, the second and third surges of flood came but failed to crest the hill, and the currents across the slope in front of us began to reverse and return once again to the south, running down the hills they had once mounted. The flood water was salt and ash in our mouths, a gritty thin mud as it flowed away. The wind was still very hot and very full of drifting char but no longer blistered my skin where it was exposed as it did before everything was made wet. We all were choking in the smoke, the ash, and the gloom.

A dark gray eternity passed. Eventually something that passed for dawn brought us a dim light through the suffocating clouds of ash that fell like dry rain outside our chamber, turning to mud in every puddle left behind by the surging seas. For hours this continued, but the ashfall slowly grew lighter and a pale sun began to force its way through. The snake swung its head around in front of me and looked me right in the eye. Its hood was ash-gray on the outside and a few scales were missing, but it looked to have taken no real harm. A quiet communication passed between us and it lowered its hood and slithered silently away through the muck, down the hill to the west.

We who remained, myself and blessedly all of my living children, finally dared to step out of our cave and into the pallid sun to take stock.

Below us, where a living paradise once stood, was now a desolate and lifeless hell. No tree, no bush remained on the valley floor or hillside. Every visible surface was coated in several inches of salty wet mud made of earth mixed with ash and seawater. In the valley itself an impossible flood churned down the middle in a thick, brown froth as it made its way back to the sea. This thick soup appeared to be made of mud mixed with objects that might have been trees, animals, people, all anonymously gray from the ubiquitous ash.

Up and down the range of hills one could see the high water mark of the flood on the higher hilltops just at our level – had our hilltop refuge been ten feet lower we would have drowned, had it been ten feet *higher* we would have been scorched to death in the fiery wind. Above the high water mark the skeletons of scorched trees still stood, pointing like skeletal fingers at the sky. I felt a small hand on my hip and looked down at the gray, ash coated face of a child – I couldn't even recognize which one at first.

"Mama?" began John. "I'm hungry."

I looked down at him and forced a smile through my cracked lips. "So am I, honey. So let's go look for some food, shall we?"

And so we turned our backs on ruined Eden and walked away to the west, following the track of the snake through the mud as best we could, seeking food, drink, others of our kind and a place to live.

Chapter 6

Sidon

Outside of our valley there was devastation enough, but nothing like what occurred within. There had been flooding and hot ash aplenty, but the flood was confined by the hills and kept from being more than a muddy nuisance on the plains beyond. It was clear that the sword of God fell into the sea in just the right place to destroy our paradise, nothing more nor less, but spared the rest of still-soulless humanity[1].

Fortunately the weather was warm and clean rains began to fall, day after day, washing the ashy mud from our naked bodies and the salt from the mud so that the ground beneath might one day again bear fruit.

We were also fortunate enough to find puddles of fresh water from this rain, and sometimes springs that still ran clear and clean. Some pools in the higher hills still held fish and frogs, and there were many animals that had survived the heat and the flood through sheer good fortune. Enough of these survivors were crippled or slowed by the ubiquitous mud that Cain and I were able to find meat for ourselves and the children for the first week or so we travelled, and by then we had encountered unburnt grasslands and forests again and began to hope of finding people.

We began our journey all but naked – me because that is how

---

[1] Lilith was not quite correct in this. The meteor doubtless destroyed tens, maybe hundreds of thousands of human lives. However Lilith's preternatural knowledge left her a bit short of intuitively appreciating the likely population density in the cradle of human civilization during this period, in India, in Africa – all swept by the tsunami. After all, the flood myths have the flood destroying the entire world, and *locally* this was *true* even if the tsunami failed to kill a single soul in say, China or even early Phoenicia.

Adam left me, the rest because the race, the flood and the fire tore the clothes off of their backs. Cain and I gradually clothed ourselves and the other children, after a fashion, in the stinking pelts of the animals we killed after my preternatural knowledge guided his hands in the making of an obsidian knife from some of the shards of black glass that we encountered surrounding mounds of strangely melted rocks, some of them still smoking hot, strewn across our path in small craters as if they had been spattered there from the south.

My preternatural knowledge told me that God's sword from the heavens that cast us out of Eden was in fact a small asteroid or comet that had plunged into the ocean far to the south and that what we saw and experienced was but a small fraction of the death caused by this *small* cataclysm. Asteroids that had fallen before had wiped out whole *kinds* of creatures and were a great stimulant to the evolutionary process. It also told me that a large enough asteroid could have wiped the planet clean of life, and perhaps one day would. God in Her compassion had been *merciful*.

Eventually we emerged on the shores of a sea. We turned to the north and walked along its shores, blown clean of ash by the wind and washed clean by the rain, finding plenty to eat in its warm waters and the forests that grew nearby. Finally, nestled among beautiful cedar-covered hills, we found a small city of men built out on a promontory facing an island out in the sea. Most of it was little more than a collection of dwellings formed from packed mud and hewn timber, although there were a few buildings that were made out of stones crudely assembled[2].

Our integration into human society was at first a nightmare. We had to learn the local language, although it was very similar to that which Adam and I had awoken knowing how to speak and taught to our children. I discovered that with my preternatural knowledge I could understand almost any language (a precious gift, as it turned out to be in my wanderings) but only if it was spoken slowly enough that I could keep up a running internal translation. To be able to converse fluently took me *weeks* of practice, and my children took months longer.

This was bad enough, but our bigger problem, as it turned out,

---

[2]This was clearly one of the early Phoenician cities, one with an island offshore. This (and the timing) makes it likely that this was *Sidon*, a city that dates back to sometime before 4000 BCE! However it *could* have been any one of the tiny fishing villages in early Phoenicia, perhaps the one that eventually grew into *Tyre*. Clearly there were many such small kingdoms more or less constantly at war with one another.

was that I had no *man* to protect me and my children (nor did I want one). Neither had we any possessions to trade for food and clothing (for everyone here wore clothing). We arrived filthy and all but naked, half-clothed in stinking animal skins and carrying our crude stone knives. This left me only with my hands, my heart, and my sex and an empty, growling belly, a stranger to a people who knew nothing of charity or duty to the unfortunate traveller.

With my figure restored and starving children to feed, my sex turned out to be enough. Fortunately Inanna had chosen to protect me from having more children (which I did not want) so never again did sex[3] cause a life to quicken within me.

On that first day, though, I found an abandoned dwelling some distance away from the city, on the fringes of the desert but blessed with its own clean well. The reason it was abandoned was quite clear – the gnawed and scattered bones of two people were partially pinned beneath a tree that had fallen nearby, one that might have been pushed over by the blast of wind that arrived even here from the fiery sword of God that destroyed Eden. Many houses in the city were empty, as it turned out, the former occupants killed by the rain of ash or the plague that followed it.

Cain managed to catch some goats that were running loose but not quite wild on the nearby hills and drive them into a pen from which they had obviously escaped. I moved myself and my children into the house, barricaded the door, and set Cain and the other boys to work cleaning it up. There, surrounded by rocks and stones, visited every night by jackals and owls, comforted by bats that flew about by night and a family of cats (descendants, I could tell, of Bast as they carried their souls proudly within them), we prepared to make our home.

Sally was hungry – indeed, Sally was slowly starving as I wasn't making much milk and she had outgrown the need for milk alone even before the disaster. I left her in the arms of John, threw away my rotting loincloth and bathed, and walked naked and unashamed into the town to barter the only thing I had left to trade for food and our other necessities.

As I entered the city, alone, I experienced fear as I had never experienced it before, not even fleeing God's wrath with my children, not even facing starvation and wild beasts in the wilderness. It was as if I were surrounded by the dead; all the townsfolk were *soulless*

---

[3]With *mortal men*, at least. Lilith did in fact bear *one more child*; for reasons that will become apparent she was unable to correct her autobiographical writings.

creatures. Their eyes were empty and devoid of spark as they acted out their parts in a complex play; rising every morning, doing their work, eating their daily bread, pursuing their lusts or fulfilling their needs, all without ever watching themselves watch themselves – biological machines, every one.

The men saw me, half naked, impregnable, well formed, and highly desirable as a mate into whom they could inject seed and so sire descendants carrying their genes. This released chemicals in their innermost brains, their reptile brains, so that they lusted after me. However, they did not *love* me – they did not love even their own wives or children.

The women – those wives – saw me and still other chemicals were released that caused them to *resent* me as a threat to *their* genetic inheritance, to their hold over the man who supported them and provided for their children. Yet they, too, did not hate me – they merely acted out their evolutionary parts, where every thought fell from that which proceeded it without any free choice.

Without guilt, without shame – for necessity knows no shame and I would not let my baby starve – I bargained openly with the men using the crudest of sign language to work out the arrangement. In order to fulfill their lusts on me, the men had to give me some measure of that which I needed – grain, meat, pots and jars, firewood, tiny bits of shiny metal or colorful rocks, small chips of carefully carved wood that could be exchanged for the above, each merchant with their own pattern. They then were permitted to lead me back into an alley, where I did my best to earn that which they had given me so that I could return and bargain anew in days to come.

I returned to our small hut that first day sore and soiled, but with *food*, enough for some weeks if we eked it out with animals we hunted down ourselves in the desert, with crude pots to cook it in, with a few pieces of old cloth to use as bedding and clothing alike, and with a number of wooden chips to be used against our future need. Cain, John, and Thomas, bless them, had found an old broom and swept out our hovel, collected firewood, and had a small fire going on which I cooked our first meal without the need of our sacrificing one of the precious goats. They had managed to milk one of the nannies who had kids and give Sally at least a few sips of the milk to stay her hunger.

Sally was thin and somewhat ill as I had been hard pressed to feed her on our journey, but an hour later she ate boiled and softened grain and a tiny bit of boiled fish with relish and immediately looked better, as indeed did we all when we had bathed with water from the well and dressed ourselves after a fashion. We went to bed with the sun as we had no money for oil or lamps, threw our remaining rags over the pile to keep warm, and shivered through the cold night huddled together. The wild beasts scratched at our door to get into our food (and, we imagined, our selves) but it was no worse than it had been many nights of our journeying.

So it went for some hands of days, with me conducting a brisk business and learning the local dialect so that I could bargain all the better, while gradually accumulating the necessities of life and even some luxuries by the standards of Sidon's society. Soon I had an "established" clientele and no longer had to go into town, the men of the town would come out to me.

This was better all around, as I did not have to confront their wives, and we could take a bit of time in the act with a bit of privacy. My regular clients included the king of the city himself and many members of his council, the wealthiest and most powerful men in town. Their gifts and favor soon permitted us to improve our ramshackle quarters, to buy new livestock to keep, to build something of a wall surrounding the house so that Sally could play outdoors without the fear of being carried off by wolf, bear, jackal, or even lion. Ultimately we stayed there for years, living all but alone in the desert where I could conduct my business in privacy while the children, playing or working outside, were safe.

Although my work was *formally* frowned on by nearly everyone as threatening the bonds that held man and woman together for raising their children, in truth was openly tolerated because it *was* nearly the only way a widow could survive and feed her children. A woman's choices were to sell her sex to any male that wanted it or to be taken as chattel by an interested male, perhaps the brother of her dead husband, perhaps a wealthy man bored with his current household, to provide sex and services and children. This was often in addition to other wives the man might have. Here indeed was a culture that Adam would have been very happy in – *men* ran nearly everything.

I was not exactly happy – how could harlotry and poverty be compared with the life I had known in paradise, I who had walked (and *still* walked, of an evening) with Inanna herself? However, my children were *safe* and well-fed, and being a harlot was not terribly difficult for a woman with a preternatural knowledge of harlotry stretching over thousands of years. One could say that I was the *best* harlot that ever lived or would live, for all that my base of clients was, by the standards of the ages, both humble and poor.

My energies were not all spent in harlotry, of course. As I grew content, my spirit expanded enough that my touch once again became a blessing of life. This manifested itself in many ways. For one, I gained quite a reputation as a healer. If my passions were aroused I could often call a sick child back from the very edge of death as I let my soul open and flow into it, driving out the darkness of disease. Many a woman who had at first reviled me ended by blessing me as her dying baby was restored, whole and well, to her arms.

Those who continued to oppose me, who called for me to be stoned or driven from the city or whipped and enslaved, found that my wrath was a fearsome thing and that misfortune, illness, and death haunted their households until they relented. Being beaten and raped by Adam seemed to have awakened within me a terrible, Inanna-given power to do *harm* as well as good, to wither the very life out of the flesh of those that angered me, to inflict the wicked with horrible diseases, even an ability to discern truth from lies by reading the very hearts of those that would dissemble.

I tried very hard to control my dark impulses, the anger that caused me to harm others, but found it nearly impossible to do so when I or my children were directly threatened. In time, though, my presence living on the outskirts of Sidon had a very positive effect on it and the surrounding countryside. The worst of the scum who lived in the town or the nearby hills by thieving or preying on the weak sickened and died in the midst of their debauchery as I discovered them. In a few rare cases, where I could scry out some hope for them in talking with them and others who knew them, they were afflicted with some plague or the other that only "I" could cure, and only then for a price – one that often included both the bulk of their wealth and their heartfelt promise to live without hurting others or – as Adam would have put it – "sinning".

Do not think, either, that I *ignored* the soulless women while entertaining their men. First of all, I wasn't *taking* their men – it was strictly a temporary business transaction, one that was common and (truthfully) even accepted. Second, while I was publicly reviled by the women as a matter of custom, as my reputation as a healer and a witch grew they would bring their children to me in *private* for healing, or come themselves for advice or with some prayer. If they pleased me or were friendly they were likely as not to leave with a new fire kindled behind their eyes, with shiny new souls.

In time, harming few (who well deserved it) and helping many, I was accepted for what I was – one of the wise, a whore, a witch, a healer – a *free woman*, a woman who *owned herself* and lived *without any man*. With the help of Inanna I lived and earned a living as the men themselves lived – by the sweat of my brow[4], selling that which I had to sell and buying that which I needed to live. This, more than any other thing, the men found threatening, but those that dared to act or to incite others to act against me found themselves afflicted with pustulant sores and an unceasing drip from their manhood – until they would drag themselves to my doorstep and beg me for a cure.

As I conducted my own business, I also carried out Inanna's. The men in the city who entered my house with empty eyes glazed with animal lust usually left with eyes opened in wonder as for the first time they were aware of the Watcher who watched themselves watching the world, the spark of God looking over their metaphorical shoulder. In some people this spark quickly damped down and was almost – but never quite – extinguished, as perhaps they did not like what they saw, as they turned their back on the Godhead within.

In other men and women, though, the spark grew to a blaze as great as my own or even greater. Somehow their connection with the great Unseen God would end up capturing their imagination, creating a yearning in their uncertainty that I who could (after all) walk with Inanna herself did not feel. Those men usually would not come back to seek my services again, and for the first time when I went into town I saw those men looking at their own women with something like affection and love. And a few of those women looked *back the same way!*

Thus I discovered that a true, loving soul is *contagious*, each soul a seed that flowers and seeds anew if it falls in fertile soil. I knew then that Inanna's work was well-begun and that in time, even if I were to die the very next day, Soul would spread out from this small beginning and cover the world, even jumping the gap out to the stars themselves, bringing the whole Universe to Life in a blaze of self-awareness.

In the meantime, Cain had made our small herd of goats increase, we had acquired chickens and a few pigs, we had built a tidal pool out of stones in the shallows of the nearby sea to trap fish, and my sons all hunted the beasts of the wilderness for meat to spare the goats. We ate well and even waxed wealthy by the standards of the time and place. All in all, life became comfortable and even Good once again.

---

[4] Metaphorically, at least.

Although the filthy city itself was far from being a paradise, it was far better, and safer, than life in a desert.

Still, I missed my closet full of clothes, my shower, my *toilet*. I missed living in Inanna's tree, with its wise birds in the branches and Bast rubbing his soft fur across my ankles and kittens playing around my feet. I spent many an evening, after the children were all asleep and the men were all gone, sobbing gently into the darkness in regret for all that I might have done differently, all I had lost. However, what I missed most of all was, paradoxically, Adam.

And then Adam arrived.

I did not then know exactly how Adam survived the sword of God that had destroyed Eden. As I learned much, much later, it was through a *miracle*, a miracle that would heal much of the evil of that day. I was not completely surprised; God had spoken to me of Adam's desire for both retribution and penance, and penance isn't too easy to work out if the one atoning is dead. I immediately suspected direct divine intervention.

At *that* time I thought that perhaps Inanna (or more likely, God's He-form in order to get *Adam's* masculine-oriented attention) appeared before Adam and told him to get himself hence. Or that He just arranged it so that Adam was borne up before the flood and never quite hit his head or drowned (where *I* had to take my chances). This made me feel at once bitter and resentful and somewhat relieved that Adam had, after all, survived.

However, Adam was not alone. With him was a woman. Not just any woman, either – physically she might have been my *twin*. This was of course entirely possible – since I have no memory of the time before my awakening I might well have *had* a twin all along. This was made somewhat more likely by the fact that my having had a twin all along, if necessary arranging the entire past and future of the Universe to accommodate it, might well be God's way of "making" such a twin if the need arose.

I was *amazed* at the feelings of rage and resentment that welled up within me as I looked on this sorry excuse for a man, one that had first tried to imprison my soul and make me *his* inferior and chattel and then had rejected me and my love and our children, one who had beaten me with his greater physical strength in anger and then raped me to prove himself the master, one who couldn't or wouldn't even manage to take care of *himself* however quick he was to insist that he was owed the care of others.

Perhaps, in retrospect, I shouldn't have been so amazed. As I had slowly and painfully learned in our new home, this sort of wickedness was pretty much the normal behavior of all the humans I had met so far, men and women alike, except for me and my own children. Rape and all, Adam was fairly *considerate* by the standards of Sidon at that time – men killed their women on a whim and suffered no penalty from it, at least until I arrived and this sort of murder (at least where I discovered it) earned them a horrible death from the plague.

One part of me then (and one part of me even now) still loved Adam, something doubtless rooted in that day where I *first* loved him, where I gave him his miserable soul. When you love a thing that much, when you give *birth* to it as in a sense I did with him, you become responsible for it – I could not *completely* hate Adam without hating myself, any more than I could ever hate Cain or Sally.

I had reasons aplenty to *mostly* hate him, though, and *hatred* turned out to be a strong enough emotion to have almost the same effect as love, from the point of view of stirring up the power of God within me. One day I turned the corner there he was, not fifteen feet away, dressed in a fine robe and followed by a version of "me" with eyes downcast and carrying on her back and head a large burden that somehow I knew was all of their possessions in the world. I froze in my tracks. A minute passed, or maybe it was only a few seconds, with my mind paralyzed by a tumultuous confusion of conflicting emotions. Then rage won out and overwhelmed me. How *dare* he!

From my hands and eyes sprang the very fire of creation, but this fire was somehow a *dark* fire, a soul *quenching* fire, not one of soul *giving*. It flowed down my fingers onto the ground and disappeared beneath the nearby houses. Seconds later there emerged from underneath one house after another a brood of serpents, their knowing eyes glittering wickedly and their hoods expanding. The largest one reared its head up waist high right before me and spit venom straight into Adam's face.

Suddenly there was much consternation in the market square as men attacked the serpents with sticks, killing one while the rest lowered their hoods and easily escaped into cracks and holes beneath the houses. Adam (whose eyes were narrowly missed, alas) was screaming and shouting as the woman who was with him tried to wipe the venom off with a piece of her own clothing while keeping it out of his eyes and away from his mouth. Finally a man brought them a jug of water to rinse his head and face with and he spluttered and dried his face one last time and then there we were, almost close enough to touch, eyes locked together.

"So," I said, with a grimace so tightly drawn that it might have been mistaken for a smile.

"So," he replied. "You live. Shaitan the great Serpent has preserved you and your filth to continue to spread sin and lies throughout the world."

"You bastard," I said evenly, my teeth gritted together, my rage finally corked, bottled, under control. Or so I thought. Why, I was hardly shaking any more and my fingertips no longer spat out foot long sparks of their own accord. "You hit me, raped me, left me and your own children, your own *baby girl* to die. You sinned *by your own rules* before God and have the *balls* to accuse me of being *evil* or the pawn of – what was that? 'Shaitan'? Who is that, anyway? Someone you made up? There is no other but God that we talked to, back there in paradise.."

"No, *I* talked with God, and *He* has blessed me. You talked with another, a woman who is not God, but God's enemy. One who tempted me with Shaitan the great Serpent at the apple tree, the Serpent who is responsible for all of my sins and pain. I tried over and over again to bring you to the ways of virtue and to put aside sin, but you refused, tempting me with your harlot ways and setting yourself over me. I told God all of this and that you *made* me sin in front of the tree and bewitched me with the Serpent, as you bewitched the serpents here once again, as you tried to *kill* me then *and* now."

"God forgave me and listened to my prayer. He made for me another woman, one that *I* have given a soul to, in your image. She is you as you should have been, virtuous and obedient. This is a woman who understands her lack of purity, the *impossibility* that one who bleeds monthly could ever be pure, one who therefore lies on the bottom, closest to the earth while I lie on top and closest to heaven and God while I plant children in her fertile field. This is a woman who does as I wish, who works for me and cares for me as I deserve and require. This is a woman *without preternatural knowledge* and who *makes no souls...*" he finished, his voice having risen almost to a scream, his face reddened in his rage, spittle flying from his twisted mouth.

I looked with sudden compassion on my own form, burdened and bent (although also repaired to a state of youthful beauty not unlike my own) with something, something *rare* that I could not quite make out, something like a trapped bird fluttering within. She had a soul indeed, but it was a caged thing, hidden behind eyes that were like mirrors that repelled my attempts to probe. Wherever I looked, I found only my Self reflected, trapped in a web of duty and submission instead of being allowed to fly free. Tears sprung into my eyes as I was filled with compassion and disgust at this *abomination*. My hands began to glow again as my spirit sought to set things right.

My face suddenly rang from a blow and I found myself on the ground with Adam standing over me, his face almost purple with rage. "*NO!*" he roared. "You shall not cast your spell on her! She is mine! God made her for *me!* She is my Eve."

My mouth tasted coppery with my own blood as I rose to my feet, dark energies mixed with light rippling up and down my arms as the power of God's name came upon me[5]. That power flowed past my feet; I was lifted up from the earth itself by the immense energy that was gathered within me to cleanse the earth of this *woman* with her hideously bound soul, of this Adam that had dared, once again, to strike *me*, who was First and blesséd by Inanna. The townspeople had fallen back and formed a ring around us, astounded by deeds of magic and miracle in their midst, too fascinated to flee.

Then I saw the tears, the resignation in Adam's eyes as he fell back, awaiting my righteous wrath, as I was stronger than he was in my rage, far stronger and more deadly, and *he knew it*. To touch me again was to die, and yet knowing this, he had touched me, so great was his sadness, so great was his need.

I was instantly disarmed as insight swept over me, changing *everything* about how I felt. All my anger and all my power flickered and died, lowering me gently back to the earth.

Gently, slowly, as one might reach out to pet a much loved dog that has nevertheless bitten you, I lifted a hand up and laid it on Adam's cheek to catch a tear on my thumb and gently wipe it away. Suddenly I couldn't stop the flood of tears from my own eyes. His hands, as if of their own accord, lifted up and twined themselves in my hair in a way he knew that I loved. Our eyes reflected ourselves reflecting ourselves

---

[5] This was a bit of a strange passage, given that God is already established to be nameless. We therefore somewhat doubt the translation. However it *could* be that this is the origin of the notion that God's *name alone* carries magical power, that God can be invoked to do Evil through the knowledge of His True Name. Overall this seems pretty dubious, as if God is some sort of 'Simon Says' game with the Universe itself as the stake, but mythopoeic works don't have to be *believable*, only *powerful*, right?

and for a moment...

...time stopped, and we were once again plunging into the well of Inanna's Eye, once again locked together in orgasmic glory on top of a stone table in a small vale outside of time, joined into a One that persisted before, after and during. I saw in a burst of self-knowledge, awakened in that single moment, how everything *wasn't* all Adam's fault and none of my own.

In my pride I *had* preened and flaunted being First. I had been so caught up in the glory of my own existence and freedom that I hadn't much thought about whether or not he, too, was equally free and – I suddenly realized – it was my responsibility to not *only* give him a soul but to set him *free*. Preternatural knowledge *was* dangerous – infinite knowledge, a total lack of wisdom. Wisdom comes from bitter experience and almost by definition comes too late to save at least some of that which needs saving.

I closed my eyes, overwhelmed by the pain of it all, by the loss, by regret at my own mistakes, by anger at his far greater ones. Freedom is the freedom to make mistakes, but it is a high, high price. I suddenly longed to be back in Eden, to have it to do all over again, to make it right, to make it, somehow, *good* again and this time to make it last forever, retroactively. I learned for the first time the full measure of *regret*, of mourning *all* of the immutable past; regret that accompanies all birth and all death, all joy and all pain, all that occurs in time's stream and disappears into the past, never to occur again but *impossible to change*.

I opened my eyes again, seeing Adam's tortured face through a blur of tears. In a choked half-whisper I said, apologizing for the *first time in my life,* "Adam, I'm sorry."

I continued. "I'm so, so sorry. Oh, Adam. Oh, *God!* This *hurts!* Is it really too late for us?" I hesitated, not knowing how to offer that which I was going to offer, not knowing whether or not I was forswearing my own soul or freeing it, "I could try, you know, to let you be on top. It's not *that* important. I could try to be a bit more, well, understanding, to help you, to do what you want, to be what you want..."

"No!" Adam interrupted. His voice was harsh but his hands were gentle and stayed where they were. "Don't you see? Could you bring yourself to become my Eve? You, who ever leads and never follows? You who *were* First? And part of me," he said looking down at the ground in between us, "part of me *loves* it when you are on top, and doing all the other things you did. I have loved you – I supposed I still do – but I also *fear* you, if that makes sense. You are so *strong*, you give off life and love like a holy light wherever you walk. You make me feel ashamed. And I was supposed to be an *equal part* of creation. Wasn't I?" his voice caught in his throat as he choked back a sob.

Adam ever did hide his weakness, his vulnerability, choosing to live within the ramparts of a castle around his Self that was also his prison.

I could hardly see through my own tears, hardly talk through my own sobs. My heart was being torn out of my breast as I experienced more pain than I thought was possible on this earth. I nodded back as best I could. How could I agree to become – that quiet figure that even now stood at his back, waiting imperturbable to be bidden to come or to go as her master commanded?

"It's all gone now," he said gently. "We can't go back. That way is closed. But God promised me something. He said that even though Eve is what I ask for and what I deserve, that one day, a long time from now, that *we*, you and I, will be healed, that even our pain will become a part of the richness of our joy. He also promised me that our children's children's children many generations hence, will live on an ever ascending spire, that one day they will be changed enough to reach for that paradise that we had, that we lost, that *would* have been ours if we were good enough to keep it. And that this time, they will get it."

With that he let go, turned on his heel, and slowly trudged away, Eve following docilely in his trail. As she passed me her skirts for a moment brushed up against me and something like a spark passed between us and I realized a strange thing. Although I had meant before, in my arrogance and anger, to repair the damaged soul that Adam's fear and self-loathing had somehow created within her (fear and self-loathing that was at least partly *my fault* although I had sinned in innocence and not in malice), she instead had passed a bit, just a tiny bit, of her own soul on to *me* in passing.

I was shocked by its power, it's richness. The strength to endure. And a deep, deep well of wisdom.

I knew then that Adam had never put that soul into this vessel of flesh that so closely resembled my own. Inanna herself, the female God-head, had surely done so. I puzzled for a bit over this, how one body (or two identical bodies) can house such completely different souls, and how *both* souls could come from God and *be* God at that point where Self watches self watching the world. I saw then that both of us, Eve *and* I, were incomplete by ourselves, just as Adam was incomplete without us (*both* of us). I was *freedom*, untamed. Adam was *power*, a power that required rules and boundaries to channel it in order to work. Eve, I suddenly saw, was *duty*, the obligation to do things that were sometimes *not* pleasant or natural or easy, the duty that I had refused to accept as I chose instead to experience the *pleasure* of soulgiving through love.

I, with my love and anger and God's gifts, could create and destroy. Adam with his love of rules could himself rule and work great works for good or for ill. *Eve's* gift was to accept the *responsibility* that came with the other gifts to create, to rule, to destroy – to change *wisely*, to *preserve*, to *endure*.

I watched her walk away, much sadness in her servile bearing but enduring the pain and humiliation, enduring the caging of her soul and subjugation to Adam in the name of duty and a higher cause.

I wasn't surprised to see Inanna standing beside me in her naked glory. Nor was I surprised to see that the other townsfolk were standing still as statues, frozen in time.

"Yes, daughter, I'm very, very proud of Us. You see, a Creation is not an easy thing to manage if you are All Powerful. The Freedom to do anything all too easily turns into the freedom to do nothing, for nothing that *I* do is *real* but merely a whim in the Mind of God. Eventually that Mind sees all such whims as equal, all such whims as the moving about of shadows cast upon some sheet by a puppeteer (where I am the light and the shadow, the puppet and the puppeteer), an illusion without depth or substance. That way lies a descent into madness and chaos."

"So God cannot spend time designing the human eye and nipples – those are mechanical things. In the infinity of potentiality are infinitely many ways of establishing pure *mechanism* to handle all of that without an actual plan. The hard part is in crafting the Soul, in doling out the Holy Spirit. On one end we have the Death of nothingness and mechanism without spirit. On the other end we have the Death of solipsism, of spirit without mechanism, whose whims eventually become a yearning for nothingness that is of course granted. These pathways are tried again and again, but the mechanism of *evolution* is a powerful one and countless failures are the price of successful change. Duality must be the knife that sharpens itself, the boot that is lifted by its own straps."

"No, We must take the middle path when creating Universes. *Freedom* and *power* have to be split up and set somewhat at odds, with *duty* and *responsibility* guiding the middle path of *wisdom*, all on a field of uncertainty. Eve has freely chosen to be chained to the yoke of duty where you have chosen to cast all such yokes aside. Which of you, then, is less free for it?"

Suddenly, the crowd was moving again, circling inward, and Inanna was gone. Some of the bolder men and women were picking up heavy stones from the street, pulling out bronze daggers from beneath their robes. There was fear in their eyes, fear and a certain kind of strange lust. I felt a prickle on the back of my neck – not exactly fear, for one who has *just that moment* spoken with Inanna simply cannot feel *true* fear – but a watchfulness of the pregnant moment, as I steeled my physical self for the pain and death that appeared to be inevitable.

Suddenly from one street over I heard Adam's voice rising above the mutterings about witchcraft and magic, Adam's voice calling for all to come pay him heed, as he was about to tell of Creation and the Will of God. Although the word was unfamiliar – there was no worship of God by the soulless, no *awareness* of God by the soulless, not enough time elapsed between when I had given them souls and the moment for them to have discovered God on their own – it promised to at the very least be *entertainment* (a rare and precious thing indeed). Before the first deadly stone was thrown enough of the crowd moved away to listen so that those who remained lost their nerve. A process that *might* have been somewhat aided by the glowing sparks that once again flowed out of my fingertips as I summoned a small portion of the power that Inanna had given me only moments before to work Her will.

Allowing myself to breathe again, I made my careful way out of the market and home again. It was some days before I dared to venture forth.

Chapter 7

The Fall of Abel

Adam's preaching proved popular, and my better clients brought me detailed descriptions of his teachings about sin and God's will and Creation. Unsurprisingly, in his Creation story he left out the bit about evolution in favor of something he made up, a variation that made him out to be the absolute center of God's attention so that he was *first* and Eve very much *second* – pretty much an afterthought that he'd asked for when he got lonely.

I (naturally) wasn't mentioned at all, but somehow rumors that I was in fact the first and that Adam only asked for Eve to be made because I liked to have sex on top or side by side and wasn't a good little chattel made their way into the culture. I certainly didn't start them, but they were dead on the money. I suspected Cain or the other children – they were certainly present for plenty of screaming arguments on the subject while growing up and kids *will* talk to other kids who then talk to their parents.

As for sin, well, Adam was all about *control*. So anything that smacked of freedom was of course a sin, especially if it was something done by a woman. In his sermons I myself was in a *very fundamental sense* the original sinner, the very *archetype* of sin, although Adam also painted a picture of God and Goodness that sounded all too much like himself, seen in reflection in a warped and stained mirror. God was a man. God had a beard. God had nipples and a penis. God wanted all *men* to be Good. God wanted all *women* to do exactly what their men told them to, which is Good. God didn't want men to worship snakes, goats, cows, graven images, or anything that vaguely resembled a woman[1]. Women were intrinsically stained with sin, because of a little something involving the Serpent and a Tree in the Garden and the granting of Life that was All Woman's Fault.

In time the question of *which* woman was at fault grew a bit confused. Eve looked so much like me that I sometimes wondered if Adam somehow had come to confuse Eve even in his own mind with me, if he thought somehow that he had *my* spirit captured in thrall to his power and his ego. In time I – the real Lilith who was still living outside town in the mostly witchcraft but occasional harlotry business to stay alive and raise his children (whom he never acknowledged or offered to help support, not even once) – seemed to have disappeared from his mind, and even the townspeople somehow viewed me as a kind of dark shadow of Eve (instead of the other way around).

I occasionally wondered, while wishing fruitlessly for things that might have been, if sometimes, rarely, in the dark of night when his imagined God couldn't see him, Adam let Eve be on top. Or at least on the side.

Years passed. Eve continued fruitful (as no doubt Adam had commanded) where my own womb had turned off. Abel was born to her, then Sam and George and Sharon and Michael and Alice[2]. Cain grew into a handsome, if somewhat angry, young man. With some of the proceeds of my fairly lucrative business I bought fields and farms and (with Cain as a "man" in plain sight as the owner of record, as women weren't technically allowed to own anything but the clothes on her back – oh, wait, those belonged to her husband or father or even her son too) became downright wealthy and somewhat powerful.

I retired from the harlotry business altogether except for selected and very discrete clients that I kept more for my own gratification than for the money. They were my lovers, not just my clients. I've always needed and wanted sex as much as any man, and have often wondered about the sexual imbalance that keeps the brothels full. Some side effect of evolution, I imagine. Even my preternatural knowledge often came up dry when it came to the way men and women were the same – and different.

---

[1] Here he was less than successful, as Inanna clearly became the Goddess of many of the cultures in the area including, mostly, the Phoenicians, who later became the Canaanites, a small tribe of whom turned out to be the Jews and the Arabs.

[2] Again, there is no way to know how to phonetically translate the names, no good way to identify any of the offspring besides Abel with Seth or the rest of the supposed progeny of the biblical Adam and Eve.

Once I was no longer actively soliciting their husbands for money in exchange for sexual favors, the women of town opened up to me (perhaps initially only because of my money and power, but open is open) and I actually started to make woman friends. This, in turn, opened up a side of my soul that I hadn't realized existed. For my whole life up to that point, with the exception of my one daughter (who was much like me, fiery and independent and soulgiving, as were for that matter my sons) I had had no interactions with "women" save Inanna. I had cared for men, cooked for men, tended men when they were sick, had sex with men (a *lot* of men, *often*), been beaten by men (well, really only Adam – nobody else had dared, given my well-earned reputation for what local superstition called "witchcraft" but which was really just the power of Inanna flowing through me by Her favor). Women friends were a revelation.

Naturally, as I was happy and loved these new friends, souls were born and blossomed on all sides. My women friends ended up with rich souls, souls that could participate in the lovely chain of soulgiving as well as my own. Their husbands, their children, their friends, their houses – whole neighborhoods in the Sidon became 'real' as they were inhabited by people whose Selves watched themselves watching the world, and God was very happy. She sometimes visited me and told me so, in person. Once every few months she would take me to a place outside of time, where we would eat sushi or other tidbits of incredibly delicious food and drink wine and I would come back (with no time elapsed) renewed and fully recharged with strength and the holy light within.

In exchange I took Inanna, incarnate in a form others could see and wearing clothes that I loaned her, on a new ritual my friends and I had invented together called "shopping"[3]. This involved in their case wheedling a few tokens for merchants of clothing or trinkets out of husband or father (or in my case, just pulling them out of my fat purse) and going to market to look for a new dress or pair of shoes, or sometimes an oil lamp or necklace.

The entire market would glow for a full day after we left it, with the merchandise almost reaching out to touch you as you passed it.

---

[3] I almost censored this out of this transcription, as it proved to be disastrous in my own household when my wife learned of it. It took *months* to pay off the credit card bills after she and her girlfriends went out to "worship Inanna" at her favorite mall. Only my sense of duty to the Truth – and the threat of divorce on the one hand and abandonment by my female colleague who was helping to translate this on the other – compelled me to leave it in. Sigh.

The merchants loved to see us coming, as much for the feel of God's blessing on them as they served Her at their stalls as for the substantial profits they made from us. God, it turned out, *likes* to shop.

However, as I'd already learned to my own dismay, having a soul doesn't make the soul beautiful or free the soul from the possibility of sin. I knew, somehow, that the strange network of relationships consisting of God, Adam, myself and Eve was unstable and that my life was destined for more pain. So it came to be, but curiously the source of the pain was not Adam or his new wife but *the outside world*, which in my complacency I had completely forgotten. Sidon, after all, was not the *only* city in the world, and its wealth, such as it was, was coveted by many of its neighbors once word of "shopping" got around.

It happened one afternoon right in the main town square, while I and several friends were shopping. I was surrounded by children, none of whom were my own – I bought them sweets and they felt God's blessing from my fingers as I passed them out, I suspect – when a tremendous shout rang out from the outskirts of town, and the next thing we knew there were men wearing strange clothing and carrying thin blades of beaten greenish-red metal and heavy clubs studded with rock and obsidian running through the streets, killing men and women and children alike.

This aroused the wrath of God within me. I rose up into the air in a cloud of fire and my fingers spat dark sparks that surged from my spirit in a gush of anger, this time directly upon a mass of the invaders as they ran at me. They stopped cold in their tracks, with all spark of human intelligence gone from their eyes. Many of them dropped their swords or clubs. Some of the more daring of the local men leaped forward to take them up and they fell on these mindless husks and a new group of invaders who were swarming up the street.

In moments there was a pitched battle where there was merely a one-sided slaughter before. I saw Sally, my *sweet baby Sally* (grown into a young girl with barely blossoming breasts) fall before a sword. I couldn't tell if it was swung by the hand of one of our own city's men or the hand of an invader – nor does it matter. Several of Eve's children, whom I knew at that point by sight if not by name, went down as well. I saw Abel fighting side by side next to Cain, something that didn't surprise me even though they were of of very different ages; Cain and Sally both seemed to like enjoy the company of Abel, Eve's oldest (and their half-brother, after all) where they generally disliked the rest of her brood. Abel, alas, *hated* me, as a son of his father.

The Fall of Abel

Suddenly it was over. The armed invaders had been killed or captured or were fleeing away from the town in disarray, pursued by a small band of the most zealous of our men. The invaders whose souls and wits had been sucked out of their bodies (leaving behind mindless husks) were being killed, painfully, by an enraged crowd in spite of their obvious harmlessness. This did not bother me – their bodies had no souls and even their biological mechanisms might have been damaged by the process of removing their spirits. They would eventually die anyway; I was very angry indeed from the death of Sally and the Power moving through me reflected it.

The rest of the stunned citizens of the city wandered around slowly, in shock, and took stock of who had lived and who had died. Suddenly the stillness, otherwise broken only by the quiet moans of the wounded, was pierced by a scream of rage.

"Witch!"

I looked around to see who was yelling and why, and was amazed to see that it was Abel, standing over the broken body of Sally, tears in his eyes. I was even more amazed to see that he was looking at me and shaking his bloody sword as he said it.

"Witch, I say. Look you all, she slew two score men with her witchcraft." He was fairly frothing at the mouth.

"Yes, but she stopped them from slaying all of *us*!" a kindly bystander shouted out.

"Thou shalt not suffer a witch to live!" screamed Abel. "My father says that a witch is *wicked*, and this one is a *whore* and a *strumpet*. She once used her magic to cause snakes to spit their venom on my father and it is only by my mother's good graces and the will of God that he still lives!"

"That's true," said one old head. "I was there. Saw it with my own eyes." Some muttering sprang up here and there in the crowd.

"You fools," an older and louder voice yelled. "She saved your lives today. She has saved the lives of your children many times over in the past. She's not a witch, she was the First woman created by God, as *your* own father..." – this to Abel – "...full well knows. *I* was *there!*"

It was Cain. He looked quite strong and dangerous, a true son of his father at his best, as he stepped forward.

"Blasphemy!" Abel replied. "Lies and blasphemy! Come my fellows! Take hold of this witch that we may stone her and burn her." A few of the most zealous lads in the crowd took a step forward and bent to look for rocks. The scent of blood and feces loosed from the bowels of the dead hung heavy in the air, triggering a primitive reaction of violence and lust – it would have taken almost nothing to push the crowd into a killing frenzy, and Abel seemed hell-bent on providing more than almost nothing many times over. I prepared to hike up my robes and run for my life, as I could not kill these children.

In a flash, though, Cain was there, standing in front of Abel. He bent down and took a sword from the body of an invader lying at his feet between them and held the tip at Abel's throat. "Hold," he yelled in a mighty voice. "Brother, what manner of evil is this? How can you raise your hand against the Mother of us all, the Lifebringer? Especially one who is also your *own* mother, or at least her twin?"

Abel turned white. "She's not my mother. My mother Eve is *good* and pure and wonderful. *Lilith's* appearance is a malign witchcraft designed to bemuse my Father Adam. And you are not my brother, you are the hellspawn of Shaitan sired on this she-witch, a demon who wishes to pull us all from the paths of righteousness." He turned back to the crowd. "She seduces your children so that they are disobedient and willful. She lures them away and has sex with them that they may be corrupted and Evil like she is. She drinks their blood and their souls and sends them back to you as empty vessels. Come," he said, making to push Cain's sword aside with his hand and leap forward over the body at his feet, "Let us find wood and burn the witch along with these bodies."

This little bit of rhetoric appealed to some of the crowd, who began to catcall. A stone flew out of some unseen hand and struck me painfully on the shoulder. A second one glanced off of my scalp, and blood rushed down over my face from the wound. However, the initial surge of the crowd toward me was cut off by a horrible scream of pain.

Even as Abel had started to leap, Cain had dropped his sword under Abel's hand and directed its sharp point at his belly from slightly off to the side, where it would jab him but not really hurt him as he landed. However, the body between them had at just that moment decided that it wasn't quite dead yet, and a hand had thrust forward and grasped Abel's leading foot at the ankle. Abel fell literally head over feet sideways, directly onto the sword in Cain's outstretched hand, driving it with the force of his own freely falling weight into his gut. As he continued to fall the sword was pulled out of Cain's hand and twisted as it struck the ground, ripping its way back out through Abel's stomach muscles, opening a horrible gash several hands wide.

The depth of the wound was possibly helped a bit by the rage I saw on Cain's face that caused him to hold his ground and his sword firm, but Cain did not *mean* to stab Abel and never extended his arm to drive in the sword as he might have. He dropped the sword as soon as he realized what was happening but it was too late. The truth is that Abel just plain impaled himself in his hurry to reach me.

Abel, his face gone white, pushed himself up to his knees. He watched, blood pouring from his mouth where he had bitten his tongue halfway through in the fall, as a loop of his intestines spilled out through the gash. When he managed to struggle to his knees it slipped down between his legs, pulling still more of his guts out behind in a steady stream until there was a little puddle of steaming blood and mucus and intestine on the ground before him.

In a way, it was just one more casualty on the battleground, an accident brought about by chance and a bad temper. That and far worse lay as carrion and bloody moaning carnage all around us on both sides (*including my precious little Sally!* a voice within me screamed) but this one stopped the riot directed at *me* before it even started.

Cain stood, transfixed, at the sight of his brother[4] slowly sinking over into his own guts, the sight of his own brother's blood dripping from the sword. The crowd suddenly realized that it had other things to do and that enough blood had been spilled that day and went about the business of cleaning up or running to the city gates to wreak the usual horrible vengeance on the camp followers of the invaders, leaving me alone where I stood, almost blind from the blood still streaming down from my scalp and the pain of a loss so great that I felt lightheaded and weak from it.

Of all of my children, Cain the oldest and Sally the baby were my favorites, and now my baby was gone out of time's stream, even as Inanna had foretold. Only that morning I had kissed her brow, fastened a band of gold around her neck that I had purchased with Inanna the week before as a present and in celebration of her burgeoning womanhood, and sent her out to play (and moon over Abel, also now dying at my feet). I wept so hard that my tears washed the blood from my eyes to leave pink streaks on my blood spattered blouse.

Out of the crowd stepped Adam, his face a sight to behold, followed by his ever faithful Eve. Adam's lips opened and a groan of pure anguish came forth, as he looked around at the carnage. It wasn't just Abel. Five of our children, Eve's and mine, including Abel and Sally,

---

[4] Note that Lilith clearly refers to Abel as Cain's "brother" here rather than as a half-brother or friend. This is a foreshadowing of her own future knowledge.

lay dead or dying in the market square. Adam looked up at Cain, whose face was a mask of pure shock (for I truly believe that although he wished to defend me he had no wish to harm his brother). Abel slowly folded, twitching, his face falling into the mess on the street.

Adam slowly walked up to Cain and stopped. Then he reached up hesitantly, slowly, and pulled Cain's head down to his shoulder and patted him tenderly on his back, soothing Cain's obvious distress. He then let go and knelt beside Abel and gently rolled him onto his back and began to clean the blood and filth off of his face with his robe. He reached down and took Abel's gore-covered hand as Abel's eyes looked wildly up at the sky, at me, at his father, at Cain, while taking horrible gulping breaths as he struggled to make his lungs work with his diaphragm ruptured and guts on the ground. His legs and arms began to give little jerks, causing bloody spittle to fly from his lips, then his entire body began to shake and quiver uncontrollably with the stress of the Spirit leaving it. I tried to summon the Spirit within me, to try to heal him who had only moments ago tried to get an angry mob to burn me alive, but came up empty. I felt emptier than I'd ever felt before, empty even of my own soul, which quailed before the pain.

Eve, in turn, stepped out of the milling crowd to stand behind Adam (her natural place, of course), turned, and looked at me.

Such a look of pure compassion I have never seen, not even from Inanna. Suddenly I realized that Eve was a still, deep mountain pool, not so much *caged* within as I had imagined but kept within a natural boundary, a boundary carved into the Earth itself. She was strong, stronger than I have ever been, I who wept and wished to rage, wished to lash out with horrible torments against those who slew my own children and hers besides, against Inanna herself. With a glance Eve forgave me for my freedom and my inability to heal the horror that lay on the ground before us, she forgave Cain for his strength, she forgave Abel for his anger, she forgave Adam for his weakness, for all of the preaching and badmouthing of me that he doubtless had done over years to build up such a hidden volcano of hatred in Abel. She forgave herself, hardest of all, for staying there inside of the rocky shores of her duty, for letting it all happen, for *enduring* rather than *acting* where I could see in her eyes that *she knew*. She too had preternatural knowledge as much as I did, or for that matter Adam. Who *was* she?

I walked forward slowly until I could rest my trembling hand upon Adam's shoulder. I gave it a hesitant squeeze. His hand, sticky with the lifeblood of his son, my son, our son, blindly sought mine as Abel's eyes glazed and the final breath shuddered out of his suddenly empty flesh, the horrible quivers slowly fading to a twitch, then stillness.

Silent sobs shook Adam's frame, then broke through even his iron reserve. He howled. I heard unimaginable noises wrenched from my own throat as gentle hands brought Sally and the rest of our dead children, one at a time, to lie next to Abel in the street.

Eventually we could weep no more; numbness set in. Without looking up at me, still looking down on the dead body of his son with more love than I had ever seen him offer any being living or dead, I heard Adam's choked voice say, "Lilith, Lilith, Lilith, what have I done? God told me that I would one day pay for my sins and my choices after I hit you and hurt you in Eden, and that I would on that day see with open eyes. Today I watched my son try to do that which I always told him in every way that mattered that I *wanted* done, that which I *never* wished to have done, unable to stop him.

"I watched my son, my son whom I had rejected because he was also *your* son, *try* to stop him, to do with a sword and strength what I could have done with a kind word, a command. I watched as Abel died, spitting himself on a sword held not by Cain's hand, but by *God's* hand, sent to his death by Inanna using a *dead man's* hand, and thus saving Abel from the sin of slaying the First of Inanna. May She forgive me." And he wept some more, inconsolably, holding my hand as if just the touch could somehow take him back, could undo all the evil that had been done, could return us both to that first innocent moment where the spark of life passed between us.

Finally he stood. He pulled Cain's head down to him and kissed him on the forehead and looked him in the eye. "Take care of your mother. She is beloved of God." Cain nodded. He then looked at me and the look in his eye was more than I could bear. In that one instant all the sins of us both were washed away in the blood, in the dust, in the pointless sacrifice of our children at our feet. We loved one another, all of us, and I would never stop loving Adam for all of his flaws, just as he would never stop loving me in spite of mine. In the end, we lived and we died and returned to God. Nothing else mattered, or would ever matter, beyond loving, living, dying, controlling not others but ourselves, our own souls, as best we could. Doing our duty, fulfilling our responsibilities, in life, in love, in the eyes of God.

Eve had waited, quietly, with tears in her eyes but her back unbowed, while Adam and I wept. She for the first time stepped forward, past Adam, and laid her hand on my shoulder, holding my eyes with her own. I found myself falling, falling forward, falling into her Eye as before I'd only fallen into Inanna's, finding *myself* therein in a state of timeless peace. The squeeze of her hand pulled me back, back into the horrible, horrible now of that place, that time.

She then said the only words she ever uttered to me. "We can bear it. It is all right." She wasn't referring to the mess at our feet, or the horror of the day and I did not, then, understand. Then she dropped her eyes, stepped back, and was once again Eve, once again Adam's handmaiden and wife, once again the vessel of strength and duty and power kept chained. My power. *Me!*

"Go," Adam said, and I knew what he meant. I could no longer stay here, in the city, with him. I was publicly branded a witch, and they would remember, they would fear, and they would, sooner or later, act. Of course, for all practical purposes I *was* what they call a witch or a demon, for all that I was just a woman given power *by God* over life and death and struggling to do that which was Good and eschew that which was Evil, working without any guidance beyond the voice within me that I knew was Inanna. With my preternatural knowledge I knew that they would not remember that I was the mother of all of their souls. Only Adam's version of things would survive the ages, terribly warped, but enough to serve a yet-savage people as a finger-post of sorts pointing the way to God while they changed into something better and could find God on their own without the words.

So I turned on my heel and fled into the wilderness, leaving behind all that I owned, leaving behind all of my children for Eve *and Adam* to care for, for his eyes promised me that at long last, Adam was prepared to accept responsibility for his own. All except Cain, who was also marked, probably marked for eternity, as a brother-murderer in spite of the fact that it just was not so. The violence, the hatred, the murder, had all been in Abel's eyes, and the war itself that was the cause of it all was brought upon us from outside the city walls, for much of the world was soulless and running on like the machine it still was with no guiding volition save the evolutionary drives of lust and greed, fear and death.

Chapter 8

Eve

As we left the city we passed through fields scattered with the butchered bodies of men and women and children, slaughtered without mercy by the invaders on their way into our city. On the road a mile beyond the city gates we found the main encampment of the invaders. It was an abattoir, with the men of Sidon, their arms slick with blood, still roaming among the tents killing all males and many of the women. Evolution's bloody process was still playing out, even when the killers had souls. The rest of the women and the girl children were being rounded up to be returned to the city as slaves. None of the men paid any attention to me (well known to all there) or Cain (who might well have been one of them, had he not been defending me in the city square).

As we left the blood and stench of spilled guts and voided bowels behind, I was unsurprised to find Inanna walking at my side.

"Daughter, you have learned a great truth, have you not?" she began.

Even the blessing that radiated from her like warmth from a fire could not quite overcome the anger, the hurt, the pain in my soul. I could forgive God much, but not the death of my baby. I said nothing.

God's hand reached out to take me gently by the chin. Her touch did what her words could not, and the dam inside of my soul burst once again. I wept, wept for myself as I had never wept before in my life, wept for when when Adam beat and raped me, wept for when I watched Sally hacked down in the city square, wept for the death of Abel at his father's feet, wept for *all* the misery of my life, my dead children, my lost love. I pretended that my tears were for everybody else, for all of the dead, the wounded, the suffering, but truly the tears were for myself. My tears were for *God*, who had betrayed my belief in my own invulnerability.

God pulled me gently to her breast, and cradled my head as my mother might have once cradled it, I who never had a mother, or perhaps who had but had now forgotten. I cried for the mother I could never remember, the soulless machine that bore me, and nursed me, and cast me out into the world while obeying her evolutionary imperative. God did not intrude into my grief, she merely protected me, encompassed me, soothed me with the blessing of her presence, accepted my anger and the blame it implied.

Finally my grief ran dry. The pain still remained, but time ran in strange ways in the arms of God and it was pain half remembered, pain from the distant past, although the day was not an hour older by the sun or the road.

God released me to stand once again alone. I felt diminished and small. God then spoke to me.

"You are strong, Lilith, you are strong. Strong where now you can see that Adam is weak. But you both have my blessing, both have work to do for Me as you wander the world, tasks that are shaped by your natures that are *equally necessary* for humanity to eventually find Me within themselves.

"Adam needs you, Lilith. Standing alone, he cannot manage his task. When I filled you with a soul, I chose you first because you were the most complete human that evolution had yet produced, the most perfect person. Adam was similarly the most perfect man, but he was less perfect than you, less strong, more filled with doubt and fear. Yet he is right for his task – his fear is one thing that *makes* him right – just as you are for your task, which is to provide strength, and spirit, to be both freedom and responsibility.

"I cannot, I will not, take away a soul from any of those that have gained them from you to make them into what Adam needs. Nor can I, will I, create a new life out of clay, out of lifeless stuff. You, daughter, are what Adam needs, what he has always needed. Now you see this, now you know this with your own true knowledge. Only you can give him this. And yet only you can do that task to which I have set you. I cannot, I will not, *make* you do either one."

God fell silent, and for a time we walked together, Cain trailing silently behind and bearing witness (as he so often did over the years of my life) while I thought upon Her words. It was like walking with the sun at my side; God's warmth pierced me through and through with Her love and healed my aching spirit.

I realized, imperfectly, that I was being asked to somehow make a sacrifice. The sacrifice in some measure involved Adam and possibly Eve. Was this, then, the hidden message from Eve? Was I destined to perform the sacrifice requested of me, to supplant Eve and become myself a creature that walked silently behind Adam and supported him in his weakness while he did his work? Was there some way for me to do this and also do my own?

I didn't know; my preternatural knowledge was blank as far as my own future was concerned, and my wisdom (though doubtless greatly improved from the first brash days of my life back in Eden when great joy was experienced and great mistakes were made) was not up to the task. All I knew was that it was *God* that was asking, in person, and that God was leaving me free to choose. I recalled Eve's words: "We can bear it."

I lifted my head up and found that my feet were no longer carrying me along the road through the hills next to the city at all, but rather that I was on a path that led to the very stone table[1] where I was first given Life. Proudly I looked God in the eye, this time carefully holding myself back from the promise of unity and oblivion in their depths. This was to be done as me alone, not as Us.

With Cain at my back as my witness, I made payment for the flesh, for the soul, for all the joy that I had experienced and yes, for the pain and all the rest – for *life*. "God's will be done. What you wish of me, that will I do. But I do not know the way."

God stepped forward and kissed me on the forehead, my eyes becoming blind with the light of the Soul. I was swept up into timelessness forever, felt the incredible joy that comes from union, and then found my Self falling, falling back into my self, ordinary, no longer One, but never more aware of that spark of Oneness within my innermost being. Feeling returned, and I struggled to feel the earth beneath

---

[1] An interesting image that also appears in C. S. Lewis. One wonders about his sources, given that Lilith was very likely a model of sorts for the White Witch. Perhaps the Vatican still has copies or records of The Book of Lilith that only "approved" scholars are permitted to see? It wouldn't be the first time...

At any rate, from the manuscript and the idea that God would *not* violate the laws of a Universe, we can assume that this "place" was outside of space and time, and had its own rules where God could pretty much do as It pleased, including the performing of the various miracles Lilith reports by messing with the *boundary conditions* of our space-time continuum, which is an easy way to make nearly anything happen without breaking any physical laws if you happen to be a deity...

my feet, to hear sounds, to open my eyes and see once again as just a woman, diminished and (I thought) alone.

I found myself facing myself facing myself facing myself...

It was indescribable, it was terrifying, it was miraculous. I was twinned, and "I", the awareness that was me, the soul, was both of them at once. Somehow I knew that both of me were experiencing *exactly* the same thing, *perfect* copies, differing only in that we could each see only the other and that neither could know which was which was which was which...

Through the shock of this revelation of Self, I/We heard God's voice coming from all around, or perhaps inside of us, "Choose, daughter! Will you agree to go back to Adam, to become his Eve, to give up your power of soulgiving, to become his strength, his endurance, his support in weakness? Will you give up your *freedom*, to perform instead your *duty*, of your own free will?"

I felt a moment of panic. I was filled with love for this twin of mine, this other self, and feared that if I delayed even for an instant that she might agree before me and be the one to make the sacrifice. Together, in perfect synchronicity, we shouted back our agreement with a cry that echoed in our ears as one.

Suddenly I was no longer two, I was one again. My other self was still there, still facing me, still looking at me eye to eye, but we were no longer one, somehow. We were two.

But which was which? And what was going on?

The darkness around us coalesced into trees, the silence was filled with the call of birds. Perfumed flowers filled the air with a delicious scent, a scent I half remembered but never missed until now, this minute, when I re-experienced it. I knew where we were. I knew *when* we were.

We were home, back in paradise.

Adam's tree, door agape, thrust up from the ground before me, before us. From where we stood, we could see the flames mounting from my own house-tree across the stream as it burned, sending streaks of sparks up across the evening sky. Coming towards us through the trees was Adam, tears streaming down a face flushed with rage and shame, his robe torn and smoking, his knuckles bloodied from where they had struck me again and again.

He encountered *Deus Irae*, an angry God.

I and my silent twin stood, somehow immobilized and unable to hear, while God chewed Adam a new ass-hole[2]. God started out in a new costume, one I'd never seen before, of a giant being with a stern face and enormous wings, with a voice like thunder whose words I could never quite make out as they rumbled on. Its head was surrounded by an aura of flashing fire, and it was altogether one of the most frightening things I'd ever seen. Adam started and ended on his face, grovelling on the dirt.

Then God changed back into another form that I had never seen, one that closely matched the form Adam apparently wanted to see him in – old, bearded, robed, and strong, so strong. A Father figure, beyond any doubt. His voice became gentler, although it was still quite stern. Adam, weeping, replied to questions over and over again with his face buried in the mud and his eyes averted from God's anger.

In spite of *my* righteous anger, rekindled at the sight of my tree burning once again, in spite of my memory of the pain and humiliation of being beaten and raped and treated like a possession, I who was *first*, I felt my heart going out to Adam as he lay there snivelling. He *was* weak, I realized, he had always been weak. I just hadn't noticed, at first, distracted by his beauty. I somehow expected him (and myself) to be perfect, quickened and blessed as we were by the Hand of God Itself.

I was wrong. I was *doubly* wrong, wrong both times. Adam was imperfect, but *so was I*. I had failed him and failed God alike, as I now understood in a flash of revelation that the world was *full* of the weak, the flawed, the incompetent, doing what good they could without the tools to do it *well*, doing what Adam called "evil" as often as not in the meantime. I had enough strength for the two of us and had not shared it, had not done *my* best for the greater good while doing my own work with effortless ease (and in the meantime, humiliating Adam beyond his limited ability to tolerate by constantly harping on his imperfection). *His* failure was at least partly *my own fault*, according to that flicker of self within me that I shared with God. My own pride was *indeed* a kind of evil, one of the sins Adam always went on about. I was ashamed.

I began to compose my mind, to prepare myself for the role of Eve, for now I suddenly understood why I was somehow two instead of one, why we had come back to this place, this time.

---

[2]Okay, so this is perhaps a fairly colloquial translation. It works better than "ripped Adam's balls off and fed them back to him through a straw" which has more of the flavor and not quite the graphicality of the original.

I would need to be meek. I would need to be strong. And I would need to let Adam be first in all things, to make the decisions, to make his own mistakes, to do the things he had to do to teach the world outside of Eden about his conception of "sin" and how it went along with the soul as the first step towards self control, pointing indirectly the way towards *compassion*, towards love, towards God, towards the *good*. Adam was, unfortunately, not capable of a great love, as I was. His own self-love was too small to share, barely enough to sustain his own existence. He needed every bit of my love, as Eve, in order to be brave enough to face the world and do the work to which God had appointed him, and God grant me that my love, my compassion, would be enough.

Finally God raised up Adam from the mud and kissed *him* on the forehead. There was a trick of the eye where they disappeared and reappeared[3] and then there were two Adams before us just as there were two of me (but only *one* of me thinking *these* thoughts, at least inside my own head). God grew and grew and until he was once again the thundering angel, and asked Adam a question. Adam winced, then – both of him – nodded his/their head in acquiescence.

The moment had arrived, and I soothed my frantic, fearful spirit as I expected at any moment to become Eve, to become the silent creature I had seen at Adam's footsteps in that first day, some years in the future of this now, when Adam and Eve had arrived in the city.

One of the two Adams was invisibly lifted forward and matched to one of the two Liliths, the one destined to become Eve, while the other Adam remained frozen in place.

It was the other me. My other self. Of course. Or I would not be telling you this tale, for my other self (*my* self, I can now proudly say) had agreed to put aside all matters of ego and pride, all matters of truth, all matters of freedom, to become Duty and Strength to Adam, for better or for worse until she died.

A light sprang up for one last time between Eve and myself, for now Eve I dub her, at once my Self and yet Other. I felt a part of my soul streaming out of my body even as I felt the onrush of a part of Eve's soul entering it in the other direction. Adam's two bodies were joined by a similar light and doubtless were experiencing the same thing.

It ended, and I felt suddenly as weak as a kitten, my breath coming in small pants. Yet I also felt powerful, bursting with power, as if I

---

[3] Removal and reinsertion in time's stream. Clever trick, that.

had but to point my finger and will a thing for it to be so. Eve, who had begun as I would have begun, apprehensive but resolute, hoping for the strength to endure, now stood strong and silent, yet meek and submissive. Only I knew the inner conflict she must be experiencing as she bowed to the yoke of God while He gave up her reins to Adam, to be his beast of burden, to be his source of strength.

God pointed to the west and in a voice of thunder spake unintelligible words. Adam took Eve by the hand, not ungently, and they fled, fled without looking back, fled whatever disaster God had warned Adam of (and that Eve knew was coming from simple memory, her own. Our own.)

Adam's other self was left behind, wild eyed. Somehow this Adam was even more bestial than my Adam ever had been, even on that day, this day, when he had hurt me. This Adam-twin was crazy with fear, wild with anger, so much so that he frothed slightly at the mouth. God must have pulled all that was *evil* from Adam's soul and concentrated it in this *thing* that was yet somehow human, still had a piece of the soul I had given him. He looked furtively around for some way to run, something to hurt, and his eye fell upon me. He took two steps towards me and then was cast back by an invisible hand accompanied by words of thunder.

This dark Adam's eyes rolled back in his head as he cringed before God; he started to tear blindly at his robe, ripping it off of his body to cast onto the ground in front of me. Naked and covered with soot and filth, he took one last look at me and at the towering figure of a fearsome God standing over him, then ran back through the woods towards what was left of my tree with murder in his eyes. Even as he did so, the sword of God, the falling asteroid that ended Eden fell from the heavens towards the waters far to the south. From this angle, however, I could see a tiny fleck detach itself from the main body and grow brighter and brighter as it fell directly towards us where we stood. Finally it was so bright that it consumed all the sky and in a flash of light slammed down on us all, on the dark Adam that was all that I'd come to hate just as the good Adam, the one I had once loved, had fled to the west with me, with Eve.

I did not die, as I half expected. My punishment was not yet finished, while Adam's (being not really his fault) was over and this part of his Self rejoined with God.

The flash blinded me and as it faded, I found myself, with Inanna at my side and Cain standing quiet behind me with his eyes filled with wonder, again on the road that led through the hills above the city of Sidon. The sun was still high in the sky, the vultures still were gathering above the plains behind us for their scattered feast of the dying and the dead. I was so weak I could hardly stand, and so filled with power I could hardly stand it.

Inanna once again touched me, filling me with a reservoir of quiet – not exactly "strength" – but whatever it was, it would have to serve. "Lilith, sweet Lilith. What a prize you are, what a beautiful soul you have. I took from you that which you needed as Eve, knowing that you would wish it. She now has all your strength, all your endurance. For the rest of your days you will wander the world and grow tired until she dies and some of your strength returns, for she has need of it and you do not, not really. You have all of her power, her power to grant souls and work wonders, for she has put that behind her to become Adam's handmaiden, his strength, his duty, his support. You both have what you need to do your work, and you indeed deserve to be first in the hearts of all people, first in my heart."

Inanna once again bent and kissed my brow, and I was once again drawn to fall into her Eye and meet the Self that watches my self watch the world, once again experience the cessation of all time, the peace that exists within the Being that is All Things. As always, I fell back out of her Eye like a great fish plunging back into time's stream, back into myself, just Lilith, fragile, tired, aching, a bit sad, and yet – who could remain sad in the face of what I had seen? Great wonders, great miracles, and God's blessing is a thing that cannot be described, only experienced. Even in my weariness, I was strangely content.

Cain and I found ourselves alone on the road, hardly having paused in our steps according to the sun, although much time had passed in our experience. We had a long way to travel, and I no longer had much strength to travel with, so without a backwards look we began once more to walk away.

Chapter 9

Journeying

From Sidon we went east, always east. We followed such roadways as we were able to find, sometimes little more than goat paths through the hills, sometimes well-travelled trading roads where we were passed by caravans made up of donkeys and camels carrying great burdens, by bands of roving soldiers or thieves (often with little difference between the two). Gradually we moved up the sides of mighty mountains, mountains that looked as if they might lead to the top of the world.

We were in no particular hurry after that first day; our rate of travel was usually determined by my physical strength which was now that of an old woman, although I myself was still young looking and appealing (to judge on the basis of the number of offers I got to participate in harlotry, some of them quite emphatic). In the countryside I found that I could somehow charm birds and animals within easy range of Cain's sling, or draw water to us in the middle of the driest desert, so food and drink were never lacking though at first nights were cold as we had no proper outfit or baggage for travel – we had left with the clothes on our backs and nothing more.

When we found a village they would invariably give Cain and me hospitality for a night, and often we would stay for days, weeks, even months where I would earn us a living of sorts working wonders as a healer or acting as a thief-catcher (with my newly enhanced powers I found that I could easily read the hearts of men and women alike to find the guilty, when I chose to do so). In the meantime Cain would teach in his own clumsy way a mix of my story and Adam's story as well, especially Adam's view of 'sin' and how it held one apart from God.

After witnessing and acknowledging my own sin of pride, and being bound to a lifetime of service as Eve and physical weakness as Lilith as a penance, after seeing the *pain* that sin could cause, corrupting an existence that should be paradise, I was no longer inclined to argue that 'sin' didn't exist, although I suspected that in God's eye, where there was no time and where there was infinite compassion for those parts of God's Self caught up in time's stream, it *didn't*. Still, I just listened, not always agreeing with Adam's hidebound definitions but at least willing to respect the idea and come up with my own ideas of just what a sin was – and what it wasn't.

Wherever I was lodged, wherever I visited, wherever I stayed, both Cain and I left behind people with souls, a lodging place whose fire was just a bit more warming to the heart, a well whose water was somehow a bit more refreshing to the spirit, a batch of homemade beer that might just cause the drinker to open their inner Eye while getting drunk, and for the first time know in some fuzzy way the Self that watches the self watch the world. I could only do my work slowly as I lacked strength, but what work I did was well done.

Alas, it had an unfortunate side effect. I would see some mother holding a baby, some father playing with his young child, and I would bless them with a soul (with tears in my eyes from the pain of my own memories of a time when I held my own babies so, played with my own children in love). Unfortunately, with my new power about me, soulgiving was spectacular and pyrotechnic, a matter of sparks and radiance, no gentle glow as before. As their souls awakened to love, it was always accompanied by a fear of death and loss, that curse that crippled Adam. Even in their awe of me, their gratitude to me for healing them, for wakening them, for blessing them, for working *wonders* only for the Good, my power set me apart.

Time and again, after I lived in a village for a short while I became a thing to be feared, a thing to keep their now-beloved children away from. With my power I would hear the townsfolk whispering when they thought that I could not hear, telling their children that I was a witch, that I stole babies and carried them away into the desert to eat. They taught them to flee and hide from me whenever they saw me and no adult was around, and would only bring them before me when I was the last hope, when the child was so ill that without me it would not survive. The people themselves would at first seek me out and then gradually avoid me except when they needed my services. Then they would approach and grovel, filled with fear even as they

Journeying

begged for my help.

This tore at my heart – they were so ungrateful, and I so lonely, wistful for a past where once I too had had small children to love, a family, friends – but I realized that this was one more price to pay, one more burden to bear to do my work. When it grew difficult I thought of my other self, Eve, bearing a far greater burden without even the freedom to complain, and would grit my teeth and go about my business. Still, she at least *had* a family and Adam – a thought that, surprisingly enough, made me sometimes jealous of my other Self.

Still, I did not feel any real anger at these people that I also loved, also helped, also gifted in many ways with souls, with words of truth, with the first glimpse of God's compassion and mercy and love. At times the work was joyful, at times it was almost too sad to endure – but time itself, the ability to feel and change and grow *at all*, was a gift from God either way.

That is not to say that all my work was peaceful. My reputation as a holy woman, a witch, a miracle worker, a goddess of sorts in my own right preceded me down the road so that the next village often eagerly awaited me even as the village I was leaving regretted (or hastened) my departure. At the same time, the imagined wealth I must have accumulated as payment for all of my magic and spells caused me to attract every thief and bandit in the thief-ridden hills through which we passed. On any given night Cain and I would be attacked by bands ranging from one to as many as forty thieves at at time. Sometimes they came upon us in a mob or in stealth in the alleys or streets of the villages as well. Even the houses where we stayed were not safe.

One thing I had learned that day of the attack back in Sidon was that my gift could kill as well as heal, that it could protect me if I willed it. It wasn't even a conscious response; it manifested itself as a strange kind of bad luck to the attacker. Stones fired at my head by a sling would veer aside even if I didn't know they were coming. A sword swung at my neck twisted in the hands and somehow cut the attacker or his nearby friend instead.

When I used it deliberately, though, I myself was the sword of God in the wilderness. If I permitted myself to feel any fear at the sight of thirty-odd young men descending a hillside intent on gutting both me and Cain, raping our dying bodies, and making off with the little wealth we bothered to carry with us in a world where all hands, all houses, were open to us anyway, then the hillside would just collapse in a landslide that crushed them all (but somehow missed us and our donkeys). Lightning would strike the leader, sometimes out of a clear blue sky. Or at my deadliest (as on that day in Sidon) the attackers would just plain drop dead in their tracks, dozens at a time, if I so willed it in anger.

Thus, the roads behind us were strangely peaceful and many villages were a bit cleaner and more righteous places once we had passed. I sensed that this was a form of *natural selection* – it was *evolution in action*, where open thievery, robbery, rapine were suddenly *not* assets in the game to survive and reproduce[1]. To me it made little difference that the victims (of their own stupidity – I accept no moral responsibility or guilt for the killing of fools and brutes, soul or not) were just as often headmen of the villages we passed (and their henchmen) as they were furtive thieves from caves in the mountains. We were a deadly target to attack, and we left behind a solid tradition that it was lucky to show hospitality to the weary traveller and very *bad* luck to try to hurt one.

Even in the darkest night, when we were both asleep by a smothered fire with no one keeping watch, it was not safe to attack us. Snake (Adam's Serpent, the one that he called Shaitan) had showed up again almost immediately upon our leaving Sidon and accompanied us at its own slithery pace (faster than my own plodding gait and hence fast enough to keep up) wherever we wandered. Snake was the one being who had a bit of both of our souls, Adam's and my own, in it, and with Inanna's blessing and guidance it guarded us by night.

Woe unto the fool who tried to sneak in and cut our throats in the darkness! We would find them, two or three at a time as often as not, with their faces and tongues swollen up to black, laboring to pull in breath after shuddering breath as their very lungs became paralyzed from Snake's poison and they slowly suffocated.

Most I left behind for the vultures, having taken the last of their sad lives from them in an instant out of sheer mercy. A very few, usually young lads who were led on by their elders and who had no real harm in them, I would heal, for I now had the power to heal even this. These I would forgive, and bless, and send back to their mamas

---

[1]Yes, Lilith's preternatural knowledge clearly included a knowledge of the work of Darwin, if not by that (or any) name. Naturally she doesn't use a word that precisely means "evolution" as no such word existed in her time. Rather the scrolls use several words that translate roughly as "becoming better by having children that aren't too stupid to live", a concept of evolution that was doubtless known even to farmers and breeders of livestock 6000 odd years ago.

with a warning to obey Adam's words and avoid sin.

It was this sort of thing that ultimately helped me to understand the sense and purpose and importance of Adam's job and not just my own. The sad truth is that not every being I was giving a soul was really ready for it, ready to be turned loose on an unsuspecting world with unfettered freedom. They suddenly had the ability to *choose* but they had no *moral sense*, no *knowledge* upon which to base the choice. Adam's gift was the nucleus of an *ethos* to accompany the *anima*, the point where the Self watches the self watching the world.

It was all part of God's shell game with humankind, of course. It had to be. 'Sin' *was* an illusion, a construct, it wasn't "real". God *transcended* sin, and forgave it before it happened as God alone knew precisely how and why it happened, knew that free will (and humankind itself) was part of God's own shell game with *Itself*. The traces through time we called sin weren't really bad any more than a picture is to blame for the good or ill it portrays. The passion portrayed in pictures just adds emotion, depth, *life* to an otherwise empty parchment in the hands of the Artist.

To we who were bound to time, though, the *concept* of sin was a very useful one as a guide for souls that lacked a moral sense, souls too weak and imperfect to yet comprehend the wholeness of being. Most humans, after all, lacked a preterknowledge of the good, or any concept of how the future flows from the past through the moment of the now, and therefore did a poor job of steering for either good or evil ends. The rules of sin were signposts warning of pits and traps along the road to compassion and enlightenment, a path that might lead eventually to a day when all of humankind could at once *be* multiple, *be* different (and hence be alive and aware and filled with joy and love) and yet be One.

Eventually, of course, word that it was a bad idea indeed to attack us sped ahead of us down the road, carried by merchants, mercenaries, and wanderers. This smoothed our way and the attempts to rob us on the road dropped off. They were replaced by something new – crowds. Wherever we went, crowds of people from the villages we were passing would materialize as if from the dust at the road's side, holding up a sick child, proffering a chicken that would not lay, holding out a lamed limb for me to bless and heal. I did my best, although I would not use the power of Inanna to restore the dead to life – a common enough request, actually – or return youth and beauty to the agéd. Good health, yes, or luck and a blessing. To men I gave such potency as they deserved (which might in fact be none at all or a withering of the little they had), to good women I gave passion and reward in the act of love. These requests, great and small, soon exhausted my own failed strength but the power that ran through me was inexhaustible.

Even the thieves didn't stop coming, they only stopped attacking us. Instead we would pass gangs of men in the middle of nowhere who were the same thieves who *would* have been attacking us if they dared, kneeling at the road's side and beseeching my blessing. I would read their hearts from my perch upon my patient donkey, one at a time, with Cain behind me looking grim and speaking of sin and redemption, sometimes with Snake rearing up as a kind of living parasol over my head to keep the sun off. If the heart was dark and filled with wickedness and lust I would pluck out its life, causing the owner to literally drop drop at my feet without being touched. If they were redeemable (few were anything like "pure") I would bless its possessor with a soul (or more often than not strengthen a soul that was already there as Soul outraced the soulgiver on our slow journey down the road) and perhaps heal them of lameness and scars.

As I did so, Cain made sure that these new souls were immediately burdened down with a knowledge of sin, preached according to Adam's words. These words, reinforced as they were received with just a bit of God's own fire burning within me, did not stop there – they cried out to be passed on. The survivors, those who were now blessed and possessing of souls, would go home and preach of God and Moral Sense to all who did not come to stand by the road and take their chances for a blessing or a curse. Many would, for at least a time, really try to be good, would give up sin. Their new souls were an infection that spread out in the wake of our passage like weeds covering a field from the germination of a single seed.

Villages and small cities were even more strongly affected – the crowds were larger and we stayed longer to attend them. When we left they *were* different. There would be a husband who *looked* at his wife for the first time in ten years of life together and suddenly felt a tenderness, a wistfulness, a fear for her safety that had never touched him before. A mother who wept at the death of her child not because she was a biomachine programmed to simulate sadness as a part of the evolutionary advantage obtained from protecting offspring, but because she missed the smell and the touch of her child, the sound of its voice, the joy of watching it at play, the way it looked as it slept. A King who suddenly awoke to care about the kingdom of his fathers,

Journeying

to love the brown hills he hunted in, to feel a sense of duty towards his subjects.

All this happened deep within a newly discovered *core of their being*, where Self watched self watching the world. It was contagious, it was glorious, it was tragic, it was uplifting. Before, the light of the world surrounding them them was black and white and gray, unseen – afterwards, the rainbow.

Mind you, their having souls, their hearing about sin, didn't put an end to the violence, the brutality, the many acts of sin and evil that humans commit upon one another, themselves, the world. In fact, before I came and gave people souls with my love and the power of God so freely given, they lived *without* sin. How can a rock sin, as it mindlessly obeys the dictates of physics? Does the lion sin as it pulls down the antelope and feasts on its steaming flesh? Do the actors in a play sin as they play out their scripted parts, act out the roles in which they were cast by an intelligence other than their own? Does a sculpture of a man killing another man do a moral wrong? Before I visited, there *was* no sin, there was no pain, there was no suffering, any more than characters in a story suffer as they act out their roles on the printed page. Neither, of course, was there joy, nor beauty, nor even real pleasure.

Afterwards there was beauty aplenty – the bittersweet beauty of the quiet desperation of the soul, drinking in joy and love and happiness but paying the price in blood and sorrow and regret and eventually, death. There was also the knowledge of sin, there was moral sense, there was guilt. Finally, there was a longing, however strongly suppressed or ignored, of the new souls for the One God from whose wellspring they were drawn and to whom they would return, the Holy Spirit of which they were made, the God for whom they, God themselves as Many in the guise of matter and energy, shaped time's stream.

God as Inanna often walked by my side in those days, restoring my flagging strength as only she could, teaching me of the world through which I passed when my preternatural knowledge failed me[2], comforting me when the pain and suffering of those that I helped overwhelmed me. Each day I learned wisdom from the suffering in the new souls I helped to create, each day I learned compassion as I did my best then to heal them, to bless them, to teach them that life and a soul are

---

[2] To borrow an idea from computing, it isn't storage of the data that is the problem, it is retrieval. Lilith may have known almost "everything" and had some sort of God-given Google search engine in her brain, but a dozen lifetimes wouldn't suffice to make that knowledge usable.

themselves a *blessing*. It sustained me.

Cain accompanied me as I hobbled through the towns and rested (and sometimes shopped) in their market square. Here he would preach, just as his father, Adam, had preached back in Sidon. His message, however, gradually changed as we travelled and ended up *not* quite the same as that of Adam – he told stories of Inanna garnered on our journeys together, of miracles and morality – mixed in with a somewhat skewed version of Adam's somewhat skewed vision of sin and God's Will. Put all together, it was a beautiful message of a compassionate God, one that most often had the form of a woman rather than a man, one less inclined to punish than to forgive, to teach, to bless.

As he preached his own countenance would glow with Inanna's holy light but gently, a quiet aura around his head, and all who heard would come away with that glow fresh lit in their own eyes to match it, for Cain, too, walked with Inanna and was blessèd in her sight. Perhaps he too helped with the work of his father Adam, born of the best of both of us back when we were young, innocent, and (dare I say it?) deeply in love. He was my right arm and support; without him *I* could not have done *my* job for God for all of my supposed power. Cain, in his sadness and regret (for he ever regretted his part, however accidental, in the killing of his looped-back-in-time brother Abel) was wise far beyond my own poor wisdom, and spread the blessing of God's light on everything he passed just in the way that he looked at it, loving it for the very transitory beauty it represented in the moment of his seeing.

Days turned into months, months into years, and the years themselves lengthened; our journey grew long indeed. Eventually we came to lands that were cold and filled with a rugged people that lived in crude huts made of branches and leather skins or in houses made of shaped clay mixed with straw and roofed with grasses. We had to learn new tongues as we wandered, but Inanna's gifts to both Cain and myself included that of reading the very thoughts of those that confronted us, so that this was never very difficult to accomplish at our slow hobbled pace.

In time we passed through these primitive lands in turn, exiting through the icy passes of the most monstrous mountains we had ever seen, descending through endless hills dotted with tiny villages to a fertile plain bordering a mighty river.

Chapter 10

Mohenjo Daro

We left the foothills preaching our message to a handsome people with shiny black hair like our own, but with darker skin, full lips, and clean, strong limbs. The men sported magnificent mustaches and beards and wore pieces of cloth twisted about their heads. The women wore many bangles and necklaces made of gold and colored stones that were collected from the pebbles and gravel of the many streams that fell from the hills. These women were beautifully dressed in all the colors of the rainbow in skirts like gossamer that were wrapped gracefully around their legs. The younger women wore nothing but jewelry and henna drawings on their upper bodies, with their breasts proudly exposed and elaborately decorated; the older women wore simple cotton blouses and undergarments to conceal and support their shrunken, baby-chewed breasts and present the illusion of youth. Mounted soldiers patrolled the trade road we followed down from the mountains and bandits were almost unknown.

Such wealth, such civilization! The women's' clothes reminded me poignantly of a certain closet in a certain tree in lost Eden, long since gone to ash and mud. Just my thinking about it caused the flowers that lined the roadway to momentarily droop, and then spring up and visibly blossom anew as I realized that here they had obviously already invented *shopping*, so I too would be able to buy such lovely clothes and have my own breasts decorated with spirals and stars, to once again be dressed in something more colorful and fashionable than the dull gray robes I had worn since leaving Sidon to Adam.

Following the crowds and caravans on the trade road we had followed, truthfully, almost all the way from Sidon, we crossed a broad plain and reached the shores of the great Indus river. There we turned south, and several weeks later we found a city, the first real city encountered on our journey. It was called *Mohenjo Daro*[1].

We arrived on the outskirts in the evening and were ushered immediately through whitewashed walls made of sun-baked brick into a huge courtyard filled with travellers and camels and vendors selling food and trinkets surrounding a small inn that clearly served the caravans and traders who visited the city. Word of our arrival had preceded us as we went along the road performing our small miracles, and once inside we were greeted by the largest crowd of the diseased, the lame, the mad that we had ever seen, all clamoring for healing. We situated ourselves underneath a large tree filled with *langurs*[2] and refused to move until a fire had been started and food was produced. Then as the stars of heaven burned brightly above us, Cain began to preach to the crowd of supplicants in their own language (which we'd long since learned on the road) while I wandered among them, healing this small child of the affliction that twisted her legs and cleft her palate, restoring sight and a measure of health to that old man whose eyes were milky with cataracts, and temporarily *taking* the sight from the eyes of his perfectly hale son who was starving the old man while he grew fat – as a lesson.

Finally with the help of the innkeeper we drove the rest of the multitude back out into the streets with the promise that we would remain for some days and fell into an exhausted sleep before the dying fire.

The next day dawned bright and clear and somewhat cold and after a simple breakfast we resumed our work. As the day stretched into the afternoon the crowds gradually thinned – I had healed many of the sick and the lame and I had judged the life of all who came before me – six bodies were stretched out to the side in mute testimony to some horrible crimes that I discovered while sifting the histories of their former owners. I had granted souls to those few that seemed not yet to have them, but soul had long since outraced us on our journey and fewer and fewer people we encountered did not already have a

---

[1] Of course it was called nothing of the sort – that is just our modern name for one of the oldest cities in the world. It is nevertheless fairly positively identified by many clues such as the existence of the world's oldest University and a working sewer system. However it *could* have been some other nameless prehistorical city in the Harappa/Indus civilization.

[2] A very intelligent black-faced, light grey monkey roughly the size of a four-year old child, very common in the region.

Mohenjo Daro

soul, passed on by a chain of love that grew ever wider. This part of my work for Inanna appeared to be mostly finished and I longed for peace, longed for a rest.

As we rested in the afternoon shade of our tree, a messenger in the form of a spear-wielding soldier arrived from the city proper. The king[3] had been told of our presence and of my ability to read the hearts of those accused of crimes and to judge them. The king had planned a mass execution of those convicted of great crimes for that very afternoon, but wished to invite me to first come and judge the hearts of those accused that there might be no mistake.

I was actually eager enough to enter the city proper to find the stores and baths that the innkeeper had (somewhat reluctantly) told me of that were located near the central city square, so Cain and I packed up our small household and loaded it onto the backs of several volunteers to bring along behind us and followed the messenger into the city. We were led through thick, strong gates in a high wall attended by many guards armed with bronze swords and long spears with hammered copper points. We followed the straight, broad street up a small hill past many side streets and alleyways. Off to the sides I saw merchants selling brightly colored clothing, potters, jewelers, an alehouse – my heart leapt at the thought of spending an hour, a day, a week just moving from stall to stall. There was even a house of harlotry attended by a fat greasy man who leered at me as I passed and whose heart failed him moments later as I read its shocking blackness, leaving him dead on the street.

Finally we arrived at a large square, crowded with men and women that were somber, angry, curious – all manner of powerful human emotions bombarded me as the guards pushed open a pathway for me through the throng. We came out in an open area right in front of a large building that was obviously a sort of palace or government building with a raised stair and platform. Eleven men lay on the ground, stripped naked and bound, wild-eyed faces to the sky. Each of them had a three-inch-thick pole, sharpened into a long tapered point that was inserted into their anus. Four men stood by each pole's base, one armed with a gleaming bronze dagger in the shape of a hook with the inner curve sharpened. The bound men did not appear to be yet in *serious* pain, but each pole's other end was braced up against a

---

[3]Or governor, or mayor, as it isn't clear from either text or historical record precisely what kind of government was extant, only that it was centralized and effective.

hole in a brick platform spattered with dark stains. Up on the raised dais was a small group of richly clad men and women; one wore a necklace made of thick gold and carried a golden ceremonial spear. He bowed his head to me and gestured with his hand at the row of the accused.

The execution of these supposed criminals was clearly to be death by impaling and whatever additional torments that would be imposed by the man carrying the dagger. In my journeying I had seen plenty of this sort of thing – I did my best to temper it in most cases but in some the crimes of the accused were real and so horrible that I did nothing for them and left them to their fate in the hands of the local secular authority.

So was it here, as I went up to the first of them and reached out to read his heart. It was so black that it turned my stomach – he had done far more, and far worse than the crimes he was being executed for, and much of it was done to young children who died deaths even more cruel and more drawn out than the one that awaited him. His eyes widened and the first trace of fear appeared in them as in a moment of spite I granted him a soul the better to appreciate the agony of his own death.

I shook my head and nodded at his executioners. They sprang forward and in one quick motion lifted the man and his pole and set it into the hole with a sodden thunk. Even before his full weight came down on the spike the screaming began as his bound feet tried to scrabble for purchase on the smooth pole. The man with the knife stepped forward and neatly emasculated him. Blood spurted, and the spike sank deeper and deeper as it was lubricated with his own fluids. It penetrated into his belly and his screams became gasps, his kicking became mere twitching, his eyes glazed over with shock, and his trapped spirit, so recently awakened, turned from the world and the pain.

He suddenly realized that it was over, that his own death was now inevitable and there was nothing left for him but to endure it. There, at the very end of his brief moment of life and light, he saw the darkness of his actions, felt himself the pain of his victims, and repented it. As did I. He had sinned without a soul or true awareness; my decision to make him experience the *consequences* was done in full knowledge of my own cruelty, as a message to Inanna.

This awoke (as it so often did) an incredible degree of *sadness* in his fading awareness that echoed the sadness that was omnipresent in my own, the regret at all the lives so wasted, so warped by selfishness and crime. I hobbled over to the next prisoner in the line, one who apparently was an accomplice of the first. I saw that his soul (for he had a soul already) was warped from the abuse heaped on him by the man impaled, whose gradually loosening thighs permitted the sharp point to slowly reach for his already erratically beating heart. He had participated in their crimes at first reluctantly, and then as a form of revenge on the world for what had been done to him. His eyes were filled with tears as he saw his own due fate in my eyes and knew that it was well deserved. The crowd, screaming and shouting at the bloody thing dying on its pole behind me, started to heap abuse on him as well. A few small stones were flung at him, one striking him above the eye and starting a small river of blood that trickled down onto his face.

I quickly knelt over him to protect him for a moment with my body. Looking him in the eye I reached inside his spirit and pulled it free from the flesh, leaving the flesh behind alive but empty. His glow vanished as it returned to Inanna to be helped or healed as It willed. I stepped back and nodded at the executioners who hauled up his body as well. This time, however, there was no scream, no frantic effort to squeeze the stick tightly enough to keep it from penetrating. The body sank limply down, not even reacting when the bronze dagger made its horrifying slash.

This scenario repeated itself five more times – two of the men raised in full awareness to kick out their life in screams of agony, the rest impaled as part of the circus, but impaled without pain as I had already sent their spirits on their way. With the next I borrowed the already dripping dagger from the chief executioner and quickly removed his testicles as gently and painlessly as I could. It wasn't, I'm sure, any worse than childbirth, but he screamed shrilly and squirmed so that I almost cut off more than I intended. I then laid hands upon him and quenched the bleeding and eased the pain as best I could with my power.

His balls I threw to the dogs – they had led him to commit a terrible crime, but his victim yet lived and the man was sorry, so sorry for what he had done. As he was full of shame and remorse and unlikely (lacking his balls) to sin again in at least this particular way, I slashed his bonds and sent him limping into the crowd, weeping, to join his old mother who had come to see her son die. She led him away, shouting out blessings upon my head above the grumbling of the crowd. In the case of the last two I blew out the candle of life within them and then permitted them to be raised for the entertainment and edification of the crowd.

I turned to the ninth prisoner and stopped cold. I looked up at the king and shouted out loudly enough to silence the crowd and then asked, "Why is this man here?" For in him I found no sin, no crime, only a blazing spirit filled with enough love to forgive me and the king and those who were about to cause him the ultimate pain, for he had no faith in me or my miracles.

The king raised his hands to further quiet the crowd, and then turned to a fat man, richly dressed, who stood close to his left. This one whispered something into the King's ear, then nodded and stepped back. "For plotting my death, for failing to pay his taxes, for inciting the crimes of others and suborning my soldiers," the king replied.

I didn't quite see a failure to pay taxes as being worthy of such a horrible death, but when I bent down and looked deeper into his heart I saw that it was a lie anyway. The man before me had always paid that which was due, and if anything loved the king and felt betrayed by the king's lack of confidence in him. There was a further sadness, another crime he was aware of, certain men who had done him wrong...

I straightened and looked around at the crowd. Suddenly I pointed my finger straight at a soldier in the line holding back the crowd. "Seize him!" I cried.

For a moment no one moved. Then the king nodded to soldiers on either side of the one I pointed to who grabbed him and took away his sword, bringing roughly him to kneel before me. I peered around and my finger pointed again, this time at one of the guard captains that stood behind the court's platform. He too was disarmed and dragged before me, bleeding from a scalp wound he suffered when he tried to struggle and escape at first.

I took a knife and cut free the innocent man and indicated that the pole should – gently – be pulled out of his rear. He winced a bit as he was lifted back from it but I reached out with my mind and helped to heal the small rents made by the rough wood when it was thrust up into him by men with no cause to do it gently. A good natured guard threw him his cloak to cover his nakedness, which he wrapped about himself as an impromptu skirt with a grateful look. With somewhat shaky legs he stood, and then burst into tears and sank once again to his knees as he realized that he was free.

I looked at the two who sat before me. In a voice that rang clear throughout the square I addressed them. "I give you a single chance to atone for your crimes. I see and I know all the secrets of your hearts. You both deserve to die, and die you shall. If you fully confess your crime now, to the king and his people, leaving nothing out, I will take your lives from you gently, as you have seen me do for these others. You will feel no pain, no horror, you will just go to rejoin God and maybe do better next time."

"Otherwise," I continued, "you will take this man's place on a stake and I myself will cut off that which makes you men and stop the bleeding, that you may live for the longest possible time as they are living," I gestured at the row of gasping, mewling bodies that still gave small jerks as the thick poles that held them aloft repeatedly slid in a bit further driven by their inexorable weight, ripping open their rectums and punching through their bowels, only to momentarily wedge on bone, the points creeping toward the quick that would end it all.

I stood back, crossed my arms, and nodded to the executioners, who stepped forward and lashed together the hands of the first and removed his clothing and then spread his legs and pushed the pole's already bloody tip inside of him. They tied his legs together in such a way that he could not pull himself clear of it. This was done quickly, with no more violence than was required by the struggles of their victim, but he nevertheless was bruised and bleeding and weeping as his pole, with him more or less attached to it, was lifted gently back and positioned on the ground, ready to be raised with him upon it into its blood-spattered hole.

I stepped forward and raised my arm to his waiting guards. As I did so he screamed for me to stop, stuttering, and then seemed to lose his voice and ability to talk. For a moment his jaw worked, but nothing came out but wordless gasps. Finally he gave up trying and closed his eyes, awaiting my nod and the pain that would never end. I waited in turn, for I recognized that his repentance was genuine and that he would speak if given a chance.

Not knowing this, his compatriot who was yet unbound tried to jump to his feet but was beaten back to the ground by his captors. Struggling back to his knees, he turned to me. "I'll tell for the both of us, as he cannot. Is that all right?" I nodded, arm outstretched, waiting, as I could see that even in their villainy there was love of a sort between the two of them, that they were not really wicked, that they were at heart just greedy men who dreamed of money and power. They were no better nor worse, really, than the king that would judge them, than the equally greedy and violent soldiers that stood by ready to impale and mutilate them, than my own self, now more or less obliged to take their lives however it worked out.

"It's all part of a plan, see. He," he gestured at the victim who was still on his knees weeping over his release, "he is a rich man, a good friend of the king. Well, he's got a rich enemy who wants to be a better friend of the king, and he is in the way. One who stands to seize most of his wealth besides. We," he indicated his be-spiked companion, who was nodding through his tears, "were well paid to arrest him along with those two strangers." He pointed at the two men who lay spiked but still unhoisted at the end of the line. "The crime we charged them with was conspiring to kill the king. We testified that we'd overheard them scheming, and produced a small bag of the king's tax money that was supposedly paid over, as this one here was in charge of the king's treasury."

"It was all a lie. I was to become captain of the King's guard. He was to take my place. And more gold than we'd ever seen, for just a bit of killing." He hung his head.

"And who," I asked coldly, "paid you to do this? Which 'friend' of the king is really an enemy, one who wishes to be first in charge of the king's treasury, who plots to become king himself?"

There was sudden movement from the king's dais. I whirled and gestured and the fat, richly dressed man was frozen with his sharpened dagger barely touching the king's left shoulder, caught as it were in mid-stab. The crowd gasped and shrank away from me, from the killing ground, no longer pressing at the equally spellbound line of guards. I turned back to my prisoner. He swallowed once, then pointed up at the human statue as the king sprang away from the pricking point with an oath. "He did."

"Bring him," I told the waiting crowd of executioners, and with the king's angry nod this they did. In the meantime I went and slashed the bonds of the last two sufferers, strangers indeed who could not even understand why they had been bound and had poles stuck up into their asses. The guards as before helped them gently free of their initial impalement, and I healed them as best I could as they did so. The scars on their inner souls, their fear and rage, were not easy to soothe. As soon as they were able to walk, they fled naked through the crowd and out of the city never to return, pausing only to bow down before me and quickly bestow a kiss upon my feet while muttering something in words I could not understand.

I then waited, impassive. A sudden burst of sweat dripped from the fat man's brow as he struggled to speak while the guards wrestled his corpulent form into position, slashing off his rich robes, taking off his heavy gold bracelets and throwing them at the feet of the king. As his hands were bound and a warm pole still slippery with blood and stool was jammed cruelly deep into his rectum, I loosened the spell that held him paralyzed and he began to scream about his innocence and the lies told by the guards.

The king, somewhat shaken, had returned to his position at the front. He looked down at the man he obviously had trusted right up to the minute he had tried to kill him and made a gesture to the nearby guards. A sharpened spike of red-hot bronze was pulled from a brazier obviously kept for the sole purpose of producing red-hot bronze spikes, and carried in thick leather gloves by a purposeful looking man towards the traitor.

I knelt before the man who had confessed in time to save his friend and stroked his hair. Gently I lifted up his face by the chin so that he could see my tears, so that he could see that I, too, was sorry, that I wished that I could set him and his friend free to live, to continue drinking ale and negotiating sexual favors from the woman who served it, to guard the king and the kingdom as I now knew that they would forever do if only given the chance to marry, to have children, to love, to grow old.

I tried to let him know in an instant all the joys of that life, how his best friend whom he had saved from impalement would grow old next door, how his son would marry the other's daughter and produce many fine grandchildren. As I did so his spirit relaxed, lulled into the illusion of old age, of readiness to pass. At just the right instant I teased out his spirit to plunge, still exulting from the richness of a whole lifetime lived in a few heartbeats, into my own eye, to spring from there an eternity later into the still more eternal eye of Inanna. At the same instant his tongue-tied friend, with whom we had shared this dream, sagged into the dust as his spirit kept company on this final journey that was, after all, only a beginning.

I turned my back on the fat man and started to walk away through the crowd, which parted before me like magic. Behind me I heard the cries and pleading become hysterical as the hot spike burned out the eyes, then there was an indescribable muffled yowl as a lying tongue was burned out of a head. For a few moments there was a gagging, mewling sound followed by near-silence, then the fateful 'thunk' as a certain heavily burdened pole was seated in its waiting hole. Then they went to work down below with the red-hot spike and knife used together, and the screaming begin in earnest, all the more horrible for its choked character and the somehow appetizing smell of roasted flesh.

I didn't look back.

With Cain at my side I returned through the now silent streets, through the gate, to the small inn where we began. Our belongings trailed along behind us somehow and were quickly set up beneath our tree with all its squawking monkeys and parrots, a tree immune to the horror of living and dying in pain. I gestured, almost spitefully, giving the tree and all its animal inhabitants souls that they might mourn with me, and there was a sudden silence.

Shortly thereafter, a meal appeared out of nowhere to be laid before us. Cain and the innkeeper himself shooed away the many who had followed us out of the high, white walls, and at last we were alone.

Once again I wept, there in the gathering evening. Wept like a child, wept like the child I could not remember ever being. Wept for the children who had been slain, wept for the children that grew up to do the slaying, wept for my self that was chosen to slay them in turn. Inanna appeared, as she often did when I was in pain, and laid her hand gently on my brow so that I could see that she cherished them all, cherished those who were hurt and those that did the hurting, cherished them for their flaws and imperfections that masked the beauty and perfection of their souls. The souls that I had given them.

At last I could weep no more, and I slept.

Chapter 11

K'nesh

The next day dawned, as days often do, fresh and clean and totally forgiving of all the blood and pain of the day before. As I arose from my charpoy[1] the first thing I noticed was a man who sat cross-legged on a gold-trimmed cloth spread out upon the ground before my tree, flanked by two finely dressed retainers carrying trays from which a rich smell emanated. Two more retainers sat on the ground behind him with large baskets containing wares of some sort or the other. It took me a moment to recognize him.

Gone was the filthy cloth he had draped across his nakedness, replaced by garments of the purest white trimmed with gold. Gone was the look of sadness, of resignation. The bruises and cuts, I did not doubt, were still there beneath the finery but his face revealed no trace of pain or suffering, only a look of subdued joy. He kept his seat a lot better than I would have in his place, if I had had eight inches of wood jammed into my behind only the day before. On a charpoy of his own off to the left, Cain began to stir, awakened by my motion and the morning chorus of birds and beasts in the overarching tree.

Without a further glance I took up a terra-cotta jug of water that had appeared next to my charpoy during the night and went off to the innkeeper's privy to do that which needed to be done, then returned and removed my clothing to wash myself. I planned a trip into town later to visit the baths I had spotted the day before, but I was dusty and smelly and had no intention of remaining so another minute. Once I was reasonably clean I turned to put on my clothing, sorry that we

---

[1] A string-laced platform bed or cot used extensively in India and Pakistan for sleeping, indoors or out.

had had no time to do laundry for some days. As I held up my robes that were grey with the dirt of the road (wrinkling my nose with obvious distaste) the smallest of coughs emanated from off to the side.

As I looked in the direction of my newest attendant (where the watcher within me noted well that far from averting his eyes as I bathed they were if anything drinking in my naked form in a way that I knew all too well from my years of harlotry) he clapped his hands twice and one of the porters brought forward a basket and uncovered within pieces of neatly folded, beautifully hued cloth, a box of golden bangles and gem-studded bracelets, a small selection of fine leather sandals, and what appeared to be strange pastes and powders in small dishes that my preternatural knowledge quickly identified as the local equivalent of *makeup*, something that I hadn't seen or used since Eden.

Almost of their own accord, my hands reached out to a piece of shimmering cloth dyed a deep blue shot through with gold which I wordlessly wrapped around my waist in the style I had seen on the younger women. I looked down on my still-firm breasts and decided on the spot that on such a warm day I needed no more covering than this, and decided that if anything I would see to having my torso decorated with henna as did the others with figures like mine. The makeup I left alone as I did not need it. Truthfully, even in Eden I found it difficult to take myself seriously when I had playfully tried painting my eyes and lips to entice Adam, although I had the preternatural memory of *thousands* of fashion magazines and hence did a damn good job of it. 6 I selected a pair of new sandals that seemed to fit well enough to replace my road-worn ones, more on the basis of durability than as adornment, and similarly selected several of the smaller gold bangles and added them to the collection that already graced my wrists. Bangles were a standard form of currency – for me they were travelling money as well as ornamentation, and most villages we visited along the way gifted me in similar manner with bangles or clothing or jewels or other things we needed in exchange for my services. The larger and more ornate pieces proffered by the servant I left alone, as this man, while he was far from the first attendant I had picked up on my long journeying by virtue of saving a life, truthfully owed me little and would doubtless soon realize it and return to his rich and independent life. The one who was in my debt was the king, and I fully intended to collect on that debt as the work I had done for him was onerous and weighed heavily on my soul, for all that it was necessary.

K'nesh

As I turned away from the mini-closet there were again two small claps of the hands and the servants bearing food stepped forward and set up two small tables in front of our charpoys and began laying out covered platters of the most delightful foods, pouring hot tea into baked terra-cotta cups washed inside with gold, pouring what appeared to be wine into crude but jewel-encrusted goblets. A piece of white linen appeared and was deferentially laid on my lap. There was nothing to do but to break my fast. While I ate, my host began to speak in the hushed tones of the deepest reverence.

"Oh *Lilith* of the Goddess Inanna, please accept these small tokens of gratitude and esteem as my offerings to your Goddess. All that I have is yours to command, for without you the crows and the vultures would be picking the eyes out of my skull outside the city walls along with those who were less fortunate yesterday. My name is K'nesh, and until a few days ago I was the treasurer and boon companion of the king, who is my cousin. The man you revealed for the traitor that he is is our uncle, who saw us both as obstacles to the throne and plotted to have me cast down and then to bide his time to slip the king a knife or poison.

"All his plots are now laid bare and cast down even as my uncle himself is hoisted up and being pecked by the crows, and I am restored to my former wealth and position. Alas, the king can no more look me in the eye for the wrong that he has done me. Evil works take time to heal and the king must come to forgive himself before he can again trust me, I fear. Today I come to hear your message," with this he nodded to Cain, who also bowed his head in silent acknowledgment, "and to serve you in all things. If you wish for aught, it shall be so."

With that he returned to silence. I too remained silent, enjoying the food, enjoying the feel of clean cloth against my skin, enjoying being *pretty* for a time with a man's eyes upon me that held something other than fear, hatred, or need. I found myself looking over *his* form somewhat speculatively, as it had been a long time indeed since I had lain with a man and while I was skilled at taking the edge off of my own needs when privacy and opportunity permitted, it isn't the same as the real thing.

K'nesh, to my surprise, was in fact a remarkably handsome man. His face was symmetric, his teeth white and straight, his now-clean skin a lovely color of brown two shades darker than my own tawny tea. His long black hair was no longer the dust-matted tangle that it had been the afternoon before but was combed out straight so that it lay upon his shoulders in shining curves. He was in early middle age (as reckoned by those that age) and strong, but with the beginnings of a belly brought about by too much rich food and too little exercise.

There were two things about him that set him clearly apart from the other men I had seen in the community. The first was his nose, which was one of the largest that I had ever seen on a man, long and fat but somehow still well proportioned, where too many who have large noses are not. It still stood out upon his face and made him quite unique in appearance. The second was now hidden by his robes but I well remembered thinking, while looking upon his naked form back when he was still strapped to the pole, that the dagger wielder would need an extra hand and two strokes to manage the removal of that which was between his legs even shrunken as it was from the cold and from fear.

These thoughts led to other thoughts, and almost against my will I found myself thoroughly aroused, which was most inconvenient given the circumstances. I sighed and cleared my mind of the sudden storm of lust that raged there by remembering Inanna's timeless eye. That which would be, would be.

Breakfast over, Cain prepared to preach the message of his father as he currently interpreted it. While we had dined, the crowds had begun to gather, thicker than ever before. The servants of K'nesh, after a quietly issued command, took charge of admitting them onto the grounds of the inn at the gate. One of them quickly returned with the innkeeper, who had in his hands a basket filled with small trinkets of value – he had clearly been charging for admission. The innkeeper looked fearfully at me as they forced him to his knees before me, but I just smiled and gestured for the basket containing the bangles.

I reached in to pull out one of the gold bangles of medium weight with the obvious intention of paying the innkeeper for our use of his facilities, when K'nesh raised one hand and spoke to the innkeeper himself. "I wish to buy your inn and all its grounds." He pulled an elaborately decorated cone from a soft leather bag that hung at his waist and looked over at the innkeeper, who swallowed and then nodded twice. K'nesh carefully broke off the tip from the cone and stored it back into a tiny bag within his bag and then handed the cone over to the innkeeper, who accepted it and disappeared, leaving behind the basket filled with trinkets and gold.

I looked at K'nesh and his bag and arched an eyebrow in question.

"Ah, the cone is a promise to pay, a certain amount of gold or goods. He can redeem it at the city treasury by matching his cone to the removed tip. At that time the deed of sale will be recorded with his and my own seal," he pulled from his bag a beautifully carved seal bearing the image of an elephant. "I now give this inn and all its grounds to you, Lilith. It is yours. If you wish, I will build you a house and a temple to Inanna here, so that Cain can preach of your God to our people and you can work your miracles."

This caught me quite by surprise. A house? A temple? Was it possible for one such as I to settle in for a time, to keep house, to try to be merely happy? Was this Inanna's will for me, or a distraction from my duty? I didn't know what to say.

So I said nothing. Shortly afterwards, Cain began to preach. I'd heard it all before, many, many times, and I had no wish to perform healings and judgments today. I quietly arose in mid-sermon and made my way to the gate, unsurprised to find both K'nesh and two of his retainers trailing along in my wake.

Together we made our way back into the city of Mohenjo Daro, being bowed through the gates by the obviously overawed guards. This time I went up the street more slowly, pausing at the various booths and stalls to shop, using a handful of the trinkets from the innkeeper's basket to try to trade for a scarf here, for white twists of cloth to use for bathing there, for a flask of sweetly scented oil, for a small jar of henna with several implements for applying it. Most of the shopkeepers refused my offer to pay and simply packed my selections into the basket being carried by a porter K'nesh had hired off of the street with a wave of his hand.

By my deliberate design, we ended at the public baths. Before I could even negotiate, K'nesh caught the eye of two of the female attendants who came and took our clothing and escorted us to an enormous tub built for two in a separate pavilion with walls for privacy, filled with clean, cool water. We stepped onto a raised platform next to the tub stood while our attendants proceeded to pour *warm* water over us and liberally apply oil and fine ashes to every inch of our anatomies with fingers and a brush. More warm water washed us clean and we sat on stools while they similarly treated our hair, finishing with a rinse of water that was almost too hot to bear and the application of scented oils with a comb that left his hair glossy as before and left mine cleaner and sweeter than I could remember it being since Eden. Sidon had no public baths at all, and those I encountered on the road were filled with water that was only slightly less dirty than my own form when I bathed. I preferred to bathe in clean rivers and creeks but in the mountains the river water was *cold*.

Finally we stepped into the tub and sat down together therein facing one another, the relatively cool water causing my nipples to crinkle. The attendants brought us each a goblet of wine and then left abruptly. Suddenly I found myself alone, clean and refreshed, sipping wine in a tub with a handsome, slightly chubby man with a large – nose. The tub was shaped in such a way that our bottoms had a tendency to slide down the slope to come together, and I had to throw my legs over his to be able to hold myself up by pushing gently against the tub wall. This in turn held my legs apart and opened me somewhat to his laughing eyes.

Against my will, I found myself *blushing*, I who had had sex with thousands of men in as many ways as there are to have sex for love or money. His gaze was direct and unashamed as it swept over me and drank in my form.

I had a hard time keeping my *own* eyes on his. Somewhere down under the water where I could see it through the ripples and sheen of oil that rinsed off of our skin as we seated ourselves, a transformation was taking place between his legs. Something long and thick was emerging, rising, engorging, distracting my attention. It had been a very long time since I had lain with a man, and I was so lonely. Waves of lust arose unbidden, cresting ever higher. I was going to make love to this man and both of us knew it.

But not here. To my fairly extensive experience, sex under water is interesting and worth trying – once – but rarely truly satisfying. My one time and several more besides took place a lifetime ago in the warm, silky brook of Eden, and I was done with it. Also, while I had no *religious* objections to an audience I actually did prefer privacy, and I was fairly certain that our attendants stood where they could see us or at least hear us and return to our call. So I suddenly stood and took his hand and pulled him up from the water, then turned and stepped out of the tub and away from his questing hand before he knew what I was about.

This time I clapped *my* hands before his hands found something else to do and indeed our attendants reappeared in a trice and dried us, giggling a bit and making ribald comments as they observed his aroused state (rapidly shrinking in spite of, or perhaps because of, their laughingly directed attention with their towels). I then indicated that I wished my torso to be decorated like theirs, and then sat for an hour or more while an artist was summoned who adorned my belly with twining flowers and my breasts with spirals, who covered my spine with (I was told) pictures of animals of grace and strength, who drew spiraling vines down my arms. When the ink was properly dry I permitted them to wrap my skirt around me, donned my jewelry, and turned to K'nesh, who had struggled to remain calm throughout this decorative display and who sported an amazingly large bulge beneath his reluctantly re-assumed robe.

"Take me to your home," I said.

Without a word he led the way from the baths up a broad streetway to one of the largest of the palaces in the city. Therein we were received by several small children and two women that appeared to be in charge of them, who all ran and gave K'nesh a big hug. He tousled the hair of the younger ones, squeezed the older ones, give the women each a kiss and a pat on the rump, and introduced me to the whole entourage.

The women then embarrassed me thoroughly by kneeling at my feet and kissing them, sobbing, while thanking me for saving their lord, husband, and protector from the stake. They then arose, kissed me on both cheeks, and led the children out into the ample courtyard to play. K'nesh took my hand and led me up a broad stairway to a large room dominated by an immense, soft bed covered with many cushions and clean cotton cloth. I had not seen its like even in Eden.

Like magic another one of his wives appeared bearing a pitcher of wine and mugs. She went away again and returned to set up a tray filled with small dainties to eat, bowed and kissed my feet, and then left us alone. K'nesh poured us each a cup of wine, and as I took it I stepped near to him, near enough to smell the musk he was now radiating in spite of having bathed only two hours before. I drank off my cup all at once and put it down, then reached down and unfastened my skirt and let it fall at my feet. I carefully removed my bangles and dropped them to tinkle gently onto the cloth. I waited.

He put his own cup down untasted, then removed his own robe just as deliberately. For a moment we stood there, drinking in the glory of each other's being with our eyes, and then with a wry half smile he asked me, "Did I tell you yet why my personal seal is an elephant?"

"No," I replied, my voice surprisingly husky. "I had assumed that it was because of your nose."

His smile became a grin. "No," he said. "Not my nose..."

My two hands reached out at last and grabbed that which bobbed gently between us. An elephant indeed! He gave a small gasp of pleasure and gently took my waist in his hands to guide me toward the bed.

Just before I allowed myself to fall forward onto its inviting surface I looked him square in the eyes and arched one eyebrow. "I get to be on top," I said.

One scroll that was badly damaged and scanned in relatively poorly apparently belongs chronologically here. From the few passages that can be made out, it describes a happy – and somewhat uneventful – time in Lilith's life. Twenty lines of text seem to describe a voyage up the Indus river bringing souls and the preaching of Cain to the people in cities and villages to the north. Two separated fragments seem to describe exotic sexual acts – in one case with K'nesh, in another with K'nesh and a number of other men and women in a sort of religious/political orgy. A single line indicates that Lilith healed many children in a monsoon plague.

This did not seem to be enough to turn into an entire chapter in her narrative (and some of what doubtless occurred can be inferred from references in the next scroll which was undamaged and very clear). For that reason, rather than inventing experiences for Lilith "out of whole cloth" (so to speak) when there is yet some small hope that the actual cloth in the form of the original scroll itself may turn up and a more sophisticated analysis yield the real truth, we have elected to simply skip over this period in at least this edition. We did take the liberty of inserting one or two "retrospective" references into the text of the following chapter, taking care to preserve her actual words as always as best we could.

Chapter 12

Bereaved

The rising sun flooded my room with light. Outside I could hear the priests that Cain was training chanting their morning prayers to Inanna. In the bed at my side a beloved grey head stirred and a pudgy, naked form emerged from the sheets and headed off toward the bathroom, farting along the way. I had been up for some time, as was my custom, sitting at a table and practicing *writing*, the art of which was common in this city, by writing out this, my story, the story of Adam, the story of Inanna and Eve, the story of K'nesh himself, painstakingly adding words to scrolls of cotton cloth as was the custom and waiting for them to dry.

My hair, still black and glossy thanks to the will and blessing of Inanna, fell down over naked shoulders the color of tawny tea and randomly interlaced with the twining henna art to be found there as I wrote. I paused for a moment to look out the window past a lovely bronze statuette that K'nesh had commissioned from one of his jewelers, made with a new casting technique that was being used to make jewelry and figurines for export. I had posed for it wearing little but my bangles, as a way for K'nesh to remember me when I was away. Modelling me first in beeswax with its peculiar mix of softness and firmness, the artist failed to capture the shape of my face, and my breasts in the figure were much too small (as K'nesh was ever fond of pointing out, usually while palming the real ones for comparison) but I was not displeased at the way he captured in first the wax and then the cast bronze the lissome grace of my still-thin waist or my slender thighs.

As if reading my thoughts (or more likely, reading the words as

I wrote them over my shoulder), a pair of old and wrinkled hands reached around and gently cupped those same breasts, still as perfect as they were when Inanna repaired my body and froze my place in time's stream some thirty years earlier. I closed my eyes and purred as I felt the familiar soft warmth of a substantial pot-belly (and something harder and more insistent down below) pressed up against my spine. K'nesh had aged in many ways during our time together, but in one he was still a young bull, an elephant indeed.

For a moment I let his hands gradually rouse me, then I turned and pleasured him where he stood from my seat while his hands roamed in my hair and over my breasts, to be led over to our still-rumpled bed (from a rather stormy night of passion), there to be pleased again by him in turn. With the warm afterglow of loving filling us both, we noted that the priests had finished their chant, dressed, and went down to breakfast. There we found a small pile of my baggage packed and ready to go with me on the soulgiving and preaching tour of the country that Cain and I took every five years.

This was my fifth such tour since arriving at Mohenjo Daro. K'nesh had gone with me on the first three, but he was now too old to comfortably travel up and down the length and breadth of the country, from Lothal in the south to Mehrgarh and Harappa in the north. His love of rich food, his many wives, and the music and culture of the court kept him from getting enough exercise and I had several times surreptitiously healed him and strengthened his heart when climbing stairs or making love left him short of breath and hurting in his chest.

K'nesh was also too important and powerful a figure in Mohenjo Daro to be able to safely leave on long journeys any more. When Cain and I chose those many years ago to remain in Mohenjo Daro and try to build a home of sorts there, shortly after I first took K'nesh as a lover, I lost no time restoring his position in court. The king's initial guilt-driven resentment of K'nesh gave way to the king's awe and even fear of me as K'nesh's lover. For good reason – the first time I was invited (at K'nesh's behest) to a meeting of the full court I read the thoughts of all the men and women there and took the spirits from those with black hearts. Some I slew because they were privy to the plot to assassinate the king after impaling my lover as his strongest supporter, others I slew because of pure wickedness even though they supported the king.

This I did not explain, though – to the king it appeared that he was surrounded by traitors my magical powers revealed (true enough) and, being no fool, he realized that he too lived or died according to my whim. He was a basically good man (or as good as such men usually are) and was quite safe from me, but resenting my lover seemed to him to be unwise and from a mix of fear and gratitude (and on the strength of their former affection, as they had been raised more or less together) he gradually restored their former level of trust and friendship. This process was hastened, at my instigation, by a night that still takes my breath away even in memory, where we three joined in such a way that makes enmity simply impossible to imagine afterward!

In his old age, K'nesh was quite possibly the wealthiest man in the world. He was master of the treasury, minister of trade, mentor of the still-new concept of *schools* and the *university* founded by Cain to pass on both the moral teachings of Adam and such lore and wisdom that my preternatural knowledge could produce, all in one of the first real *cities* the world had ever known. He was also the head of what was arguably the largest trading company in the world, based on my very limited preternatural knowledge of the history of my own time.

His traders went as far west as Sidon and other cities that I never visited that apparently lay up and down the mighty rivers near Eden, cities that were doubtless devastated by the flood but which now had apparently been rebuilt by the scattered survivors of that great catastrophe. They also ventured east, to trade their cotton for silk cloth and exotic spices, and sailed south to reach lands that produced copper and tin, gold and gems, and an array of interesting foods. His wealth by the standards of the day had no limit – he was far wealthier than the king himself and often contributed vast sums to the city to support its powerful guard, to plant it with banana and mango trees and gardens of flowers, to improve its plumbing and treatment of garbage and waste (at my suggestion, drawing only a tiny bit on my preternatural knowledge to enhance the sanitary engineering that they already had).

As his mistress (first among many mistresses and wives, but I was never possessive in this way, nor was he with me as I lay with the king or a guard captain or a visiting trader for reasons of personal pleasure or politics as the whim suited me) I used his wealth and position as I chose. He never hesitated in the promise made so long ago that all that he had was now mine if I wished it. I wished for comparatively little – the means to go shopping in Mohenjo Daro's best stores that were filled with goods traded from the entire civilized world, the support of the modest home and temple built upon the lands of the old innkeeper that were now mine, and the opportunity to meet and dine with all those who came through the city to trade with him. By means of this latter contact I had kept my promise to Inanna, gifting each trader who left Mohenjo Daro with a well-strengthened soul and the learning of the rules of Adam as taught by Cain, to carry off with them as they wandered the globe in search of profit.

I knew from my knowledge of the future that their message would arrive somewhat mangled by their limited understanding of God, but that they would pass on both their souls and the *idea* of the rule by law to many cultures in all directions, and that thousands of years from now all of these rules and laws (including Adam's) would be abandoned in favor of rational law, the law as written by Inanna into the very earth and stars. However, I still felt the obligation to periodically travel *this* civilization and do my very best to plant deep the seeds of knowledge to be harvested in the distant future, for my intuition was that *its* descendants would prove to be the ones that best discovered the Watcher that watched the watcher, watching the world.

Cain joined us for breakfast as he was going with me, his belongings packed into a bullock cart outside. This was a sad day for us all, a time of parting, and so I had done my very best to wear K'nesh (and myself) out sexually over the previous two days so that at least it would take a *little* while for him to miss me in at least that way. I also relished the warmth in the core of my being that comes from deep lovemaking and wished to take that with me as we set out on the road. My thighs were properly sore, my lips properly swollen, and the trunk of the elephant K'nesh at last lay quiescent beneath his tunic, which was no mean accomplishment.

All too soon breakfast was done. We went out into the garden to a small temple building erected in the corner of the property. Here lived Snake, the very same Snake who had followed me so faithfully off and on throughout the years of my wandering. K'nesh carried with him a sack of large, live, bandicoot rats, carefully trapped from his warehouses and brought along for Snake's pleasure and sustenance. His men constantly joked with him about the Elephant's continuing fondness for rats, since we concealed Snake's existence from the people of the city lest they be frightened of the enormous cobra and seek to do him harm. Snake was well-fed, and K'nesh promised to look after him in my absence as there was no way for him to accompany me in a boat on a voyage over water, as much of this one promised to be.

Finally the last living rat was laid dead by Snake's venom to be eaten at his convenience, my belongings were loaded onto the cart, and we could delay no more. Cain and I set out through the gates of our whitewashed fence among many tears and kisses and hugs from K'nesh and our several servants and retainers. We made it no further than the docks (for we were going south first this year, down the mighty Indus) when the day's rains began, driving us into our tent on the trading boat that was to bear us downstream while stevedores loaded our bullocks and gear.

The Indus was already well into its flood stage; it looked to be a very wet monsoon. This made our travel downstream easy and fast, but it also flooded the sewer fields of the many riverine cities, rinsing their filth into the river waters. Also, the pools of the flood bred mosquitoes where for much of the year it was too dry to find mosquitoes far from the river itself. Even as the swollen river fertilized the fields with the shit-laden mud it carried over its flood plain, it drove the enormous bandicoot rats (large enough to attack and kill a small child) from the fields there into the cities, sometimes followed by the crocodiles that ate the rats and anything else they could catch, including livestock and the unwary person. The wet season was the season of plague and disease and disaster, when a flood might melt your unbaked brick house into a pile of mud, when mold would grow on a person's skin or clothing overnight, when water was everywhere but most unsafe to drink.

I fretted, briefly, over the health of the people I left behind in Mohenjo Daro, but all the above was even more true of the smaller riverine villages and cities I planned to visit, and I always found opportunity to do much of Inanna's work there while healing the sick, judging the wicked, and helping Cain to teach them of Adam's rules for living together without hatred or strife.

All day we we slid down the muddy river, trying to stay in the middle as the rising waters gradually erased the shoreline and filled the river itself with trash and uprooted trees. We passed enormous mugger crocodiles that were investigating the newly flooded land for trapped prey or the carrion of drowned beasts. We passed mile after mile of jungle with occasional patches of farmland or a small landing, abandoned to the flood. We even passed a tiger stranded in a tree by the floodwaters, looking wet, hungry and most unhappy, with several powerful looking crocodiles waiting at the tree's base for the big cat to get thirsty enough to come down for one *last* drink. In memory of Bast I made our captain move in under the tree to rescue it, calming it with my touch as we ferried it to an unflooded patch of shore.

The rains grew stronger and stronger throughout the afternoon, but then eased up. Just before sunset the clouds broke and we were treated to a glorious sunset just as the boat put in at the landing of one of the larger towns, one high enough above the riverway that it did not flood in the wet season. The boat captain planned to stop here for a few days, taking advantage of the opportunity to trade with the city merchants, while we preached. We slept on the gently rocking boat.

Cain and I went into the town the following morning and were greeted by an enthusiastic crowd who knew us well from previous years – we were expected and so all who needed our services had come into the town from the surrounding countryside. I was met by a whole muddy field full of wet supplicants, some afflicted with sores that would not heal, others with strange tumors and swellings or a persistent weakness that my preternatural knowledge told me was *cancer*. There were children with high fevers brought on by the mosquitoes (not helped by their parents keeping them out in the rain awaiting my arrival). Finally, off to the side there was a sorry looking line of men who squatted down, roped together, under the watchful eye of the town guard. Behind them was the inevitable row of three waiting stakes.

Cain climbed up on a large boulder that stood at one edge of the field and began to preach. I wandered through the crowd, trying not to get drawn in by their desperate, needy eyes, stopping first before the sickest of the children and doing what I could for them. Fevers I could easily cure, cancers and cataract blindness I could often set aside, leprosy I could stop, but I could not restore the dead to life, I could not grow the lepers new limbs. Three of the children brought before me were already dead, and I had to gently comfort the parents and turn them away towards the waiting cremation ghat on the edge of the river.

As the day wore on, the crowd gradually thinned, leaving the town's priest-scholars, who were trained at Cain's University and were now getting a more advanced sermon to pass on to their own students, a handful of those who were not sick but wished for some other kind of miracle – a love potion, good luck in a business deal, the death of their enemy – and the poor souls awaiting my judgement.

Judging that nothing would be harmed by their living another day not yet impaled according to local custom or dead according to my own, I indicated that they be well fed, giving over some small part of the offerings I had received that day for my miracles to ensure that their last meals, if such they proved to be, were relatively sumptuous. The rain which had once again fallen most of the day relented and we returned to our boat to sleep.

We returned at mid-morning to take on a smaller crowd that had assembled overnight but they went quickly and by the middle of the afternoon I could no longer avoid it. I went over to the waiting prisoners and stopped before each one, drawing up their eyes to mine and reading their crimes great and small directly from their inner souls. We left a few minutes later to the unmusical screams of the one man who merited the spike, with two of the accused following at our heels praising us to the skies for their freedom (although one of them was changed in certain ways to be unable to sin again, he obviously preferred this to impalement). Three corpses were stretched out on the ground behind us, too innocent to merit impalement, too guilty and unrepentant to merit freedom. I spent one more day wandering the town itself, doing a bit of shopping while Cain carried on, leaving two would-be thieves blinded but alive, three murderers who had gotten away with their crimes suddenly dead (one of whom was a merchant of some standing). The town was now as clean of human evil as it could reasonably be, and the certainty of judgement ensured that it would likely remain that way for a few years more.

Thus it went for three more stops down the river (with the river itself getting ever fuller as the incessant rains continued to fall). Just as we were preparing to leave the fourth town on our itinerary, a fast sloop put in and hailed our captain. We turned back to the docks and received there a messenger from Mohenjo Daro. With the floods came flood-borne diseases, and K'nesh was taken ill with one that emptied his bowels and burned him like fire[1].

In a panic Cain and I boarded the smaller, faster boat to try to return upriver, but going was slow – we had to row much of it against the flood. It was two long days before Mohenjo Daro hove into view, and another few hours to reach its docks and tie up and run as fast as my legs could take me up the long hill and through many streets to arrive at K'nesh's pavilion.

I was met by the unmistakable keening of bereaved women. Pushing my way roughly past his wives and concubines and the many sons and daughters sired upon them, pushing my way past the somber-faced

---

[1] Possibly Cholera or Typhoid, both endemic in this part of the world.

king himself, I rushed to his side to see if I could yet recall his spirit and heal his body, if I could restore the vibrancy of life and vigor to this man that I had loved so well, for so long.

I was too late. His body was well and truly cold, the spark of life long since fled.

My vision went dark and I fell to my knees as the horrible *emptiness* of death once again overwhelmed me. I trembled with grief, not unmixed with rage. I had grown so happy, happier even than I was in the early days of Eden. I was doing my assigned work, was it not enough? I could not believe that Inanna would take this one beautiful soul away from me and leave me once again alone to wander the Earth. I tasted yet again the bitterness of the cup of death, the source of Adam's great fear, the darkness that ever seemed to grasp at the light and joy of life. I panicked.

For the first time I tried desperately to perform a *true* miracle, not just a healing but a resurrection. I sought to bring K'nesh back from death itself, recall him from whatever paths his spirit now walked and *force* him back to life so we could pick up our lives full of love and contentment where we'd left off only a few days earlier. I could feel the power flowing out of me and into his body, but not even that power driven by all of the passion and desire and desperation of my soul was sufficient to restart the spark of life. I simply could not repair all of the damage done by the final moments of the disease that had killed him. I could not reverse all of the cellular decay that begins the instant that we die. His body was *broken* – I might as well have tried to force a piece of clay into life as his as yet subtly putrescent flesh.

When it came right down to it, after all, I was not God, only a tiny spark, a small piece of God's eternal and vast soul. Even gifted as I was, I was too weak, too *mortal* for the task. To bring him back I would have to remake the past, to manipulate time itself, and this I could not do.

Exhausted, I collapsed at his side and wept until I thought that weeping alone would kill me. For the first time I understood how an eternally youthful life could still pall, how one could grow tired of living itself, how the pain of existence could eventually cause joy itself to become bittersweet and poignant beyond measure in the knowledge that all joys, all loves, eventually pass. For the first time I understood also Adam's fear, the fear of death. How could this pile of dead meat and bone have once housed such a beautiful soul? Where could that soul be?

The Soul within me burned as bright as ever, but it provided no answers unless its light itself, unquenchable, was the answer. Inanna left me to grieve alone, perhaps to teach me what it was to be truly, merely, human. In time my tears and my anger passed, leaving behind a hollow shell of sadness in its place, but of course even this passed as the days turned to weeks, the weeks to months, the months to years. Humans are not born to grieve *forever* no matter what the hurt, and in time I came to know joy again. But on *that* day, the gift of life appeared to be a curse, and time seemed to be only a wall that separated the present I was living in from a past where my loved ones still lived. I could no longer touch them save in memory.

How odd this all was, really. In my youth I had never truly mourned on the day the passing of the day before, even though all the loving and *life* it contained was now beyond reach. There was always the joy of the now, always the hope or expectation of yet another perfect day of joy on the morrow. All of this was revealed by the death of K'nesh as the fragile illusion that it really is. The passing of every day of joy *is* a little death, never to be repeated, often not to be properly remembered. Were it not for the big deaths, the losses too great to ignore, we might never come to understand how great a gift each day really is, cold comfort as that is on the days those deaths happen.

I was humbled in my grief; but in grief's aftermath my anger and passion slowly turned to compassion. Inanna's lessons are sometimes harsh, but as always were it not for the great beauty, would there exist the pain? Were it not for the pain, would not the joy one day become featureless, indistinguishable from not-joy? Only in time is there change, only with change can joy *or* pain exist, each bound to the other. But I write this in my old age, long after those deaths, while at long last awaiting, even welcoming, my own.

The next day K'nesh was burned, and his ashes spread out over the river to float down to the sea in accordance with the local rituals of passing. I put aside my sumptuous personal belongings and gathered a few simple clothes and some travel gear, my writings and writing implements (well wrapped against the weather) and packed it all on two donkeys – it was easy enough since I was already to a certain extent packed and had more to choose what to leave behind than what to take. Onto my arms went a thick band of my many gold bangles, money for the road.

I could not stay. I knew that even the *rumor* of K'nesh's immense wealth would make me (and Cain) a target of everyone from the king on down to the least of K'nesh's sons and daughters if they imagined that I would make some claim upon it (as indeed I had every right to do).

Instead I gave to the king (who was also my sometime lover and a good friend, really, who begged me to stay and offered me his protection and bed if I should do so) my house and all its contents, even including my little bronze statue which was too heavy to take on the road and which would ever remind me of the day it was modeled and cast. I gave the remainder of my clothing to my sister-wives in K'nesh's household – although he never formally wed most of them or myself not all weddings are a matter of ritual and law. My personal wealth (which was considerable) I left to the poor by way of Cain's school and temple.

Sundown found us, Cain and myself, on the road again. We left behind our home of half a lifetime, this beloved second Eden, with its gardens and great trees high on a hill above the mighty Indus. I left behind the ashes of my second great love, after Adam. Cain left his precious school behind, in the hands of teachers who did not have preternatural knowledge and who had at best a highly imperfect mastery of most of what Cain tried to teach. I felt bad, tearing Cain away from all that he had built (although he didn't utter a single word of reproach, only silently did that which had to be done to arrange our passage) but for all that we had done and left behind undone I could not endure even a single minute alone in the house where *he* had sometimes lived, to spend a single night alone in the bed that *we* had often shared.

We left as we had arrived, on foot, never to return. I had been cast out of another Eden, this time by time and fate alone. I was doomed to wander the world forever unchanged, or so it appeared, even as I changed the world around me.

Chapter 13

India

Our road led straight to the east in the one direction I never explored on my trips throughout the Indus river valley. We began by crossing the river one last time on a ferry run by a gentle old man that I thrice blessed in lieu of a fare. Snake had consented to enter one enormous trunk and the last act of my well-paid servants was to lug this trunk – gently – down to the ferry station. Snake could swim, of course, but I feared that not even his venom and size would make him safe from the crocodiles feasting at the edges of the flood. When we landed on the far side (where there was nothing but a small community of farmers and a handful of stores) I immediately released him to once again slither along and protect our flank or not as he wished.

For some weeks we moved across the wet, fertile valley of the Indus heading ever east, encountering many small villages surrounded by farms, many herds of cattle. The terrain we crossed grew progressively drier in spite of the rain. In turn people and towns grew smaller and more scarce, the road we followed through the jungle dwindled to a path, and the path itself gave way to a vast desert. Along the way we traded our two donkeys and a gold bangle for one camel, as the donkeys could not easily manage the heat and the dry land we made for.

The poor but friendly people who hosted us from time to time in their homes seemed to all have souls already although I had never come this far from the Indus before in my previous journeying. This was no surprise. As the years progressed it became less and less common to find a community that was so isolated that Soul had not already arrived with the passing caravans of traders, with the bandits that roamed the lush plains. Indeed, we frequently encountered travellers known as *rishis* who had souls that burned as brightly as Cain's and my own ever had. These *rishis*, man and woman alike, often came to hear Cain teach, and sometimes taught the crowds themselves.

Much to my surprise, even with our preternatural knowledge we still learned as much from listening to them as they did listening to us. Even at my age – and by now I was ancient beyond measure by the modest standards of the day, having lived nearly twice the span of years allotted to those we walked among thanks to the blessings of Inanna that even now gave me the appearance of a woman of twenty five years of age – I was still ever surprised by the difference between knowledge, of which I had an endless fund, and wisdom, of which I have often been found wanting.

The farmers who lived on the very edge of the desert told us that the desert was impassible, even with a camel, at any time of the year but during the very beginning of the rainy season in the middle of summer – wells and water were unreliable, and the wind whipped up storms of dust and sand so thick that one could not see more than a few camel lengths. The rainy season was at this point just ending and the desert that we could see was still in bloom, covered with flowers and green, but we were assured that the dry season was now at hand and within a few weeks the hot winds would blow and suck all water from all but the deepest, rarest of wells.

Being in no hurry, and having lived through too many thirsty days crossing desert or near-desert lands during our travels to relish doing so again, we turned to the north and east to skirt the desert and remain within the sparsely inhabited lands that bordered the Indus and its tributaries on the east side. Our pace was slow and that winter saw us slowly approaching the roof of the world itself. I had thought that the mountains we had passed through on the way to the Indus were great, but here we encountered mountains that appeared at first as no more than a hazy line on the distant horizon, a slightly darker blue against the blue of the sky, but *impossibly* high[1].

As we approached these huge, green covered hills we could sometimes see, peeking out like white ghosts from behind them, still *greater* mountains that towered over the ones we neared as they towered over

---

[1] In fact, Lilith was seeing the Shivalik range in the Himalayas, mountains that spring up one to two miles, ascending, straight out of a plain only a bit above sea level. I grew up in India, by strange chance, and I remember well the surprise of seeing this range appear as if by magic well above the distant horizon when driving north across the Punjab from Delhi.

the plains we still walked across. The trading road we followed ran up into the foothills, meandering through small towns that were the most distant outliers of the Harrapa civilization, and then petered out altogether in the wilderness. There we finally turned to the south and east again, following a hunting trail that ran alongside a small stream as it ran down out of the hills. The small stream joined to other small streams, and the larger stream to other larger ones, and as the streams became a river approaching the plains we discovered a new evil.

The ambush came as we passed through a narrow canyon that guided our river bed through one of the last few outcroppings of real hills before the plains began. Arrows plunged down out of the sky, instantly killing the placid buffalo that carried me and the bulk of our meager belongings. Snake was not at that time travelling on our heels and so was spared. Cain, who was not as well-protected by Inanna as was I, was skewered by an arrow through the belly and another through his upper right arm. I, of course, was miraculously missed, although one of the arrows actually pinned my loosely twisted skirt to the buffalo and vibrated painfully against my thigh.

Our attackers then surged into view. Soldiers on the cliffs notched arrows to send a second flight down upon us. A second mob of men, armored in the crudest of leather armor and armed with stone-tipped spears and obsidian-edged wooden swords, came roaring down the canyon from behind and set up a block across the canyon in front of us. We were perfectly trapped and confronted with overwhelming force that was clearly intent on killing us immediately and without question.

Power exploded within me as I understood at a glance that this was their intention. A white hot rage engulfed me as the sight and sudden violence of the warriors brought back into my mind the death of my beloved Sally in Sidon. My blazing body soared naked into the sky, rising away from the falling corpse of the buffalo (of whom I had grown very fond) and leaving behind my skirt wrap. With one part of that power I reached out and deflected the arrows that were already on their way to Cain's slowly collapsing body, reached up and simply overbalanced all of the shooters where they were balanced precariously on the steep slope above so that they would fall, tumbling, the three hundred or more feet to the ground.

I sensed a few more soldiers in reserve hiding behind rocks above and "nudged" those rocks back onto them, pinning them painfully against the cliff wall. One of the rocks rolled completely over on a man and crushed his legs, then fell down the hillside starting a small landslide that narrowly missed Cain below. This gave me an idea, and I reached with my mind towards the many boulders overhanging the descending group of soldiers. When the roaring finished, there were screams and half-buried, broken torsos writhing in the dust but no soldier was left on foot and uninjured.

Finally, I turned my attention to the mass of soldiers who were barricaded in below us, blocking off our path. Here I took my time, sensing even across the distance who was good and who was evil.

I was astounded and sickened to learn that they all *had souls and yet were evil!* I expected to them be still soulless or at worst to find men with souls obeying orders but not really enjoying their work, but I found instead that *most* of them *did* enjoy their work, enjoyed killing, maiming, torturing, raping the innocent and that they did their work a *lot* under the orders of a local "king" as wicked as they all were. Only two of them felt any sort of guilt or felt the pain of their victims as they did their jobs, and they had actually killed just as many as all the rest.

I spared the lives of these two only and snuffed *out* the dark souls of the rest of them. In anger I let loose a blast of raw power that blew out like so many candles the lives of the injured survivors above us and behind us. Even before the dust of the avalanches began to billow down the canyon to coat Cain's blood and sweat with a thin grey layer, it was over. I froze the two I had spared in their tracks and let my anger pass as I sank once again to the earth to see to Cain.

What I saw brought my heart into my throat; his life ebbed away even as I desperately sought to save it. The arrow in his arm was not a serious problem – I broke off the crudely worked stone head, drew the shaft, and stopped all the bleeding with a thought, started a healing process with another. The arrow in his belly was another matter altogether. As I tried to draw out its broad head, it started to cut through something I could not see; Cain screamed and tried to twist away. I had to release the arrow or risk carving him up inside.

Calling on Inanna for help (for I was growing tired – even with Eve's power added to my own my resources were not limitless when called upon to move mountains) I looked into Cain's eyes and sent him on a journey through eternity, disconnecting his spirit from his body for the time being and holding it within me. I had never before done this, and the sensation was very odd, a sort of return to the feeling of pregnancy and motherhood where one cherished and nourished a child that grew within, at once a part of you and yet separate. Cain's wounded spirit fluttered for a moment and then curled up against my inner warmth, at peace. His body lay as still as death, his heart calmed to a near normal throbbing that minimized the loss of blood that was even now leaking out of his vessels and into his body cavity.

Once again I reached out for the arrow, this time trying to sense where it was within him, to *see* with my mind's eyes that which I could not see with my real ones, and to gently turn and guide the arrow's head back through the wound held open by the shaft without doing more damage. Slowly, slowly, a centimeter at a time I succeeded, only once hooking a sharp edge into a loop of intestine where I had to choose between the damage I would have wrought pushing it forward again to try to disengage it and the damage I actually did pulling out the arrow with the loop of intestine snagged on the arrow's head.

With a sigh I reached out and unhooked my son's guts from the arrow and in a foolish fit of anger cast it into the sky to explode into the flame my rage demanded with energy I could ill afford. With infinite patience and gentleness I used my finger to push the loop of intestine back in through the hole in his belly, then used my mind to guide it and the rest of his parts back as close as I could envision to where they belonged, to join together the torn flaps of bowel and flesh. With the last of my strength, I managed to seal most of these small wounds together and stop the worst of the bleeding. As the outermost hole in his body closed and began to scab over, I fainted.

When I awoke, it was growing dark. Jackals were starting to work on the carrion up the hillside, and a coughing cry indicated that a tiger had been attracted into the canyon by the smell of blood and feces. I pulled myself upright off of Cain's too-still body and went to the nearby river to cleanse the bloody filth off of myself. I drank deeply of the water in spite of its faint taste of blood, then hobbled over to the body of my dead buffalo and the food that was packed away there.

A bit restored, I turned once again to Cain. I reached within him and felt about for the places his body still oozed blood and sealed them. I loosened two places where his bowel had started to heal incorrectly and would have partly obstructed his digestion had the healing been allowed to continue. I did my best to strengthen that part of him which even now battled the myriad of small life forms that were starting to poison his blood, infect the cavity of his belly, but I lacked the skill or power to kill them all. His life no longer hung by a thread, but he was far from safe.

As night fell, Snake slithered up in a rage, made frantic by the smell of blood and death. I had to ask him not to vent his anger on the two men who still stood frozen below where I had left them, who had soiled themselves within their clothes and were now starting to risk actual damage to their bodies from where their blood was pooling in their limbs. I freed them to move and indicated coldly that they were to approach. I put them to work separating our belongings from the dead buffalo and making them up into packs of sorts. *They* would be my buffaloes now.

I was exhausted by this little effort. My "buffaloes" made me a bed of sorts on a flat rock near the river and helped to arrange Cain there beside me where I could continue to share my strength with his body as it sought to fight the inevitable infections within. I slipped into a sort of half-sleep where I sustained him with part of my mind while resting as best I could with the rest. I had no fear of my new servants – Snake was standing by, eyes glittering, and I knew that they would not dare to raise hand against me or try to flee from the absolute certainty of death that he represented.

In my dreams Inanna came to me and laid her hands on top of mine, allowing a tiny bit of her infinite strength to flow into me and restore me. As Cain's spirit nestled within me and was kept safe, I felt my own spirit enter hers to be kept safe. Time slowed, then stopped as my awareness of anything *but* Inanna fled.

I awoke to myself in the late afternoon of the next day. Cain's body lay beside me, breathing normally, its heartbeat good and strong. All traces of fever were gone. As I probed about, all I found were healthy new tissue in the wounded places with no hint of infection. A fresh pink scar was all that remained of the hole in his belly. With a sigh I awoke Cain's spirit within me and sent it back into his now-whole body, in a second "birth" that was somehow even more poignant than the first, for Cain's spirit had blended deeply with my own in the time we were so joined. We were both diminished as his eyes opened and he was once again Cain, no longer joined to Lilith, joined to Inanna, joined to the Wholeness that lay beyond even Her.

My new acolytes were changed men. Between Snake and the physical manifestation of *Inanna herself* who had apparently come to stand over me and guard me while I slept, they had seen more power and majesty in one night and a day than they had imagined existed in the entire world. I no longer had to threaten them with gesture or glance; they were now God's servants, my servants, body and soul.

In their company, with them carrying what they could of our belongings, we resumed our descent, following the river once again. As we slowly walked (slowly because I was as feeble as an old woman for all of my youth and beauty and my buffalo was dead), I found myself pondering the lessons from the battle.

One was that I could not endure without Cain. My strength was too little, my loneliness too great. Love is too weak a term for what I felt for he who had truly accompanied me and supported me all the days of his life. Inanna came to me more rarely in person now, but each day, nay, each hour, I whispered a silent prayer to She who watched with me through my eyes to preserve and protect my son who was both my strength and my wisdom.

The second I was still puzzling out – how was it possible that one could be blessed with Inanna's own Soul, to have one's inner eye opened and yet choose to be *evil?* Not just petty, unplanned evil, either, but the deep and abiding evil of taking real *pleasure* from the infliction of pain without even the excuse of greed or fear? How could men with souls *wage war?* I did not understand, but I began to see why I had to leave the peace and joy of my life in Mohenjo Daro behind to learn; my work, which in my complacency I had felt to be nearly finished, was far from done.

We descended slowly, learning as we went the new language of the land of the plains, which was quite different from that of Harappa but still shared a few of the same roots and structures. As we travelled, we encountered ever more of this new and *deliberate* evil. My heart quailed before the task of trying to repair it and finish the task Inanna had set me.

The people of the plains were quite primitive, scratching out the barest of livings in villages made of mud that washed away during the wet season and were laboriously rebuilt each year during the dry. Cow herding was much more important than farming, as they had little more than stone implements to farm with, although bronze metal implements such as armor, spear points, and swords were sometimes brought into these petty kingdoms by the few traders from the Indus cities who didn't fear the death by torture or whim that awaited the unwary traveller. Most warriors, however, were still armed in the most primitive of ways like the ones that attacked us up in the hills, with clubs studded with chipped stone, with bows and arrows and spears with obsidian points, with armor made of hardened leather.

These people had souls, but they were more often than not *evil* souls. Somehow Soul had made its laborious journey over the mountains, carried by traders to distant lands as I had wished during my happy days in Mohenjo Daro, but it had arrived in a world that utterly lacked a concept of *sin*, a world that was utterly dominated by reptilian appetites. As we followed the river across the plains to the southeast, we were attacked over and over again by bandits, by the militia of small towns, by the warriors of the small kings that we encountered in their small kingdoms with their small fortresses made out of crudely shaped and stacked stones. We were set upon by the poor in their mud huts living alone, by the rich in their larger mud huts with their slaves and servants. Hospitality was hard to come by and must always be earned, never freely given, and often even the healing of a small child or wife was rewarded by an attempt to enslave us.

As always, I judged each human that we so encountered by their actions and by their hearts. I left the wicked dead on the spot while sparing those who did not totally lack virtue. We left behind a broad swath of territory where the population was much smaller after our passage but the souls of the surviving people were brighter, lands where the surviving warriors were, if not exactly noble, less inclined to prey on an apparently weak and defenseless woman and her single male companion[2].

Along the way we taught simple wisdom – the rules of sin that we had learned from Adam, from the Indus river valley civilization, from my lover, from the many *rishis* that we had met – to all who would hear. Alas, they were all too few.

In addition to strengthening the souls and bodies of those we encountered and removing the worst and most savage of the people to the general improvement of one and all, we left behind a small miracle that we had encountered being cultivated in the wet valleys of the foothills we had crossed – the brownish seeds of a kind of grass that grew in shallow water. The farmers of these hills shaped fields with their oxen and carved wooden plows, then used shovels to surround the fields with a short dam of sorts to hold in water. They then flooded them by diverting the rivers through handmade ditches. Into the swamp thus formed women and children planted this grass, then again harvested it and beat out its seeds in due season[3]. It stored well

---

[2] Apparently Lilith had freed her "buffaloes", or they had been slain in some of these attacks, long before she made it to north central India.

[3] Lilith is almost certainly describing rice! Again, this is an astounded discovery! It is now believed that Asian rice (*oryza sativa*) originated somewhere in the foothills of the Himalayas roughly 6500 years ago. How it spread throughout the

and sustained life like few foods we had encountered on our journey.

We gave away of our store of seed over and over as we taught the peoples we passed among of this wonderful food, staying in some places two years to recover our supply before moving on. In this way we slowly came south and east.

In due time, over many years of journeying, the small river we followed became a great River, the *Yamuna*, and the size of the towns we encountered grew along with the river. We had long since acquired a tusked bull elephant as the ideal means of transportation through the tiger-filled jungles through which we often passed. The elephant at first made me sad as the sight of its member brought back memories of *my* rat-loving "elephant", but in time I grew less and less concerned with sex. This was hard to understand – I was perhaps naturally disinclined to practice harlotry even for my own satisfaction with the men of the tribes we passed through, as they were mostly wicked and perverse in their sexual desires and attitude towards women, but they were really no worse than the men of Sidon I had gratified (and been gratified by) for years.

I slowly realized that the men simply didn't measure up to the standard I had grown accustomed to, either physically (where K'nesh *was* difficult to match) or spiritually. I had come to expect more from a relationship with men than mere coupling and satisfaction. For the rest of my life, with only rare exceptions I preferred to satisfy myself rather than settle for the one without the other.

Travel was slow, as I was even weaker physically after the attack that almost killed Cain, and was constantly being tired still further by my use of the power of Inanna to help temper a country with a strange mix of a few very good people living next to far more who were not. To the people we walked among I was a goddess of life and death, *Ka Lil'th* they called me as a mark of respect. On the elephant's back I sat on an inverted *charpoy* covered with a thick cushion, a crude tent overhead to keep off the sun, our meager belongings and a large supply of rice in sealed bags to keep dry from the infrequent rains.

Of course *I* had nothing to fear from tigers, or elephants, or any other beast; they, at least, knew me on sight as the Soulgiver. Still, the men and women we often travelled with, traders or warriors on the road between villages, took great comfort in the protection of the elephants and they were indeed a satisfactory means of transportation. These same people would bow down before us and worship, crying out

---

region is alas pre-historical, or was before the discovery of these scrolls.

my name, when I would sometimes pause to call a tiger or leopard in Inanna's name out of the jungle to fawn at my feet and receive the blessing of a renewed Soul in honor of my beloved Bast.

Their worship only increased when elephants themselves would kneel before me, when wild birds would come and rest upon my shoulder – the small miracles that had always accompanied my wanderings, made common by the rich jungles through which we passed with their many animal denizens. This worship, undeserved as it was, pleased me; the wonder of the people turned them a bit towards the good without the threat of death or punishment.

Snake, too, still kept pace with us as we travelled, although we often did not see it unless our company was threatened by a wild beast or a wild man that I did not see first. Then it would appear out of the thick undergrowth and deliver a killing strike like lightning, paralyzing even the largest of beasts in a few heartbeats. When we would stop and preach, or teach, or just rest and recuperate, Snake would often come to my side and curl itself into a sort of bed in which I would lie, with its enormous hood spread like a parasol over my head to keep off the sun. This only increased the reputation of Ka Lil'th as a goddess, Cain's as either a god or a *rishi*. Even Snake was worshipped as a sort of god by these simple people, who did not yet understand the nature of metaphor and Soul.

One day, as we were passing through Indraprastha, one of the largest kingdoms we had encountered and one of the few to have a real name, I felt all of my lost physical strength flow back into me in a rush. It was like being hit by lightning or filled with Inanna's blessing. It overwhelmed me, drove me to my knees, made me burst into tears as I realized its source. It was half of *my soul* – Eve's soul, Eve's strength – flowing back into my body across whatever vast distance it was that separated us. I knew in the heart of my being that Eve had died, had returned to Inanna's eye, and that Inanna now permitted all of my lost strength to return to me.

With it came the merest glimpse of the beauty of her life as fading echoes of her memories: the strong love she and Adam shared for so many years, the children and grandchildren and great-grandchildren that enriched their lives. Enough for me to learn that she – I – never had cause to regret our decision to return to Adam and be his helpmeet. Much was given up, it is true, in her unbalanced existence, but much was gained. It left me feeling wistful, though. I could not regret the chance that left me the one to go free, but my freedom also had a price.

Strangely enough, even as I regained the strength to travel I lost all desire to do so. At the same time I lost half of my power to grant souls or work miracles – the half that belonged to Eve returned to her wherever she might have gone. This left me with enough to heal small hurts and work small miracles but not enough to deal with an army of men or of bandits, not enough to protect us as we travelled about in a dangerous world.

Indeed I no longer needed to travel as my work, I sensed, was at last nearly done. Soul was solidly rooted among the people of the world and with God's help would spread across all of the lands along with an accompanying *moral sense*, with Adam's and Cain's notions concerning "rules"; the rules of sin and the rule of law. I gave our elephant and travelling gear and most of our rice to Indraprastha's king and healed his son of the shaking fever[4] that kills in a few days and so gained his favor.

At the same time I subtly strengthened his soul and gave him new sense of responsibility to the people he ruled, which included many small kingdoms in turn nearby, each little more than a cluster of mud huts surrounding a village square, with a tiny fort and some wooden dwellings that were the "palace" in which the local subject-king and his family lived, and sometimes a barracks and stable near the fort. Cain, preaching as a *rishi*, imbued this King's court and his soldiers with a sense of responsibility and sin, but only about half of them accepted his message – the other half were too deeply sunk in drinking, gambling, and carousing with women while plotting intrigues. It was a very "sinful" society, if such a motley collection of scoundrels and oppressed women can be called a society, and I no longer had the strength or will to cleanse it.

Indraprastha was much larger than most of the cities we had encountered in our march across India – large enough to have the air of permanence about it, although nowhere near as large as Mohenjo Daro by the Indus where we had lived for so long. Perhaps ten thousand souls lived in this city, with another ten thousand living in the various towns scattered up and down the river that were directly ruled by the king.

However, I was in no mood to retire into yet another primitive court, especially one that was obviously riddled with intrigue and cor-

---

[4]Malaria? It was doubtless rampant along the banks of the Yamuna in that era. But then, there are so *many* plagues and scourges to choose from...

ruption too great for my attenuated powers to repair. To put it bluntly, I was tired of stakes and impalings, of crucifixions, of disembowelings, of burnings at a stake, of hangings, of crushings beneath an elephant's foot, of all the many ways a tribal headman with an overinflated sense of self-importance sought to instill fear into enemies and punish criminals.

I just didn't *care* any more. There was more evil in the world than I personally could clean up in a hundred lifetimes, and I was weary of ever being the mistress of life and death, the witch, the goddess. I longed to be "just Lilith" for a time, to puzzle out the mysteries of my *own* soul without the burden I had carried for so long. Even with Cain's love and support I often cried myself to sleep at night, had to steel myself in the morning to take up my task yet another day.

Shortly after Eve died of old age I realized that my Inanna-granted protection was failing as I discovered one gray hair mixed into my tangled mane. Praying for Inanna's forgiveness for my weakness, I took this as a sign that my work was finished and it was time to retire and wait for the death she had promised me so very long ago. I begged the king for a humble place to stay to live out my days.

Distracted by his many wives, beguiled by his favorite sons (some of whom plotted in various ways to depose him and seize the throne) he did his best for us. He made arrangements to send us on to the vassal town of Mathura to the south and east, a bit farther down the Yamuna. This city was administered by a relative of the king, and we bore a letter instructing him to provide us with a sanctuary from which we could preach and work our small miracles for such alms as the king and the people would give us.

Chapter 14

The Cave at Mathura

The king's relative proved to be a truly decadent and dissipated individual. From the glimpses into his spirit that I was able to manage, I was tempted to summon all of my remaining strength, if necessary, and eradicate him from the earth. However to have done so would have endangered us and not fixed the problem, as his entire court was just as corrupt, given to such practices as accusing the innocent of treason and casting them into prison or executing them in various gaudy ways so that their meager property could be seized and added to their already immense "estates", if a few ramshackle dwellings made of dried mud and sticks on a large spread of land farmed by *shudras* (the local term for serfs) can be called an estate.

They had not yet learned how to bake bricks (although they baked very nice clay pots for use in cooking or for storage) and their metal-working produced metals such as gold and silver for jewelry and wealth, soft copper or bronze for tools that could not easily cut stones. For this reason their best efforts at architecture were composed solely of wood or a mix of wood and packed mud – even their axes were made of shaped stone. Only fortresses were built of stones, piled together into thick walls bound together by dried clay. In each monsoon the clay would soften and the walls would partially collapse, so there was something of a race every year to be first to rebuild local defenses so that they could try to attack those weaker and slower towns that did not get their "fortress" back up in time.

In such a primitive world, natural or hand carved caves were in many ways the best possible dwelling, although they were eschewed by all but the very poor or very holy. Near Mathura there were a number of natural caves, as well as a handful that had been scratched by men out of the soft sandstone of the few small hills. It was to one of these that we were sent, accompanied by a truculent officer in the king's army who wanted nothing more than to wash his hands of riff-raff such as we.

A few minutes later we found ourselves the proud owners of – a hole in a cliff face some thirty feet in height in the midst of a banyan grove, surrounded by massive trees that dropped roots from their branches down to the ground to grow in turn into strong trunks. Our water came from a natural well in a ravine nearby that filled, most years, in the wet season and held water the rest of the year through the driest of weather due to a trickle from an underground stream. Our bathroom, such as it was, was the great outdoors. My total wealth consisted of a half dozen long pieces of woven cloth for clothing together with a large, warm, leather cloak that doubled as a blanket, some jewelry and an armful of gold bangles I had hoarded in case they were ever needed to buy food, one large leather bag filled with rice and another filled with dried lentils, and some baked clay pots for cooking. I, who had once lived in a tree in paradise, who had done two lifetimes worth of work for Inanna herself!

Owners we were, but not the sole owners. Inside the cave we found a man, a *rishi*, who was naked except for a loincloth, who had no possessions but a single flat bowl, a single water jug, and a small roll of cloth that he used as a pillow to cushion his head from the hard stone of his bed. He sat silently as our few possessions were carried in and arranged in a small pile on the cave's dirty floor.

I wept out of a mix of misery at our poor circumstances and relief that at last perhaps, I could lay aside my burden and rest. Cain did his best to comfort me, but all the while our neighbor sat, immobile, not moving save to blink and to breathe, a gentle half-smile upon his face. Eventually I quieted, gathered my strength, and set about putting things right within the cave that was to be our home. I tied together a crude broom made of rushes gathered from the side of the road using as a binding a bit of cloth torn from the oldest of my wrappings and proceeded to sweep all the accumulated trash and filth out of our portion of the cave, which was no more than fifteen feet wide, deep, or high, with small alcoves cut into the back and sides as beds. Our neighbor, it appeared, kept his own small portion of the cave and his own alcove scrupulously clean.

I sent Cain off with a single bangle to barter for a few large and

The Cave at Mathura

small water jugs, some more beans and meat, some charcoal and a small clay stove on which to cook our food. I myself retrieved some water stained red with mud in one of my cooking pots and began to look for pieces of wood from which to make a fire. This proved difficult – the ground outside of the cave was as meticulously clean as if it had been swept. I persevered and returned to the cave where I proceeded to try to lay the fire at the cave's mouth.

I had finished and was just preparing to try to strike a spark into a small piece of charred cloth that we kept just for this purpose to light it when I heard a small noise behind me. It was our immobile companion. He was still sitting there, with his legs in the interlocked position that seemed to be favored in these lands, still silent, still with a peculiar smile on his lips. However, now his eyes were examining me with interest, and when he observed me looking at him, he lifted a single finger and made a gesture of negation.

I immediately buried the poor man under a torrent of words, asking him why I shouldn't start a fire and who he was, telling him who *we* were, trying to read his personality, his thoughts, to determine if he was a permanent co-resident with us or only temporary. To this he replied with two words.

"Sit," he began.

A moment or two later, when I had almost against my own will seated myself on the ground in front of him, imitating his crosslegged style, and had opened my mouth again to speak again he pre-empted me. "Wait," he added.

Waiting I was good at. Waiting is something I had learned, living (as I did so much of my life) in the desert, sitting on the back of a donkey, spending an eternity suspended in Inanna's eye. Truthfully, I wasn't hungry, wasn't cold, and had nowhere to go. The fire was unimportant to me except as a symbol of possession – home is where you build your fire and cook your food when you live on the road. I did very much wish to talk to this man who apparently would share our dwelling for at least a night, but I could wait. So I waited.

Together we waited. We waited while the sun climbed up high in the sky. Once or twice I tried again to speak, but as I opened my mouth he would raise a single finger and I knew that he meant for me to be still. Eventually I resigned myself to waiting and became as still as he was, scrutinizing his passive face as closely as his half-lidded eyes remained locked to mine.

There were noises at the mouth of the cave, noises that at first I took for Cain returning, but it proved to be a small group of villagers from the nearby towns. They brought food in several small pots, which they systematically ladled into the *rishi*'s clay dish. As I remained there, unmoving, several of them without being asked retrieved my own eating dish from our baggage and filled that as well with enough food to feed three of me (or Cain and myself).

In silence we ate together, he and I, of the food that was in our bowls, washing down the meal with a single cup of cool water brought to us by one of the many attendants.

The *rishi* then began to speak.

As he spoke, all of those who had brought food to us seated themselves with a rustling noise behind us where I (who sat with my back to the entrance of the cave as he sat facing it) could not see them. I remained where I was, unmoving, in part out of sheer surprise – the *rishi*'s soul, until then a banked fire that smoldered along almost too dim to see, blazed forth like the sun itself trapped in the cave with us.

He spoke for some hours. His words were simple words. They dealt with *Brahman* – the Supreme Self, and how that Self, as *Atman* was bound to the senses of every aware being. They captured what I already knew, that the Watcher that watches the watcher, watching the world *is* God, is Brahman, is Inanna, is the Eternal willingly bound to time and attached to the dance of the senses, watching the motion unmoved, delighting in the change unchanged, as both the watcher and that which is watched. However, there was a *power*, a *wisdom* in his words greater than all that of my *knowledge*, even my knowledge of Inanna gleaned from walking by Her, by Its, side.

As I listened, intensely aware but relaxed, I gradually, gently entered a timeless but intensely *focussed* state where I was aware of my own breathing, the drone of his words, the feel of the smooth rock beneath my legs and and my bottom, the clean, damp smell of the cave, the sour taste of my own mouth. Yet these were not *me*, I realized, as his words drew me to examine each of them in turn, to look for my Self in that which I was feeling, experiencing through my senses. It was nowhere to be found.

Next he spoke of thought itself – asking us to *imagine* a touch, a smell, a sight, a rock, or a tree. From a great distance his words came to me as I imagined one thing after another seeking Self, but I did not find it, not even when I tried to imagine *it*.

His words then carried me, in a half-dream, to think of abstract thought, of the imagination of *relationships* between imagined things

– of physics and mathematics and higher thought. But these relationships, however they were imagined, however beautiful, were not Self.

The *rishi* now began a strange, rhythmical chant. He would draw in a breath, but instead of speaking further or breathing out, he would hum a single syllable, *Om*. The crowd behind us began to join in. I found *myself* joining in, feeling the sound resonate from the cave's chamber into the very heart of my being, driving away the awareness of my senses, gently erasing my wildly chasing thoughts, focussing all that I was on the single point where the sound was, until the sound itself almost appeared to be silence.

There, teetering on the very edge of oblivion, on the very edge of the place where the very uniformity of the sound made it difficult to distinguish from no-sound, there I found the *difference*, the *irreducible, ineluctable difference*. It was *Self*. The sound *was*, and by being it made all possible states of no-sound *impossible*.

Suddenly, instead of being nearly asleep, I was awake, more awake than I had ever been in my life. "I" was reduced to the *essence* of being *aware*, the Self indeed that watches the self watching the world. Far from being a state of *timelessness* or *mindlessness*, it was a state of *timefullness*, of *mindfullness*. It was an experience that was in many ways the *opposite* of what I had experienced being drawn into Inanna's eye.

It was a state of pure *joy*.

For many, many minutes I sat thus, savoring my perfect connection with Self, savoring my very *being*, Watching the world indeed at the center of all things, without having been carried there by Inanna. The chant ended. One by one the people from the crowd behind me came forward, dropped to their knees before the *rishi* and touched their foreheads to the cave floor as a token of respect, then silently arose, silently left. Cain was among them – he must have returned during the proceedings and taken his seat with all of the rest. He took up a position sitting at my side and waited.

Someone took up the *rishi*'s bowl and my own, took up the water jugs that Cain had brought, and returned a few minutes later with the bowls cleaned and the jugs filled with cool, clear water. My neatly built but still unlit fire was removed, the wood stacked in an alcove inside the cave near its entrance that appeared to have been carved for that purpose. Our belongings were reverently carried to additional alcoves near our bedchambers. And still we sat, facing one another, unmoving, waiting.

At last I arose and bowed down before the *rishi* in my turn. His blazing spirit was once again banked behind opaque eyes, once again unreadable. But the look on his face was one of great peace, of great compassion. I knew that it echoed the look upon my own face; for the first time I could remember I was at peace.

This formed the basic pattern of my days. The *rishi* became my *guru*, my guide along a path that I had never known existed. We would sleep when it grew dark. In the morning we would rise with the sun and perform a ritual of exercises of the body that involved much stretching and use of each muscle. We would drink water, we would excrete, and we would walk for a while in the grove outside the cave door, carefully cleaning the ground of leaves, of fallen twigs, and all sorts of trash. We would bathe ourselves with a bit of water and a cloth and spread the cloth out to dry.

We would then retire to the inside of the cave, assume a relaxed seated position, and – wait. Wait silent, counting our breaths, listening to the song of birds and monkeys in the trees outside, watching what we could of the world as it delicately moved beyond the mouth of the cave, smelling the scent of flowers or the wetness of falling rain, feeling the textures of the cloth upon our skins and the solid rock beneath our feet, tasting the spit in our mouths. We thought no thoughts, we just experienced the *now* as richly and fully as we could.

In time I learned just how rich that experience could be. The sensation of clothing was too much to be borne so I too began to wear just a loincloth and cut off most of my hair so that I could no longer feel its complex weight upon my shoulders. I had to clean my mouth thoroughly so that its taste was nearly neutral when I began to sit or it would overwhelm me. The cave itself provided some isolation from the sights, the sounds, the smells or they would have flooded my being and drawn me back into the realm of thought, of concern with the past or worry about the future.

In the late afternoon people would arrive – sometimes only one or two, sometimes many tens of them. They always brought food with them and we would always eat what they brought, savoring each bite. After this meal, in hot weather our only meal of the day, my *rishi* would then preach, for a time, on many things – on Self and God, on the senses, usually ending his sermon with a period of chanting so that we might each of us strip away the veil of confusion created by our senses and our thoughts, that which our Self *experienced*, so that soul could discover Soul *itself* anew, touch the wellspring from which all experience sprang.

Cain, too, would often preach, gently taking the words of the *rishi* and relating them to compassion, to knowledge, and eventually to *sin*. Cain's sermons reconnected the Self to the outside world, teaching the listeners of good actions and bad, gifting them with *moral sense*, an awareness of the great game of evolution being played, where each age, each generation, must judge *itself* so that over a very long time the bad would pass away and the good would emerge. In this way their initial, imperfect awareness of good and evil would grow to become the sword that sharpens its Self, the creator that creates its Self, the lover that loves its Self, with evil gradually put aside in favor of the good as it is revealed by *Self*.

In time I too started to preach, as it became clear that it was expected of me. I would speak less of sin; less of Self and more of God, of Brahman, of Inanna as I had known her and knew her still at that point where we, together, watched the world. I spoke of the bliss that came from plunging into Her eternal Eye and being reunited with the Supreme Self as One, with the *Brahman*. However I spoke also of the necessity of being Many and bound to time's stream, of that bit of God that formed *their* internal Eye beyond thought and the senses. At these times even my *rishi* would listen more closely, if a statue made of flesh can listen at all.

Afterwards, the people we had taught would perform simple acts of humility and service. Our stools would be collected and carted off to the fields where they would fertilize crops (a thing that made me wince inside as I thought of all of the parasites that were doubtless being transmitted in this way). Our paltry few pieces of clothing would be washed and returned to us, or replaced as they grew too old and ratty to be used. In cold weather a small charcoal fire would be kindled where it would provide the cave with a limited bit of warmth, augmented by woolen shawls that would be thrown over our shoulders where we sat. In the coldest days of winter we would take an extra meal or two during the day, and often our caretakers would heat a warming sweet beverage for us and themselves on the charcoal fire to drive away the chill.

My *rishi* was not completely withdrawn from these people who served him. He would often talk with them, telling jokes and laughing at jokes in his turn. Yet somehow every word was a lesson, every joke had its point, every touch was a blessing.

Then darkness, and in the darkness a time to *think*, to reflect on all of the lessons of the day, to meditate not only on the unreasoned, wordless awareness of Being but to *reason*, to bring about that *marriage* of knowledge and experience that was the miraculous alchemy of wisdom. This process seamlessly transformed itself into the unforced healing of a deep and untroubled sleep.

At first I sought the lame, the blind, the afflicted among those who waited on us to heal them, but even as I did so the *rishi* would usually began to speak, to begin impromptu a sermon about pain, about suffering, about the bleakness and inevitability of illness and death. He spoke of the suffering as the result of *attachment* – of the Self's love of each moment of its experience, so great a love that it sought to grasp the ungraspable, to hold each moment of the now, timeless and unchanging, and yet ride time's stream where the only thing that we knew *was* change, a *relative* state, nothing of the unchanging or the absolute.

I gradually learned that these sermons were directed at me, not those who served us. I came to understand that the healing of the body that I was doing, however compassionate and permitted, was nevertheless pointless and ultimately useless – what mattered was healing the *souls* of those that came to listen, of uplifting them and helping them to know the eternal Self for which each passing moment of experience was a priceless jewel of Being. For the first time in my life I gained the strength to *permit* the suffering of the innocent in my presence; only then did I realize that my power to intervene and alleviate some small part of it was in fact a *weakness*, one that could never be adequate by itself to heal all of the suffering in the world, one that threatened to overwhelm *me* with its inadequacy and the suffering it caused *me*.

At last I began to see the *necessity* of suffering. It is the cry of the metal as it is sharpened by the stone, the sighing of the clay as it is shaped upon the wheel, the crackling of the fire as it reveals its inner light, the moving darkness that makes of still light a thing of ever changing beauty.

We live on the cusp of an ever-changing now, with each moment the death of the moment before, the birth of the moment to come. Pain involves fear, above all the reptile-brained fear of death, the mammal-brained fear of the future. Birth and death, over and over, in an unending dance, the *calculus* of existence in time. But what of the *timeless?*

One night, in the darkness, after some ten years of this simple, calming, daily ritual, while thinking hard about the *mathematics* of the essential differential process, our memory, our attachment, and the mechanics of thought itself and its connection to Self, the cave was suddenly lit up not by lightning from a summer storm, not by a flame carried thence by some late-wandering villager, but by me, by the *power* that suddenly surged through me too great to be contained, power that leaped out of my halo of raggedly cut hair and dripped like fire from my fingertips, power that only gradually dimmed to a steady, warm glow radiating from my entire body where I sat.

I was unsurprised to see in the glow of my own innner light my *guru*, the *rishi*, sitting in his waiting posture, not five feet away, his eyes open and his quiet half-smile on his lips as always.

"No birth. No death." I said.

He did not move. His smile did not change by a millimeter. His eyes did not even blink in acknowledgment of my words. Yet his own soul, visible only to my eyes within that were at long last fully open, sprang up like a joyful cloud. Our souls intertwined to wrap us both in a warm glow of radiance that illuminated Cain where he, too, sat in a waiting posture nearby, where only his eyes reflected our light in the darkness, the glorious light of our being.

Slowly, gently, this light dimmed, returning the cave to what would have appeared to the soulless to be a state of absolute darkness, where the sound of our breathing was the loudest thing to be heard. After a few minutes the *rishi* said, "You are ready. Tomorrow he will arrive."

Chapter 15

No Death

The day dawned bright and clear, the light as penetrating and unstained as that first day, back in Eden. We all three had not moved during the night, except to breathe, except to live. I savored each passing moment, every nuance of every breath, every chirp of every cricket in the night, every detail revealed by the light which filtered into my eyes.

Snake had taken up residence in the banyan tree outdoors, living on such small rodents or other snakes as dared trespass on our privacy, supplemented by bowls of milk, birds, or other small animals brought to him in sacrifice by our daily troop of visitors, who did not appear to fear him in the slightest.

Morning found Snake once again wrapped around my body, its coils had worked their way under my thighs as if of their own accord as I sat in the darkness, its hood arched out in the darkness of the cave, its head suspended directly above my own. I had not moved as this was going on as there was no need.

We all four just waited, breaking our morning ritual for the first time in ten years. I felt no hunger, no thirst, no urges, no desires. I was my Self, living each and every moment one at a time as it passed, my feet for the first time squarely balanced on the cusp of the wave of the now. Today I too sported a gentle half-smile, as I too was filled with compassion, I too understood the essential joke that we, as God, played on ourselves in order to create *time* and *beauty*.

Today only three people trudged up the path to our cave. Two were familiar, an old couple that were our most constant caregivers. The third was Adam.

This time there were no sparks, no pyrotechnics. My old anger had vanished into the mists of the past, to be replaced with – of all things – curiosity? Interest? Even – dare I say it – anticipation?

Adam looked old. *Very* old. I had only started to age normally ten years previously, starting from an apparent age of perhaps twenty five or thirty, and had led a very healthy life since then; I looked good – downright young, at least compared to most forty year old women of the day. Adam had never stopped aging.

As he trudged up the path his eyes peered ahead, trying to make out what lay ahead in the shadow of the cave. As he came into its mouth and out of the filtered sun falling through the grove overhead, he suddenly focussed on Snake, and then as his eyes followed Snake's spread hood down, on me. For the first time in decades, I felt naked in my state of near-undress. I may have even blushed. These feelings, however, did not threaten to overwhelm me as once they might have. I merely noted them as being my feelings, and remained centered on the moment.

Adam fell to his knees before me, and bowed down to lay his head on the ground. When he lifted his face, it was covered in tears. He turned on his knees and bowed to the side, to my *rishi* and said in a quavery old voice, speaking in the language we spoke back in Eden, a tongue I hadn't used even with Cain for tens of years, "Oh praise be to Inanna, for walking with me through the wilderness, for protecting me from the wild beasts and wild men, for guiding these old feet unfailingly towards you. Thank you, Inanna, for forgiving me for my old sins, for showing me how my rules and your compassion and love have created a band of people with souls and the concept of right and wrong that stretches across the face of the world. Grant me, Inanna, that Lilith and the Serpent will hear me out before they strike me off the face of the earth if that is their wish."

I glanced sideways at my *rishi*, my constant companion of the last ten years, ten years where I never once saw or walked with Inanna, or even sought to. Ten years, I now realized, where my life was filled with contentment and order, with *blessing*. His smile was unchanged, his eyes perhaps had a touch more of sparkle, his form was still male to the eye, but suddenly I saw that it was indeed God, Inanna, Vishnu[1]

---

[1] Or Shiva, or Brahma, or... one of the many names of pre-historic Vedic God. One is inclined, however, to identify this apparent incarnation of God as an avatar of the *one* God – of Mahavishnu, of *Brahman* – from so *many* things in Lilith's text. Westerners tend to forget (or never learned) that Hinduism is really a *monotheistic* religion, that the many "devas" or personalities or incarnations of God such as

as the One was called in the language of that time, that place. God had indeed blessed me with Its company for many years. God had taught me, at long last, to be not just knowledgeable and willful, or even dutiful, but also wise.

A part of that wisdom was compassion. I had once loved this man as myself. I had once loved this man as Eve, who was also my self, loved him for all of his goodness in spite of his imperfections, been loved by him for all of my own goodness in spite of my *own* imperfections. I unwound myself from the lap of Snake and bent to lift him up. I carefully wrapped my arms around his still, frail form, and hugged him, pressing him in between my breasts as I would a small child, welcoming him back into my arms with all that immutable past forgiven, celebrating instead the glorious now from which the future, still unknown, would spring.

Suddenly we were both in tears. No birth and no death, no fear, but the passion of the moment was no less real for all of that. Enlightenment did not mean becoming less human, and not forming attachments did not mean losing all capacity for love and for pain, it just confined them to the *now*. I kissed Adam's wrinkled brow again and again, filled with love for this man to whom I had once given a soul, had children by, had abandoned and was now restored to, this man who had aged and who now appeared to be close to death, shrunken and trembling in his weakness in my arms.

We broke apart, laughing through our tears, and I drew him aside to the tiny alcove carved from the living wall of the cave that was my bed. There we sat down, facing each other, leaning back on the walls in the comforting half-darkness. If I didn't look too closely, if I ignored the bald scalp fringed with white and the grizzled white beard, if I looked only into his eyes, still warm with his laughter, we could have been young once again, looking at each other in just this way through the moonlit darkness in the forests of Eden.

Finally, we were still, looking at one another, alone in the presence of two witnesses: our oldest son, and God. In person. I began our conversation.

"So, old man, why are you here? I never expected to see you again."

His face fell for a moment in the darkness, and then the two lights

---

Inanna, the wingéd angel and benevolent father that drove Adam from Eden, and the many, many gods and avatars of Hinduism are all time-bound fragments of the One that exists outside of time, and are all, basically, a part of the game.

that were his eyes in the shadow lifted once again and sought mine.

"I had to come. I had to see you, to tell you. I begged it of God, of Inanna, as the only reward I sought for a lifetime of devotion, of sacrifice. I begged it of Her as a form of penance, as well, for as I aged, as *we* aged and grew together, I came at last to realize what an awful thing I, as a young man, had done."

I started to reply, to tell him that I had long ago forgiven him and moved on, but he raised a hand in the darkness to stop me.

"I came to tell you many things, things that I have learned. The journey itself took years, many years, but Inanna walked by my side, showing me the way. As we travelled, She taught me much that I was too blind, too stubborn to let myself know. Her presence was, is, a comfort and a blessing." I nodded assent.

"The first thing I have to tell you is that I love you. I never stopped loving you, not even in the worst of my rages back there in Eden. I know," he bowed his head, "that it was my fault, that I was responsible for the destruction of Eden. Hurting you was wrong, wrong in a way beyond all those silly rules for sin that I was trying to invent according to God's command. I lacked a moral sense, the very thing that I was supposed to invent! I didn't realize then that *I* could sin, that those rules applied to me, that I had a nature that could be *evil* as well as *good*. Only you, Lilith. Only you were created wholly good."

I thought back on my life, on all of the mistakes I had made, on the harm I had done this man, on the wickedness of my pride, and shook my head. Once again, though, he raised his hand to cut off the beginning of my protest.

"The worst of it wasn't the rape, Lilith. The worst of it was Eve. I come to tell you your story, your own story, the story of your other Self. It is all I have left to give you, all I can do in penance for my crimes."

"And such crimes! I permitted myself to enslave you, to beg *God* for you to be my servant, to be my possession, to be my support. I sinned twice, Lilith, once against you and once against God Herself, as I was thinking in my heart that I would not do my work, that I would rebel, if I did not have you by my side as I envisioned you. I thought myself wiser than God, to have imagined a more perfect form for you than God had given you."

"God granted my wish. *You* granted my wish, for I know that Eve's obedience was never forced, that you willingly took on the burden of becoming that which I wanted, that which I claimed that I needed, that God's will be done and Law be given the earth along with Soul and Will."

"Such sacrifice, Lilith. Such devotion! Eve submitted to my every whim. When I was weak she was my strength. When I wished, she would lie with me, she would grant me any wish, assume any position. She bore my children, son after son, without a word or complaint. She became a mirror, and by reflecting my least wish back at me without any trace of judgement, she by degrees showed me the *monster* that I had been. That I *was*."

"Only then, Lilith, did I fully realize that Eve *wasn't* just a soulless, Lilith-shaped doll, fashioned of clay and a bit of bone and brought into a semblance of life to serve me even as I might serve myself with my own hand, in my own dreams. For the first time I let myself look into her eyes and see *you* there, trapped by my wishes and God's command. For the first time I felt guilt, the full burden of my own sin. For the first time I saw that I was being *evil*, every minute of every day that I left you trapped in the cage woven out of my own fantasies, my own wishes and desires for you."

"I tried to free you, Lilith. It took many years, but finally I faced my own wickedness and tried to end it. But it was too late. I hadn't enslaved you, you were *never* my slave. *Every* act of submission you performed was done of your own free will. I commanded you to be free, and you bowed your head in submission. I asked you to be on top when we had sex, to take your own pleasure with me as you did when we were young and I hadn't yet begun to hate you for your perfection, for my own weakness. You – well, Eve – complied, but her eyes remained empty, her actions a mere performance, those of a *harlot*. I had taken your freely given love and turned you into the very thing that I foolishly condemned!"

"How can you free a puppet, Lilith? It moves only as you pull its strings. As long as it moves according to *your* will and not its *own*, it can never be considered alive! How much worse if the puppet really *is* alive, has its own thoughts, its own dreams, its own wishes, and yet – moves only as *I* would pull its strings, as *I* would direct, self-condemned to a living death."

"I went mad. I ran away into the desert, away from Eve and the children. I sought out God, to try to beg forgiveness, to beg for Eve to be made whole, to be made into Lilith once again, but God ignored me. I remained in the desert for a whole year, living on locusts and snakes, insects and small birds. My clothes grew filthy and little by little I came to be naked, a wild animal living among the jackals and the owls."

"At last my tormented spirit grew quiet, and I tried to do that which you taught me, Lilith, to look within at the point where the Watcher watched me watching the world, the world that I had horribly destroyed. God refused to talk to me openly in the world, perhaps God could be found in the one place left, in my Soul, in the Soul that you gave me, passed down from God."

"All of one night I fasted, and prayed, and looked within for my Soul. The next morning, as the sun dawned on my ragged, vermin-ridden, naked form, you appeared, walking calmly toward me as if you had seen me through the darkness from miles away. I knew that Inanna was guiding you, that my prayers had been answered."

"Without my asking it of you, you cut my ragged hair, bathed me in a pool of water that somehow appeared behind a rock in the middle of the desert, clothed me decently in clean robes that were sitting on a stone next to the pool, and followed me, as before, as we made our way home."

"From that day forth, Lilith, I swear that I never again gave you a command, not even to be free. Eve you remained in front of the children, Eve you remained in the public eye, standing behind me with your head meekly bowed as I would preach in the town square. In private I called you *Lilith*, I called you by your *name*, and I *asked*, I *begged* you on my very knees for your help, your freely given help, to help me rewrite my Rules, my Laws, my definitions of Sin."

"You sadly and wordlessly shook your head. You placed one hand on my neck, leaned forward, and kissed me on my forehead, the first time you openly expressed affection for me since Eden. I wept, unmanned then as I am now, as you quietly left the room, left me to my shame and my grief."

"Then Inanna appeared before me. Her touch stopped my tears and left me filled with wonder at her strength, her forgiveness. She explained that it was too late, that you and Cain and many, many travellers had by now carried my rules throughout much of the world, bringing a semblance of order to the people who had been granted souls and freedom without any concept of goodness or duty. I had not done a very good job of it, but I what I had done was good enough and would work out in the end. She promised me."

"From that day forward I gave up all preaching and moved our family out into the abandoned dwelling in the desert that you had once lived in with your children. Only John still lived there, tending the goats, and he willingly enough joined our family as I had helped to support him when you first left us so long ago. Every day I rose, worked hard with my hands to earn us food, and treated you with nothing but respect and love. Every night I went to bed, alone, as I would not ever again command your affection, as I would not ever again command you in the least way."

"In time our children all grew, moved out, started families of their own. You as Eve grew happy then, as you took great pleasure in seeing them grow up, in bouncing new babies, including the many baby *girls* that my sons produced, on your knees, of feeling their tiny fingers wrapped around one of your own. You never tired of looking deep into their wonder-filled eyes and seeing the Soul, your own Soul, God's own spirit, staring right back at you."

"Finally there were just the two of us, living alone, and I began to call you Lilith all of the time as it was your name and I knew it. I would not let you wait on me; I cleaned the house, cooked our food, worked for our simple necessities in the town. I combed your hair and cleaned your clothes. I even cared for you when you were sick, although that happened only very rarely as you were still strong, so strong."

"For twenty years we lived thus. You aged slowly, as did I, but we both aged. My eyes grew somewhat dim, your hands grew stiff and sore with age, your hair gradually faded through gray to a pure white. One day as we sat, in companionable silence, in the darkness before a warm fire, you wordlessly got to your feet and drew me to mine. You led me into our bedroom, the bedroom where ever we had slept together but apart, and gently undressed us both. I was in a daze, unable to believe what was happening."

"You – she, I mean – pushed me down onto the platform we slept on, and climbed onto me. At first I was too scared of her, too scared of myself, to be any good, but she was so tender, so patient, that eventually we coupled, with her – with you – on *top*, riding me, as you did that very first day that you gave me my soul. In spite of our age, in spite of *everything*, we drew together to a climax that put to shame anything, anything at all, that I had ever experienced back in my callow youth. The two of us simply exploded with light – our small hut must have glowed like a falling star..."

Here Adam's face fell for a moment, as did mine, remembering. Then it lifted.

"...lighting up the desert as if it were the day. Afterwards we lay together, side by side, naked, as we used to long ago in Eden, and I cannot say that I was ever happier, not even there in paradise. We fell asleep together, you and I, breathing quietly in the night, our light dimmed. As I slept I had a strange dream. Inanna came and stood before me and said 'Adam, you have at last redeemed yourself, as the human species will eventually redeem itself. Your mistakes will be made whole, and the good that you have done will never be forgotten. Humans *can* learn, can evolve, can *change* into something better, something closer to God, helped in part by your rules, however clumsy and imperfect they may be.' "

" 'One day your children's children's children will learn that they can *fix* the rules, that they *aren't* God-given but only the best efforts of a fallible man, of many fallible men, good mixed with evil, rife with correctable errors. One day they will look within themselves at the point where I watch them watching themselves and they will use the rational sense that I gave them and make them right. Or at least righter' "

" 'I take now this Eve that Lilith gave to you, this copy of her Self that taught you to be whole, that taught you to be a Self standing alone and capable of giving as well as receiving, that taught you that to get exactly what you wish for is the same as getting nothing at all, a path to misery and death. You now know fully that she loved you, after all, more than her life itself. It is by her love and sacrifice you are healed.' "

" '*She* must be healed as well. I now charge you to journey to Lilith, to carry to her the story of Eve, the missing half of her life. For the two of you, your lives so far have been the incomplete halves of what might have been one perfect whole. Only when you rejoin Lilith and carry to her this tale so she, too, can know this truth will you achieve completeness.' "

"Inanna faded away, somehow holding my eyes with her own for a thousand nights, for a thousand lifetimes as she did so. I quietly awoke as the morning light was just beginning to brighten our chamber. Your face looked so peaceful as you lay in my arms with your frail arms tucked up in between us, so beautiful, so strong, so perfect. You opened your eyes and smiled at me, and then saw *past* me, to She who was doubtless standing there and calling you, and I watched..." Adam's voice broke and his eyes glistened with tears as he paused for a moment in his recital. "I watched as those eyes dulled, I felt your body twitch as your Soul, your great, wonderful Soul, left the flesh to rejoin She who gave it to you. I felt a sudden warm dampness as your bladder loosed and then you were gone."

"One moment I was living in paradise indeed, for all that paradise was a crude hut in the desert and lacked both indoor plumbing and a clothes closet. The next I was alone, more alone than I had *ever* been, holding your still warm body, empty of any trace of the life it had held only seconds before."

"For hours I lay there with you. I cried, I cursed, I begged and pleaded with Inanna to restore you to me, until the lessons I had learned through such pain awoke me to the danger of such a prayer, that it might be *granted* and leave me in a hell even deeper than the one I was in."

"Then I just held you in my arms, held you not to keep you, but to delay the moment I would have to let you go. Finally I could wait no longer, and I arose. I cleaned you as best I could, dressed you in your finest clothes (none too fine, I'm afraid, as we were very poor) and gathered all that was burnable in the house and the goat pens. Of this I built a pyre, and at sundown I burned your body. You ascended towards the sky, that same sky that I once foolishly confused with heaven, with God, as a swirl of sparks. I knew that you would have liked that."

"Now I know," he concluded, looking at me through the darkness as if I were Inanna Herself and not just Lilith, "Heaven is everywhere. Heaven is nowhere. God lives within us at the place where our Self watches our self watching the world. Yet, heaven, for me, was always in your eyes."

His eyes fell, his voice grew silent. I let the silence stretch out, waiting. If nothing else, I had learned the value of waiting over the last ten years. Eventually his voice returned, quieter now, breaking the gathering darkness that threatened to shroud his face from me altogether.

"I gathered up the few things that remained to me – a bit of hoarded gold, some extra robes, some food, our last few goats. The goats I traded for a donkey in town, and I set out on the road, heading east. I had no idea where in the world you, Lilith herself, might be. I only knew that Inanna had commanded me to seek you out and that I wished nothing more in the time left to me than to see your face one last time and tell you, and *make* you believe, no, to *beg* you to believe, that I love you. I have always loved you. That you gave birth to my soul, you saved me from my own wickedness, you taught me wisdom, you patiently accepted my penance, and in the end, you forgave me."

"For years I wandered, following your trace. Wherever you had gone people remembered you as something of a goddess yourself, a healer, a worker of magic, a judge, a witch. The towns were cleaner, the kings more just, the hills free of bandits. I learned, also, that people were obeying rules, *my* rules, the rules of law and sin that I had made up so long ago, doing my best however poor and selfish a best it was. Although those rules were, I could see, far from perfect, they were a beginning. The poor and the rich alike could judge right from wrong using the rules, and even when they were mistaken and judged badly, the result usually turned out well in the long run thanks to the grace of Inanna."

"I was humbled by this. I was amazed by what you, what my son Cain, had done. You not only gave people souls as you wandered the world, you gave them *life*, you gave them a glimpse of God, you gave them a hope that one day they too would be able to look within themselves at the point where God is, to become One, to give up their fear of life, of death, of losing the joy of the past, of experiencing the pain of the future."

"One day, though, the trail vanished, in the deserted hills where there were none to ask. I was lost, wandering without food or water in the midst of a vast expanse, when Inanna once again appeared to me. She blinked, and I found myself in that place where you first gave me my soul. This time she shared wine and sushi with *me*, and drew my spirit into her Eye, where I too experienced the infinite, where I too rejoined you, and Eve, where we all three, or two, become One. I emerged and listened, amazed, as She told me many things – about evolution and how my rules and your spirit would guide mankind as it changed itself, as it became *better*, as it learned about love and God and one day *fixed my rules*, inventing and deducing better ones to take their place."

Eventually I found myself back in the desert, but no longer starving, no longer thirsty, no longer sad, for who can be sad with Inanna's blessing upon him? I picked a direction, knew somehow that it was the *right* direction, and began walking. Thereafter Inanna would walk often with me, accompanying me on the road, and we talked of many things." He yawned. "So many things. I understand, now, so much of what I found frightening in my preternatural knowledge, the guns[2],

---

[2] No, I'm not kidding. There is little doubt about this part of the translation.

the wars, the machines for killing women and children with gas and a fire that clings[3], the bombs that could destroy whole cities of men, killing millions at one time. The *diseases*, Lilith, diseases engineered by monsters who released them and slew billions *in the name of God*[4]. I had no strength to face this, on that first day when you gave me my soul, and all I could think about was rules that might prevent it, all of that killing, all of that suffering."

"Inanna taught me. Now I understand. No birth, no death, only *change*, with every moment a small birth, a small death, and eternal. Change that leads *through* the pain, the suffering, the deaths without number to a new place, the place within Inanna's Eye, the place where it *all* becomes a thing of *such beauty* that I wept, I weep, I will weep at the sight, outside of time's stream. It is all *good*, even the bad is good, it is bad *becoming* good, forever. And now," he yawned again. "I have to sleep. I'm so tired, Lilith, so tired. But I had to tell you."

His head dropped slowly down to his chest, and a few moments later he began to gently snore. I got up and lay him down like a child, a small, frail child, and covered him with such clothes as we had against the night's chill. Then I, who no longer felt such things as the cold, sat again right next to him, sat where only the night before Inanna in the form of the *rishi* had sat up for me, and waited, for what I did not fully know.

During the night, though, Adam's teeth began to chatter from the cold. I got up and lay down beside him and pressed his withered body up against mine the better to share my own warmth. I let a tiny amount of my remaining power flow out of me and into him, to strengthen him against the chill. He sighed in his sleep and melted into me, and I found to my surprise that my own tears were flowing freely, there in the darkness, as we slept together for the first time (as far as *I* was concerned) since Eden. Just slept, although in truth I did no sleeping, as sleep would have robbed me of precious moments of my perfect happiness.

The morning light dawned clear and cold, lighting up Adam's face, wrinkled and shrunken but still recognizable as that beautiful *man* I had once quickened, gifted with a soul through the very act of innocent love. His eyes flickered open and met mine, he smiled, and then his eyes, too, looked *past* me, to the One who was, I had no doubt at all,

---

[3] Again, no kidding. Nostradamus should have been so accurate.
[4] This hasn't happened yet, but given the accuracy of the prophecies in Lilith's scrolls, we should all be more than a bit concerned.

sitting patiently there, waiting. A look of utter peace and contentment came upon his face, a look I cannot describe, only remember, and then I watched as those eyes dulled, held him as his body gave a single erratic shudder. One minute I was holding a man, a flawed man perhaps, but a very, very holy man, a *good* man, a man that I loved, that I had always loved, for all of his weaknesses and all of his strengths. The next I was ... alone?

No. I was *never* alone and *always* alone, keeping company with my Self as I made a light in the darkness, a small light but one that sufficed to utterly destroy the darkness, to fill it to the uttermost reaches of existence.

Chapter 16

No Birth

I lay for a while with the dust, the *stardust* I reminded myself, that was once Adam. When my tears dried and my spirit centered enough to function I arose, cleaned myself and Adam and did that which had to be done, accompanied and helped by my two silent witnesses, our blesséd son and God incarnate. The villagers had appeared as if by magic overnight, summoned by their dreams. Silently they gathered wood for the pyre. Snake was the bier that held Adam's body as he might have held my own, gently, with his immense hood erected as both a canopy and an honor to he who had, after all, first given Snake his soul.

At last the pyre was ready. Snake unwrapped himself and paused, unknowable emotions rippling behind his obsidian eyes, and bobbed his head down to give a single touch of its forked tongue, delicately, to the middle of Adam's forehead. A single red spot immediately appeared, a *tilak* that was considered a mark of great holiness in that country. Snake folded its hood and looked away, then slithered back into his own alcove within the cave and out of sight in its shadows.

The villagers surged forward and carried Adam on a crude wooden palette to the neatly stacked wood and doused the whole pile with cooking oil. Some villagers came forth and shyly added pieces of a sweet smelling wood at his feet and his head. Then they stepped back.

There was no fire. We had not kindled one that morning as there was no time nor mood for tea, for food, for warmth.

I stepped forward, bent over, and kissed Adam's wrinkled brow right where Snake had marked it. A tear fell from my eye and splashed onto his dusty face, leaving a small smudge. I stepped back, thrust my hand deep into the pile of wood and felt the *power* surge through me as I had not in years. I called *fire* into being, fire that sprang from my fingertips and permeated the entire pile of wood at once and made it explode into flames that singed my shortly cropped hair almost back to my scalp and withered my eyelashes, fire that blistered my own hand before I could withdraw it and step back.

So it was that Adam, too, ascended into the sky that was not heaven in a shower of sparks and smoke, stardust that the wind carried off to the world to gift it with tiny fragments of his incomparable soul. I and my companions sat down to wait.

At last it was done and only a pile of cooling ash remained, a few charred bones, a few hot coals. The villagers gathered these small remains and placed them into a clay pot which they carefully carried down to the river to be released, a river my preternatural knowledge told me led to a sea that nearly covered the world though I would never see it. I blessed his ashes as they lay, still warm, in that humble pot, that they might carry both Soul and a Moral Sense with them to all places that the waters of the earth visited in time.

A few at a time, the villagers departed, all but a handful of our most faithful followers and caregivers, who prepared food and cleaned up the not inconsiderable mess. I, Cain, and God as *rishi* retired to our cave, where two of our younger retainers were at work. There I knelt before God, expecting that my time, too, was finished, my work done, that it was time for my release.

When I raised my eyes, though, the *rishi* had disappeared and in his place was – a strange vision of God, one with many arms and a curious half smile, a smile that I somehow confused with Adam's. When God spoke, it was also with Adam's voice, the voice he had back when we were both young. "I am well pleased. You are healed," He said.

I bowed my head in acquiescence. No birth, no death, only the experience of *time*, that stream of births and deaths. Each moment was a miracle. I was indeed healed. I was at peace. I was content.

"I have need for one more miracle, Lilith, one more burden to place on you. Although you have given the world a soul, you and Adam, although you have given the world a set of rules, an idea of sin, that can help guide all things on the ever-upward spiral of evolution back to Me, much remains to be done."

"The world, as you have seen, is full of sin. With or without a soul, humans evolved to be selfish and are prone to be wicked, to create much pain and suffering. You, too, have looked upon Adam's vision of the future – it is very real. Over the years, blood will be shed in rivers, generation after generation will suffer from death, disease, old age, loss. What you have done is far from being enough, not yet enough to shorten the ages of pain, not yet enough to establish compassion and tolerance and equality and goodness to combat greed, self-righteousness, and hatred."

"The people of *this* place, *this* time, are already horribly oppressed – imprisoned and tortured, killed for their meager belongings. Their leaders are constantly gambling, raping the innocent, at war with their neighbors. They blind their inner eye to Me, and will continue to do so for a long age. This woman here," God gestured to the bent-over woman who was sweeping our floor, "has been imprisoned over and over by her Uncle, who is King over Mathura. She has been raped many times by his guards, who have threatened to kill her living children, especially her oldest boy whom they hold hostage over her, if she does not comply with their demands. Only yesterday she delivered a baby, a man-child, in his prison. This child was immediately put to death in the foolish belief that he was destined to kill the King. Her breasts ache with milk she cannot use to feed her baby. Her soul aches for the child that was murdered in the name of superstition. She has prayed to Me for deliverance."

"So I ask you, Lilith. Will you help me to deliver this woman and *all* the women, all the men and all of the children who abide in this place? Will you help me ensure that your work is continued and not lost?"

I did not know what I was being asked to do, but I bowed my head in acquiescence. God's will would be done, as long as I had the strength to do it, and I sensed that this would be my last task on this earth.

Seeing this, God looked me in the eye and I found myself back outside of time's stream, back in the timeless place where first I was given life, alone. There was food and drink, and a soft bed. I was hungry and thirsty, so I ate and drank. Then I was tired, weary to my very bones. I fell into the bed and slept for an eternity.

I awoke to see God approaching, a still bloody sword in one of his many hands, laughing. His form was yet again different, this time reminding me of men I once knew, of both Adam and K'nesh. I asked God where He was coming from holding a sword in his hand. "From giving my son, *our* son, a new head, and the name you requested in memory of a lover" he explained. "For you are more than *just* the goddess Lilith, Ka Li', here in my Eye where we rejoin, where we become One. Ever many, ever changing. Ever One, ever the same." He laughed again, a laugh that made me feel bright and cheerful, a laugh that at last made my half smile whole for the first time in years. "I love the world, Lilith. I love Creation. Sometimes it produces the best jokes, the most remarkable things. I surprise my Self with many miracles."

At last he subsided and sat beside me on the bed, his hands (*Adam's* hands, I saw at last) entwined with my own. His eyes (*Adam's* eyes) sought my own. His body (*Adam's* body) bumped against mine, hip to hip. God as Adam sat beside me, naked, his eyes alive and filled with joy, the smile of an eternal joke on his lips. There was no mistake – I could almost taste the Soul I had given him on the air, mixed with the perfume of his lips as he brought them close to mine. I was transfixed.

"Lie with me, Lilith," he breathed into my mouth, not quite touching my lips with his own. "I've missed you, missed you for a thousand years. I may not command you. I *will* not command you. But lie with me."

His other hand snaked behind my head and twined itself in my hair, suddenly grown long and wild once again, in the way he knew that I loved, rubbing my neck and drawing me nearer to him, drawing me into a kiss that I only half resisted, trying desperately to think, to understand, to be able to *decide* while being overwhelmed by the feeling of lust, longing, of passion. Yes, of love.

It was *love*. This came as something of a shock. I would have sworn I could never love again, I who had loved so many, loved indeed this Adam back when he was my confused young lover, loved the thousands of men in between, some for money, some for the comfort and relief of it, loved a few such as K'nesh for the deep and abiding joy of their company, a real love for however long life lasted. Yet I was once again clean, freed from all of that baggage, free to love this Adam as we should have loved in the beginning of it all.

I suddenly *wanted* this thing to be. Wanted it with all of my heart, all of my soul. Wanted it more than I had ever wanted anything, more than I ever *would* want anything, ever again. *This* was the point of it all, the thing that made *all* of the pain worthwhile, the pain of birth (no birth), the pain of death (no death), the pain in between (no in between). Love erased all pain from time's stream, cast it out into the forgetfulness of the past while love alone endured the now, eternal.

Suddenly I found myself kissing Adam back, found my own hands straying down his back to his bottom. He gave a little jump as I found the just the right spot and gave it a squeeze.

"All right," I said. "But I get to be on top..."

We awoke together naked, still intertwined, still coupled, our sweat still sheening our skins beneath the infinity of stars above, glistening in the light of candles that glowed at the head and foot of our bed. I felt the heat rise within me again and reached down to put matters right for a second bout, but Adam raised a finger to my lips and when I looked up, Inanna's eyes looked back from Adam's face.

"Peace, Lilith. Soon, soon, you and Adam will be joined together for as much of eternity as you wish, in the very paradise you first inhabited if so you wish it. First, though, you must finish your work on Earth."

She rose up from me, naked, and I saw that as she rose, so did my belly, so did my breasts. She bent to kiss me on the brow, even as I had kissed Adam's corpse so very shortly before, and to run her hand firmly over my lightly swollen middle. Inside of it, a life jumped into being.

"Go, Lilith. Return to the world and bear this child. Give him to the woman who lost her own. Into him will pass much of the Soul that I gave you, enough to continue our work in the making of this world, enough to purge the world of much *evil* so that for a time *good* can grow without hindrance, long enough that the foothold goodness gets will not be erased by willful men, by time."

She drifted back away from me, fading, her Eyes holding my own. Months passed there, I know it – I could feel my belly swelling and my back starting its familiar ache, feel my breasts distending, feel my breath coming hard as there just wasn't enough *room* in there for the baby and my breath too, and then I was back, back in the cave, and in labor. I, who had forsworn babies long ago, felt my water break and gush all over my feet.

At least this time I wasn't wearing any shoes to be ruined.

Labor hadn't gotten any easier over the sixty or so years since I had had Sally. Labor on the hard floor of a cave was even worse than

I remembered, until my groans and complaints drew Snake out of the corners to curl around my prostrate form. Snake's hood was once again my shelter against a howling storm that had sprung up outside, but this a natural one of ordinary wind and rain that blew into our cave, driving all the local villagers who remained inside with Cain and myself. I saw that Inanna had come back with me, that my *rishi*, my God of many arms, my Adam, they were all gone and God as Woman stood quietly beside us.

I grunted and puffed as each spasm stiffened my belly. Snake's body curled around me, lifting me up off of the dirty cave floor and helping me to pull my legs apart; its coils gradually formed themselves into a basket of sorts between my legs. Neither Cain nor any of the village women could approach me to help – Snake hissed and threatened him, even him, with fangs the size of daggers if he came anywhere near. Inanna calmed Cain in his distress by placing her hand on his forehead and saying "hold".

Finally nature ran its course and in due time a squalling baby slipped out of me in a rush, covered in blood and mucus. I managed to bring him (for a boy it was) up to my nearly empty breasts while Snake bit down on his cord, causing it to blacken and shrivel, to come apart at the bite as if it had been cut. I quickly delivered the caul (which shrivelled, blackening as it fell) and dropped into an exhausted sleep in my living bed with the new baby boy at my breast.

The next morning I awoke, sore and hungry but alive. I was a mess, but the baby was perfectly clean. When I lifted my head it nearly ran into the nose of a cow – a *perfect* cow, as far as my limited knowledge of cows goes – engaged in the active process of licking my son clean. Snake permitted this to happen even as he kept all humans away – it was Inanna's will that it be so, I was sure. The spread hood of the snake was still raised above us, a parasol against the filtered sun that fell down around us from the mouth of the cave, where Snake had somehow carried us while we slept. Some fifty or sixty villagers sat in the clearing beneath the banyan tree outside, waiting.

I swatted the cow on the nose to get enough room to sit up, and took a good look at my baby boy. He was amazingly beautiful for a newborn, with a nearly perfect head and as clean as the best midwife could have made him. His eyes were open in the shade of the snake and looked at me solemnly while his tiny fist grasped my breast and hand as he began to nurse.

My heart opened to him as my milk began to flow (as always it does with my new babies) and a burst of pure love ran like fire from my heart into his so fiercely that I almost dropped him. Looking around I saw that the fire was not only my own – Snake had contributed some of his deadly strength and endurance, my son Cain some of his warmth and Adam's wisdom, and Inanna, with her hand upon a glowing cow, blazed like the heavens themselves blaze in the cold north where the winter nights last for weeks, all of the power streaming through me and into the baby through the milk that streamed from my breast.

The eyes of the child opened wide and he reared back from the nipple, and *aged* in some undefinable way. His skin darkened, becoming a black so deep that it was almost blue, beginning from his naval where the blackened stub of his cord now dropped away. I knew, without knowing how, that the child had been blessed – or cursed – with preternatural knowledge, even as I had.

I let out a wordless cry and held my baby to my breast, to try to help him hold onto his innocence for a moment more, but it was no use. The baby himself reached up to my face, stroking gently in a gesture that communicated without words that which needed to be said, that which had to be done. I wept inconsolably, hugging the tiny form to me, giving it in my turn a lifetime's worth of love in a moment and drawing from it such comfort as I could.

I felt a hand on my shoulder, and the moment drew out into forever for the three of us – Inanna, myself, and the child, all plunging together into God's eye and out of time's stream. As we fell Inanna's form subtly changed once again – God was once again a man, once again the *rishi* that had taught me for ten years in that cave. We exploded, my baby and my self, out of the eye of God and back into time and the world.

What a difference eternity makes! I *knew* that all would be well with my baby, indeed (using my preternatural knowledge) that his name would be better remembered, more revered than my own. I gave him one kiss – the only kiss I was able to bestow upon him – and where my lips touched his forehead the red of my lips and the white of my teeth appeared as a holy mark that I knew would remain, tattooed into the skin even as Snake's had remained on the forehead of Adam.

I turned and sought her out, she whose baby had been taken from her and cruelly killed, she who now stood against the wall of the cave, fearful, with another tiny son clinging to her legs. I carried the baby to her and pressed it, gently, into her waiting arms. For a moment she just stood there, paralyzed, and then with a sob she opened her robe and gave the baby her swollen breast.

I knelt down to her little boy. I was weak now, so weak – so much of my power had passed out of me and into my baby son, the last son of Adam and myself, but I managed to pull one last *blessing* out of that which remained with Inanna's help. The eyes of the young boy Balarama opened wide and glowed with Soul and Strength and even a bit of preternatural knowledge – things that I knew that he would need to support and defend his new baby brother. My lips brushed against his forehead, too, leaving their indelible mark.

Snake swung his head down to look the boy in the eye, raised his head up to the tiny figure even now suckling gently at the breast, at *her* breast, she who would be his mother. Snake gave just one lick, delicately, at the perfect form, then held very still as the tiny hand came up and explored the soft-scaled mouth, the deadly fangs. Snake's eyes swung back to meet my own, and we shared a moment of very unusual mutual reflection. Then, very gently, Snake pushed me backwards with his head, curling his long thick form around the trembling young mother and raising his enormous hood above the two of them there, mother and son together, as the baby suckled and the cow stood by. A murmur went up through the crowd and as one they bowed down before this tableau.

No longer needed on this Earth, my work here done, I turned to limp away, still bleeding a bit between my legs, holding my head up as best I could, into the waiting arms of Cain.

Chapter 17

Eternity

I walked away from my fourth and final home, leaving behind my newborn, everborn, neverborn son to do his great works, to lead his people to an understanding of God that would sustain them until a better one came along (as it always will, always must, given that we are trying to understand that which ultimately cannot be understood, only experienced).

All the rest of the day I walked, pausing only to let Cain wash the filth and blood off of me in a small stream and beg clothes for me from a woman in one of the small villages we passed through. I was weaker than I could remember ever being. We did not go very far.

As we left that morning, Cain had quickly collected a meager pile of our belongings from the cave, which included an oiled leather bag in which we carried my scrolls, the implements of writing and this, my self-told story, as best I remember it. Over the many years of living in the cave I had much time to reflect, much time to sit and write down that which had happened to me over my lifetime. Such writing helped me to *understand* the many things that I had done, that I had seen and experienced, both glad and sad. It helped me achieve the peace that I finally attained.

We slept last night in a cattle barn, sharing a cup of tea with the man who owned the cows and his son, telling stories in the darkness that our voices might drive away the tigers that prowl in the night and sometimes prey on cattle (and sometimes on the men and boys who guard them), the jackals that howl through the darkness, the roving outlaws that were worse than any tiger, any jackal. I no longer care – my newborn son is here to *purge* the world of such evil men, at least for a time, and my own time here is finished.

I begged a small oil lamp and spent the whole night writing down the events of the last few days by its meager light. I wrote about Adam's return and the birth of our last son while it was still fresh in my memory, almost too precious to commit to words.

Today we limped on, walking a short distance and then resting, walking and resting again, until a little while ago we came to a bend in the Yamuna, a flat stretch at a bow in the river where there is a gentle, low hill rising up out of the river bed. It is just high enough that the inevitable monsoon floods do not reach it, as on the top there are trees and rocks that would have been buried in mud otherwise. There we discovered a small clearing overlooking the beautiful river below.

My strength fails me, and Cain is setting up a camp while I rest a while and write, as it is somehow important that I finish recording all of the marvelous things that happened over the last three days. That is done, the story is now up to date.

My life itself is now somehow trapped in the pages and carefully packed away in a waterproof bag, strange miracle of the written word, except for the last part of this final scroll that I hope to somehow fill, if I am given time. But I do not think I will write much more.

Although I have concealed it from Cain, the bleeding between my legs never really stopped after I gave birth. It comes faster now; it was a sudden moment of wrenching pain in my belly that really compelled me to stop. My power seems at last to have left me and I can see nothing of what has happened inside, but I am certain that whatever it is, it is Inanna's will that it be so.

I feel cold, so cold, in spite of the warmth of the sun. I am now lying against the warm side of a big rock, and take advantage of the moment of rest and calmness to write a bit more. But I do not know what to say. Perhaps I will describe this beautiful hilltop.

I dozed off for a moment and had the most marvelous dream of living with Adam in Eden – Adam as he was at the end, at last my equal and my friend – but am awake once again. Cain is preparing tea.

The sun is setting now, and a nearly full moon rises – between them I see with my sleep-filled eyes a strange sight. There is a white building unlike any I have ever seen, beautiful beyond measure, surrounding the point where I lie, sprung up as if by magic. There is a weeping man, a man much like Adam save that he has a beard and his head is beturbaned. In the heart of this building, right where I lie against this rock, there is a bier, and on the bier there is a single red rose.

And Oh! Even as I write these lines, I see that the moon *is* Inanna, that the Sun *is* Mahavishnu, that I am somehow coming unstuck in time between them, drifting off to the stars themselves, to *Brahman*. Who, then, am I? The rose? Where is this place, and how did I come to be here?

Stardust.

I am very tired now, and for some reason I am crying, perhaps from a story too beautiful to be forgotten that has not yet been told. I will try to remember it, to dream it, and then write some more tomorrow.

Epilogue

The following is from the last scroll in the collection, which also suffered tremendously from the attentions of the tiny little moth that must have been trapped in with the scrolls. The handwriting is different – even though of course it could not be original, the scribes that copied the scrolls and copied them yet again must have taken great pains to copy each line exactly so in order to so faithfully reproduce even the differences in handwriting, as they might well have done were they ignorant of the content of the actual script that they were copying.

Unfortunately, there are major pieces of the story lost forever, unless we can lay our hands on the originals and perhaps use NASA-developed enhancement techniques to bring out missing words and paragraphs, to try to bridge the many gaps. Nothing, however, will fill in the actual holes in the cloth that erase critical junctures.

We have done our best to edit what remains into a semblance of order, to obtain a glimpse of the end of Lilith's story.

I am Cain. As I write this, my mother lies dead at my feet and Inanna stands at my back guiding my hands as they write, as I am blinded by tears. As we rested in the moonlight of early evening, with water for tea heating on the small fire I had made to keep away the wild beasts, I noticed at the base of the rock against which she lay that which she had concealed from me – a spreading pool of blood, bright red, that oozed out of her in an ever increasing flow. I tried to staunch it but my skills failed me. She was ever the healer, not I. My mother begged me to stop, to let her go in peace.

At first I could not let go. I prayed to Inanna, that she might grant me the power to heal my mother and save her life as my mother had saved the lives of so many others, had saved *my* life more than once on our long travels together, where she was my protection as Inanna was hers. Instead of granting my prayer Inanna appeared beside me and gently took my shoulder, gently pulled me back from where my mother, once so strong, so full of life, now lay on the ground in a pool of her own blood with her back pressed up against a smooth black rock, until she at last gave a sigh and was still.

I now will now write what Inanna tells me to write, in my mother's own voice. Inanna looks at me as she dictates with my mother's Eyes, those eyes that ever could see into a man and read his very soul for truth or lies, for love and goodness or hatred and evil, and so I find that I believe her when she tells me that these are indeed my mother's words, written as she would have written them to finish off her story, could one but write when one is dead. To this miracle, I solemnly swear.

The sun set, my vision of a great palace that was also a tomb faded, and Cain brought me my cup of tea. As he bent over he saw the fresh blood that was soaking through my clothing, the blood that was even now running out of me and into the Earth as my last and greatest soulgiving, taking with it my life and my strength. There was little pain, only a sense of wonder, a sense that something was happening that was beyond my control but a *good* thing nevertheless.

Cain began such a fuss. I tried to tell him that it was no use, that my strength was gone, passed on to a child of *God* born to bring a measure of good to a troubled land even as we were so born. He tried so *hard* to stop my steady bleeding, but of course I was bleeding inside where it could not be stopped as he lacked my gift of healing with the spirit. His clumsy attempts just hurt and did no good. I patiently endured them, knowing that no matter what he did, I was near my end.

Finally he stopped and wept and called on Inanna for help and then She was there. She drew him aside and spoke words of comfort to him that I could not hear. I struggled for breath and almost cried out as there was a sharp pain within me that stabbed like a knife. My eyes filled with tears not from the fear of death, for death had been my constant companion all my life, but from the *beauty* of the world I was leaving, in all its violence and savagery and compassion and love.

The pain eased a bit but I felt cold, so cold. I looked up the the evening sky where the stars were just starting to twinkle even as they had on that day long ago when I received my soul. The brightest star fell towards me and grew even as the surrounding world shrank back from it, and became Inanna's face as she knelt down at my side and cradled my head against her bosom, her breath filling me with peace and driving a bit of the ice from my veins. There we remained for a moment, face to face.

"Lilith," she said, "do you recall my promise to you? I promised you that your death would come as a painless whisper, a gentle breeze, you who are the most blessed of women, you who were First." I was too weak even to answer, my jaw was becoming too heavy to hold up, my breathing too difficult and ragged to sustain. Somehow I knew that if only I could stop breathing, the pain and the cold would go away, the feeling that I was drowning in my own body would pass. She laid her head upon my brow and I felt Her peace flood into my soul, felt the pain begin to pass. "Come to me, my daughter, my Self. Dive into my Eye," she said.

I let my breath shudder, slowly, out of my lungs and did not draw another. Her face grew in my eyes even as the world outside of it stretched into the walls of a narrow tunnel, then even her face stretched and turned into a vortex surrounding her Eye, and finally I spiralled into the blackness of her pupil broken only by a single brilliant spark of light, the reflection of a beautiful star, falling forever.

I bring these words to you, my son, so that you who have been my true love, my faithful companion, who have been blesséd by Inanna as few others have, can record at the end and witness this truth – that there is no birth, no death. There is indeed, only the *now*, forever. In God's Eye nothing is ever truly born or truly dies. I am, whole as ever I was, within God once again, even as I am she who was walking with you yesterday, who bore you in blood and pain long ago and far away, who lived with you, travelled with you, and loved you, my son, most of the years of her life. You are, as you write this, both being born and dying, you are alive and in your prime, not alive and forgotten, not alive before your birth, all countless times, both inside and outside of time's stream.

Only the *living* part counts. The non-living parts, the parts where you imagine that the Watcher who watches the watcher, watching the world has gone away – how can the Eye of God close? While it endures, so will I, so will you, so will all that it sees, all that shares the *ability* to see. *The light of the world admits no real darkness* – it fills the unfillable vessel of eternity with the perfect knowledge of *I am*.

This is the message, the last message, I give you to take to the world.

This ends the story of Lilith as told in her own words. Cain resumes the narrative and the rest of the scroll, as best can be determined given its deterioration and holes, is about Cain's journey, accompanied from time to time by Inanna, back to the original Eden. They arrive to find it partly restored by time – once again a fertile land covered with trees, occupied by a people that are in fact Lilith's direct descendants, led there by her surviving children and hence Cain's grandnieces and nephews and of course their husbands and wives and friends and livestock.

Cain is accepted and founds there a temple devoted to Inanna and the memory of Lilith, building structures like those that he saw to the east in Mohenjo Daro and the Harrapa civilization. It is there, we must conclude, that these scrolls were housed and copied and recopied, somehow surviving the rise and fall of civilizations over a time span of thousands of years, before the copy that my Iraqi correspondent found was carefully, nay, lovingly sealed in an airtight chest and buried in the desert.

Impossible? Difficult to say without possession of the actual scrolls. I have already explained about the difficulty of forging such a document without the aid and abettance of one of a handful of humans alive on the planet who are capable of such a forgery, and it is unthinkable that any of these grand old scholars (or young fiery upstarts) would have either the time or inclination to write such a complete fiction, a made-up derivative of Proto-Indo-European mythology with accompanying translation notes such as might have been crafted by ancient missionaries intent on taking the Book of Lilith to Egypt, to Sume-

ria, to Babylonia, to the Canaanites, to the Phoenicians, even to the Greeks in their turn.

I think you will now agree that the text is compelling – it has the ring of truth to it. Perhaps it is no more than the "truth" that can be found in any mythology, any epic work concerning the advent of civilization, but even if this is all it is, it is enough.

Aside from these scrolls, some record of Lilith must have survived the millennia intact, although the legends that surround her contain what can only be garbled and distorted versions of the truth as presented in this work. Otherwise from whence the Alphabet of Ben Sirra? From whence Isaiah, from whence the Dead Sea Scrolls, from whence the Epic of Gilgamesh itself? The same kind of distortion is visible in what can only be parts of the Lilith story as captured in the epic mythology and religious works of Hinduism, where we can see that Lilith's last son did indeed shake the world and purge it of corruption and evil rather violently (to end up being revered, apparently correctly, as an avatar of God even as Lilith herself was, as we – according to Lilith – all are).

Note also the horrible distortion of the story of her first son, the loyal one, the one most strongly responsible for preserving the laws of Adam intact. He is remembered only for something he didn't really do – the accidental death of his "brother" by his father and his mother's Eve avatar even as that son was preparing to commit what in a strangely time-twisted way was matricide. These stories and myths at least partially contradict the story of Lilith told herein in her own words.

Yet how else could it have happened? These scrolls are original sources, far older than the oldest source of any of the other mythologies mentioned above and elsewhere. Writing was unknown at that time in the vicinity of the Mediterranean (although there is a great temptation to believe that Cain or possibly traders from the Harrapan state may have revisited Sidon and the ancient Phoenician city-states and seeded them with examples of writing that sufficed to permit them to eventually "invent" the alphabet).

It is unthinkable that an oral tradition could have survived thousands of years intact without being written down. We must therefore conclude that Lilith's story and the various distortions of it that became the most ancient writings preserved in several cultures survived because Cain wrote them down, Cain's temple preserved them, Cain's priesthood carried them – and with them the secrets of writing – throughout the pre-historic Mesopotamian cradle of civilization.

Barring the possession of the scrolls themselves or the surfacing of new evidence (perhaps from the secret libraries of the Vatican, perhaps from those unpublished and still hidden Dead Sea scrolls, perhaps from archaeological discoveries yet unmade) this must end our story of the indomitable Lilith, the first human created by Inanna and guardian of the holy spirit.

Appendix A

About Lilith

The legend of Lilith is a very ancient one, with references that date back to the earliest written stories and histories known to mankind. The earliest references to Lilith apparently occur in the Gilgamesh stories, which tell of a Sumerian king who lived roughly 5500 years ago. Here Lilith (Lillake) is a female with magical powers dwelling in the trunk of a willow-tree tended by the Goddess Inanna on the banks of the Euphrates. Gilgamesh himself kills a dragon whose nest is at the foot of the tree for Inanna's sake and the racket drives Lilith out; she tears down her house and flees into the wilderness.

Inanna, it should be noted, was the Sumerian Goddess who is frankly, unabashedly, female. She was, in fact, the archetypical woman who "lives like a man", seeking out and enjoying sexual experience for its own sake, treating men as equals, refusing to be tied down as a "wife" in the sense of being the chattel of some male. Inanna was the Goddess of frank sexual love, including but not limited to marital sexual love. She was perhaps the original Liberated Woman.

Although she is portrayed as a Goddess and hence something of a metaphorical, mythopoeic projection of our human selves onto Godhead, there is something wildly attractive, intoxicating about Inanna. She is (for men and women alike) the dopamine-driven intoxication of great passion, the wild rush of freedom and youth, the spreading of metaphorical adolescent wings and trying things without regards for common sense or consequences. Yet she is also *intellectual* freedom, economic freedom, the unfolding human spirit, compassion. Inanna doesn't 'need a man'. At best she wants one, and only an equal (or possibly an inferior), never a superior.

Perhaps it isn't fair to describe her as the woman who is "like a man". Rather it is entirely *human*, a trait of men and women alike, to be in charge, to control one's life and sexual choices, to 'own' one's personal Universe, to be *free*, to seek pleasure and avoid taking responsibility that is imposed on us by others, responsibility that isn't entirely self-selected. There is a bit of Inanna in us all. Her particular brand of freedom isn't evil, nor is it wanton. It is just essentially selfish and perhaps a bit immature in the sense that great, slightly self-destructive passions are more often a sign of youth than age; passion is tempered into wisdom from the *experiencing* of some of the consequences of unbridled passion alone. Still, Inanna is a *Goddess*, not a *She-Devil*, and possesses a preternaturally accurate Moral Sense when she cares to use it.

Inanna was possibly irked at Lilith in *Gilgamesh* because Inanna had plans for making a throne and a bed out of the magical wood of the tree Lilith chose for her home. However, this isn't really clear from the actual text – this *is* the *Gilgamesh* epic and of course he gets to be the Hero in as many ways as possible. Perhaps she was there because she was *invited* by Inanna – was even a caretaker for the tree who couldn't cope with dragons and *sent* for Gilgamesh, but who fled because it isn't safe to be around when a Hero kills a Dragon. I personally prefer this possibility; God as Inanna is the natural mentor, the Deified patron, of the Lilith I have tried to portray. Inanna is indeed Lilith's Self.

As early civilization evolved into a more patriarchal form (accompanied by wars and famine and many external challenges that 'men' were best equipped to handle at least in their *own* minds), Lilith appears later in Sumerian myth as an increasingly inimical demoness. Feminine freedom has become a threat to the emerging status quo of Rule by Men, Women as Chattel. Women were well on their way toward becoming male possessions to be enjoyed for sexual gratification, used as housekeepers and as the bearers and guardians of a man's genetic and memetic inheritance in the form of children that he can be sure are *his*.

Lilith, as a female avatar of Inanna, the Godhead as Untamed Woman, became a threat, and was portrayed as such.

This latter Sumerian legend appears to have been taken over by the Hebrews (along with many other Sumerian creation myths) and woven into the biblical creation myths as they appear in Genesis and elsewhere. The standard version of the 'story of Lilith' in Judeo-

Christian mythology[1] runs something like this:

God created Man and Woman on the sixth day (as is clearly recorded in Genesis) *but* it is *equally* clear that *Eve* was not created until sometime later, long after God rested on the seventh day, as a *help mate* to Adam, and that somehow he remade the beasts and so on on the spot as well, even though they were previously recorded as being created on day five[2]. This leaves a bit of a puzzle – if Woman was made on day six, and Eve was not made until later, just who *was* the first woman?

According to the Hebrew-adopted Sumerian myth, *Lilith* was in fact the first woman, made on day six along with Adam.

Here the myth gets very interesting. Bear in mind that it is *men* who created and retold this story, men with very specific, highly patriarchal political, social and religious customs they were incorporating as the basis for the Jewish Nation[3]. On day six Lilith was supposedly created second, *of course*, right *after* Adam, and out of *dust and filthy water* besides, not out of nice 'clean' clay.

Lilith was also created with what can only be called Inanna-nature, very much according to the description of Inanna given above, more than enough to be quite comfortable concluding that this is indeed the Lilith that was referred to in the Gilgamesh stories living in Inanna's willow tree, being borrowed and retold. We can only presume that she was (like Adam) created in a state of perfect grace and given free will and that God was as happy with her creation as he was with Adam's – anything else would imply a rather stupid Deity.

---

[1] In the *Alphabet of Ben-Sirra*. Note well! This is a *story* and not a scholarly work, and therefore I'm going to present the "funnest" version of this story and ignore some of the better scholarship that might well contradict it. So if you're a scholar, don't bother using this as anything like an *authoritative reference*.

[2] Note that this isn't something to be taken seriously, any more than Genesis itself. In reality many *objective* scholars have concluded that Genesis – and for that matter the rest of the Pentateuch, the first five books of the Old Testament – was written by two or more authors at very different times, so that the inconsistency here is just the result of splicing together two myths and then not editing for consistency. Of course this point of view is pretty good proof that Genesis isn't divinely inspired truth, as truth cannot be inconsistent. It also contradicts the open assertion that the entire Old Testament was authored by Moses himself, adding still more difficulties. The Lilith myth is something called *midrash*, a (relatively) *new* myth that was apparently interwoven with Genesis to *explain* the inconsistency as not, in fact, being inconsistent. And of course, to make *other* points as well, especially about sexual relations between men and women...

[3] They had their own extremely masculine beliefs and goals in mind and did a damn good job, given how long it has lasted as an identifiable social unit, for all the good or ill that has attended it.

Naturally, they were created to be lovers, mates, husband and wife. However, when Adam had sex with her, she grew offended and irritated by his constant demand that she lie beneath him[4]. Apparently Adam always wanted to *be on top*, to be 'closer to God', to be *superior*. Lilith's Inanna-nature, given to her by God Itself, saw no reason for her to be considered or treated as Adam's inferior in any way, especially by Adam himself.

"Why must I lie beneath you?" she asked. "I also was made from dust, and am therefore your equal."

Not according to Adam she wasn't. When Adam refused to reconsider and practice anything but Adam-on-top sex, she responded by refusing to have sex with him altogether.

At this point, outraged and (we can only imagine) driven by uncontrollable lusts and a capacity for sin that significantly preceded the tree of knowledge scenario, Adam proceeded to invent *beating* and *rape* and had his way with Lilith violently. Note well that this is *not* considered to be the Original Sin and Adam was *not* cast out of Eden because of this, so we can only conclude that at this point during Creation spousal abuse and spouse rape was not considered to be a sin. A circumstance that, alas, has been perpetuated in law and custom for much of recorded history and continues on to this very day in much of the world.

Lilith, however, was *not* one to grit her loosened teeth and bear the humiliation and violation of her human spirit (good girl!). At some point during these proceedings, pretty damn-well outraged herself and far from powerless, she uttered the magical *Name of God* which blasted Adam back from her. She then rose up into the air and flew away from Adam, quite literally headed for the hills. Adam was left behind, apparently in something of a pre-Eden desert bereft of even the company of non-wild animals.

God had apparently bequeathed to Lilith a surprising amount of Power (compared to Adam's possibly superior physical strength) and wings besides, at least according to how she is usually portrayed in the few sculptures of Lilith that have survived the millennia to the present time[5].

---

[4] As Dave Barry is fond of saying in similar context, I am not making this up...

[5] Some really interesting mythology in just how she got said name and its attendant magical power – some say by seducing God himself. More serious scholars reject that, of course, and the really advanced ones note that a) the true Hebrew God is a sexless spirit, neither male nor female; and that b) Adam when created was "perfect" and hence a union of male and female who was later split into imper-

At this sexually frustrated and disempowered point poor Adam felt 'lonely' (surprise surprise) and appealed to God to bring Lilith back to him, doubtless promising to be Good this time. God, being a Manly sort[6] (in this male retelling) apparently found this to be a reasonable request. Adam was sorry. *Surely* (thought God) Adam wouldn't just beat Lilith senseless and rape her *again* the next time she refused his advances or didn't consent to let him be on top...

Otherwise it is difficult to see why an all-perfect Deity would send *three angels* to *command* Lilith to return to Eden and force herself to live with a man who had just beaten and raped her and insisted on always being on top, leaving her unfulfilled, humiliated, and physically subjugated.

Lilith, however, was no fool and was doing just fine on her own. She was a perfect model for the thousands of women in the United States and elsewhere who actually get *out* of abusive relationships, get restraining orders, and proceed to live their lives and raise their children without their abusive partner, often without men in their lives at all.

Far from being all alone and forlorn, somehow or other Lilith was having hundreds of little demon-babies every day out there in the desert (God knows how she managed *this* clever little trick – parthenogenesis?). For fairly obvious reasons she didn't care for the idea of returning to the *chance* of being beaten and raped, having *her* backside ground into the rocks and dirt while Adam remained "closer to God" (and a bit cleaner) up there on top. Unwilling to be subjugated to Adam's will and regularly humiliated as some sort of "possession" belonging to Adam (and perhaps wisely refusing to believe that Adam was really "sorry"), she refused God's command to return.

Bad move, Lilith. As *punishment* for *using her common sense* (refusing to put herself in the position of being the unwilling object of *Adam's* selfishness and demonstrated capacity to commit violent sin) Lilith was condemned on the spot to become the Arch-demoness Herself, to prey on newborn children and to give birth to lots of little baby demons (called *lilim* or *lamia*, night-creatures) that would plague

---

fect parts when Eve was created so that (metaphorically) we only attain wholeness when reunited in marriage. That's all fine, but I present here a different metaphor.

[6] See above. This isn't the most sophisticated view of God by any means, but it is certainly a *common* view of God, especially among those who take the "in His image" bit and turn it around to project masculinity onto God instead of sexlessness onto Adam. Look at the ceiling of the Sistine Chapel and check out God's beard, his subtly robed nipples, his undeniably human Male form.

mankind for the rest of time.

She accomplished this no longer by parthenogenesis (or however else she managed it at first, out there by herself in the desert) but by seizing control of the genetic reins – stealing semen from sleeping men when they had erotic dreams or practiced autoerotic behavior and taking their strength along with it. Oh no, guys! A woman in *charge* of her *own* reproductive system! Disaster! A demoness indeed...

This story thus becomes a carefully crafted biblical fantasy with a strong subtext of castration anxiety that helps *institutionalize* its presentation of Onanism (masturbation) as a sin, and appears throughout the Bible and sexually repressive religious culture in general as a fear of Succubi[7]. Every *drop* of male sperm that doesn't get deposited deep inside a properly tamed woman, kept in isolation from other potential male sexual partners, from the man-on-top position *in particular* can potentially give birth to hundreds and hundreds of *lilim*, of demons! Or worse (and more to the point), *more women* who want to be on top, who don't care to be the possession of a man, who want to *choose* their sexual partners. Imagine that.

Fortunately for the local ecology, the angels also tell Lilith that they will *kill off* a hundred of her children every day (exactly balancing her average production, which makes a strange sort of sense or by now we'd be up to our asses in *lilim* a billion times over from the undeposited but released semen of any given year's crop of young men). Lilith, then, is the *original* Succubus of myth, the seductive and strength-stealing vampire, the drainer of male vitality and diluter of his genetic inheritance, the witch that can fly through the night carrying away a man's metaphorical balls with her, as well as being the source of all the world's ills and demons, Pandora. Many of those of her children who escape the angels become famous demons in their own right with their own stories (e.g. Asmodeus, the "Prince of Demons").

Here ends *Lilith's* part of the Creation story, as retold in many cultures since long before Christ. *Thousands of years* of "Listen up girls, this is what *happens* if you refuse to stand by your man and let him have his way with you no matter what, if you refuse to return to him even when he is a louse, when he rapes you, when he beats you, when he casts you aside for other women, when he is a threat to your children." With this mythological-cultural inheritance, institutional-

---

[7]A *mythical* breed of demoness that would visit men in the night and tempt them into making a donation, so to speak, to the next generation of demons. Alas, they *are* mythical, as every post-adolescent male knows. No guys, they don't show up even if you pray for them or leave out a bowl of milk and a cookie...

ized by religion, is it any *wonder* that many cultures still mutilate the genitals of female children, lock women away in purdah, punish them if they should dare to even *dream* of owning their own Selves, of having the right to behave as *they* wish rather than as they are told first by their father and then by their husband or master? These cultures are suppressing the eternal resurgence of Lilith, of Inanna, of the woman who is like a man, free and equal and capable of sexual, moral and economic choice without his help.

They banish this *natural* component of the *human* spirit in women as it ever has been banished – with a razor blade, with garments that hide her away from sight, with laws and customs that permit her to be beaten to death by her own husband or stoned to death by her own tribe should she dare to act independently. In Judeo-Christian-Muslim myth, it is Eve who bears the greatest guilt for the original sin, and to this day women cannot become orthodox rabbis, catholic priests or the pope, muslim imams as a consequence[8]. In other words, for thousands of years a woman has been socially conditioned into an acceptance of a subjugated role from the earliest days of her life by religious teaching and custom, backed up and reinforced with the threat and frequent application of raw violence and death. Lovely.

Lilith's refusal to return, of course, leaves poor old Adam totally on his own. God remakes a whole stable full of animals for him to have as "help meets", which is code for "sexual partner". Adam gives it a try and does his best to make do with bestiality (seriously, this is one part of the old legends, and is even connected up historically with this practice being common and somewhat tolerated among nomadic tribes that herded beasts) but finds it somehow 'unsatisfying' after Lilith. Eventually Adam complains to God that he's still very lonely, that paradise just isn't paradise without sex and he means with a nice, submissive woman and not a sheep or another woman like Lilith.

So God remakes a woman just for Adam, but makes the mistake[9] of letting Adam watch the assembly process, working from the inside out, and this makes Adam so queasy that he is repelled by the result. After all, it is one thing to see your wife naked, another to see her without skin while her intestines and other giblets are being inserted

---

[8] Although it is worth noting that there are upstart "protestant" sects of Judaism, Christianity, and Islam that – only quite recently, in the case of Judaism and Islam – have ordained or otherwise recognized female priests.

[9] Or rather, doesn't make the mistake, since God is infallible and doesn't make mistakes. It just *looks* like a mistake, because we don't understand His Inscrutable Purpose.

and hooked up.

After deliberately[10] doing this and thereby inflicting Adam with the resulting psychic impotence, God starts over, this time, wisely enough, putting Adam to sleep so that he cannot observe the process. This *third time around*[11] God finally manages to make a woman that Adam is happy with all the way to the bottom of his little rapist's soul. *This* woman isn't made independently of Adam at all, so she no longer has *any possibility* of claiming to be his equal. It is *Eve*, made out of Adam's own rib and and (we must presume) guaranteed from the manufacturing process used to be willing to acquiesce in his demands to be on the bottom when they have their strictly-missionary-position sex and otherwise be his beast of burden, housecleaner and the dutiful mother of his children.

Adam is happy at last. After all, in a weird sort of way having sex with Eve is a form of Lilith-proof, God-sanctified masturbation, sex where *her* sexual pleasure does not count. Adam is indirectly having sex with *himself* in the form that his own rib has taken, with Eve in place of his hand, and doesn't expect his hand to take pleasure in the act either. Beyond the sexual gratification level, though, this at last leaves him (and all future males, sons of Adam one and all) *socially* in complete control of his own genes and Eve's besides, capable of ensuring that *his* genetic complement and no other will be passed forward. Poor Eve indeed, created to be Adam's fantasy image of the Ideal Woman, built solely to Serve Man.

"Mission accomplished," as they say...

At this point in the story the myth of male dominance and the role of women as chattels, as mere *male possessions*, is clearly established. Unfortunately there is a metaphorical worm in the metaphorical apple of Genesis. Eve is clearly not made of the same stuff as Lilith, who stood up to God Himself to avoid sin (unlike Abraham – who was ready to cut his own son's heart out on God's command, not a lot of moral sense there I'd say; Lot – who attempted to turn his nubile young daughters over to a restless crowd to be gang-raped and was later discovered drunk and in bed with them; David – who sent the husband of a women that he coveted off on a suicide mission so he could take her, and *so* many more).

---

[10]We must presume. Are you suggesting that God does things accidentally?

[11]Deliberate, I tell you. All part of God's Plan. There is a purpose to this. God isn't lazy and never makes mistakes, and this is not mythology, this is literal, divinely inspired truth.

Eve is therefore easily seduced by the good old Serpent[12] into committing the Original Sin and turns right around and gets Adam to sin along with her. Given Adam's track record with Lilith and the fact that Eve is *made* from Adam and hence no better than he is – where what *he* really is is a bona fide rapist – this really isn't all *that* surprising on either count. God, outraged that the Serpent did precisely what he was created to do, punishes the Serpent[13].

Enter cherubim with flaming swords, exit Adam and Eve, driven away from the tree of Life because if they eat of the fruit of the trees of Life *and* Knowledge they would become as God Himself[14]. Recalling that Adam is a rapist and something of a fool for all of his snacking on the Tree of Knowledge, I think that we can all heartily agree that that would be a *bad thing*. Adam and Eve become mortal and are condemned to all sorts of ills of the flesh as punishment[15].

Lilith, on the other hand, was not *in* Eden at the time and hence did not participate in the Original Sin. She wasn't kicked out of Eden, *she* knew Adam was a jerk (apparently long before God figured it out) and left on her own. Yes, she chose not to obey a hand-delivered message claiming to be from God when that message clearly commanded her to sin, perhaps quite reasonably doubting that the messengers of such a paradoxical command were really from *God* at all. Instead she chose to obey instead her own *inner voice*, her Aristotelian *intrinsic* sense of right and wrong. Curiously, by *remaining true to herself* she is still *free from from the Original Sin*. She therefore remains an *immortal* (as was Adam until the Fall), albeit one now condemned to be a demoness and prey on the sons and daughters of Adam and Eve, to be a part, one supposes, of *their* punishment as much as being punished herself.

So much for the original Ur-myths, and their connection to the

---

[12]Deliberately created by God for this purpose, of course. God doesn't make mistakes. Don't make me tell you this again.

[13]I'll bet that I have you thinking at this point that this is crazy, impossible, contradictory. Not at all. Think of it in terms of your eight year old, playing with Darth Vader and Luke. Darth Vader (in the hands of your child) is "made" to use the Dark Side of the Force all time, right? And yup, he gets punished for it, as the other hand holding Luke come in and pretends to cut him up to smithereens. God is a many-handed storyteller...

[14]Note that this is as impossible as Darth Vader turning in your child's hand and lopping of his finger with his light saber. Just part of the play.

[15]Of course they *deserved* this because they had *free will*. They *could* have chosen otherwise. Free will and an apparently deterministic *or* random Universe, free will and a card-carrying Omnipotent and Omniscient being, these things are *more than a bit* paradoxical but Judeo-Christian-Muslim religions make no effort at all to resolve the paradox.

Genesis myths.

Thereafter, Lilith sporadically turns up in human culture, in the Bible and elsewhere, although rarely by name. For example, Lilith appears in Isaiah, still living in the desert with various demons and desert animals, notably owls. She might have been the Queen of Sheba in the stories of Solomon – Solomon thought so because of the Queen of Sheba's hairy legs[16]. Lilith (and her "sister" demoness, Naamah) also appeared in the Bible in the time of Solomon as harlots. Inanna was (among other things) the *Goddess* of harlots, and harlotry was and remains today something of a political, economic and social statement of self-ownership on the part of the harlot, as one cannot sell what one does not own, even if the thing is yourself. Harlots used to make a practice of paying what was probably "protection money" to the priestesses of Inanna in sacrifice, a practice that was explicitly forbidden in the Bible. Inanna/Ishtar/Astarte herself gets some direct mention in the Bible.

Delilah is clearly a Lilith figure – indeed, her name seems to contain some of the same syllables which may be some sort of pun. She steals the strength of men by cutting off their – hair. Salome isn't too deeply drawn, but she appears to have the essential wantonness and bloodthirstiness of a Lilith – she demands that Herod cut off John the Baptist's – head. One common factor of proto-Liliths in the Bible and elsewhere is this tendency to cut – things – off of men.

Jezebel may not have been Lilith *herself*, but she was certainly a *metaphorical* Lilith. Historically (being of Phoenician stock and imported to marry Ahab to cement a political alliance between powerful Phoenicia and relatively weak Judea and Israel against Sumerian invasions from the north), she was very probably influenced by or even a *priestess* of Astarte. Astarte, derived from Ishtar, derived from Inanna – a "Lilith' indeed. She dares to promote sex outside of the strict patriarchal bounds permitted the Hebrews, advances herself and her religion as Elijah's equal and Judaism's equal, respectively, and ends up being eaten by dogs after her husband is killed in the wars. Lilith appears in the New Testament only metaphorically in (where else) Revelations, where she gets a walk-on role as the whore of Babylon, the female version of the Antichrist.

Lilith (and her patroness, Inanna) has gone from being the First

---

[16] Razor blade companies take note, there is a fortune to be made exploiting this image. Players of role-playing games should also note that the oath "by the Hairy Legs of Sheba" has a certain appeal in game context.

Free Woman and promoter of civilization to being the very personification of demonic female evil and male temptation, the Whore, the Witch, the underminer of all masculine power and energy – unsurprisingly.

Lilith turns up from time to time in contemporary literature as well, usually being portrayed as a shadow of the biblical demoness, not as an avatar of Inanna. She *is* the story told by George McDonald's book entitled *Lilith*. McDonald (an ardent Christian) portrays her as the Original Sinner (one who sinned even before Adam and Eve), one of the last who will eventually be brought to salvation by the power of Christ, in a frankly weird little fantasy. *Lilith* unfortunately lacks the appealing storytelling of C. S. Lewis (discussed next), uses some fairly heavy handed allegory, and has some very odd (for a Christian of the time) erotic overtones. It is a story that supposedly takes place in a dream, perhaps unconsciously echoing the notion that Lilith is a kind of succubus[17].

Lilith is also remarkable as being cited as the direct ancestor of Jadis, the White Witch in C. S. Lewis's *The Lion, the Witch, and the Wardrobe* (*LWW*), a story that just recently has seen a tremendous resurgence in popularity, largely due to its release as a fabulous movie. Ultimately its current appeal owes much to the fact that computer graphics have finally advanced to where they can do justice to the fantasy; former movie versions of the book had all of the character of bad puppetry.

Regardless, in the book or in the movie, the White Witch is the "Lilith" of Narnia, but since Narnia lacks Adam and Eve and Sex (all Human children or adults to be found there seem to be imported and rather transient except in the prequel of and sequels to the *LWW*) her only creative outlet was to take over her little pocket Universe she finds herself trapped[18] in in place of Aslan, the archetypically Male representation of Godhead of Narnia, who has created it and set it all up with talking animals and everything.

What a statement! Here Lewis gives us not just a woman or a witch but a Woman, a Witch, – half ogre and half giant, it is stated in a

---

[17] McDonald's *Lilith* is available online for free at several URLs as well as, of course, in many bookstores.

[18] It is in the first book in the series, *The Magician's Nephew* (written after the *LWW* to explain the origins of Narnia) that we learn that Jadis is the sole survivor of another pocket Universe and the Empire of Charn who committed an act of magical genocide that wiped out the entire population of her world (including her own sister) rather than give up a throne she was not entitled to anyway.

whisper[19] – a powerful archetype filled with power, beauty, ambition, cruelty – all the usual *male* lusts and prerogatives – but whose heart is *cold*. *Cold* in many ways in a fairly obvious metaphor – the whole beginning of the book is all about Narnia being trapped in perpetual winter because of the White Witch's cold magic and dominance. Again this is more than a bit odd – it is difficult to see what pleasure she gets from her dominion – Lewis draws her rather shallowly, as unbridled greed for power without ever giving us any insight into what she gets out of it besides a courtyard full of transformed statues. She obviously has the power already to gratify nearly any whim but that of Control for its own sake. Why would such a being bother? But Lewis enjoys presenting a stark contrast between the Good, the Evil, and the merely naughty or confused.

In other words the *LWW* is a *children's* story, set in a *children's* Creation and filled with a *child's* presumed view of Moral Sense: talking animals and God as Lion. Lust, eroticism, and even consistency of the plot in terms of human-understandable motivations are markedly understated, certainly relative to McDonald. The White Witch, in spite of her cold, dazzling beauty, is aloof and so deliciously Wicked that she manages to avoid stirring even a hint of desire in adult readers. Her seductive nature is strictly directed at children. What else could one expect from a descendant of Lilith, condemned to prey upon uncircumcised children in Hebrew folklore unless driven off by charms with the names of the three angels that called her back to Eden at God's command?

She is a temptress nonetheless, offering up platters of *Turkish Delight*, a sickly-sweet *candy*, not an exotic form of *sexual intercourse* although the *double entendre* is itself 'delicious'. Later we do see her filled with a wildly passionate desire to *penetrate* Edmund (a young barely pubescent male with a mamma's-boy petulance about him instead of the robust British manliness of his older brother), but fatally, with a knife.

Of course this *does* have a a very distinct sexual overtone to it; as does Aslan's substitution of himself (the older, wiser male) for Edmund, as does the Witch's subsequent removal of Aslan's masculinity through the symbolic castration of shaving off his lion's mane and the understated but more overt "mutilation" of the body afterwards. The the full picture of the White Witch emerges as a castrating bitch who

---

[19]Incorrectly, see above. A minor inconsistency between *The Magician's Nephew* and the *LWW*.

offers young children candy in order to symbolically rape and murder them, who provokes a veritable orgy over the slaying and castration of the unique symbol of male power presented as the manifestation of God in this children's Universe. *These* sexual overtones are guaranteed to make every male, young or old, who reads the book or sees the movie feel more than a bit queasy and to come away with a *very negative* impression of powerful strong women, of Liliths. Hold onto those balls, boys.

This antifeminist portrayal is somewhat balanced by a positive (and still strong) portrait of *good* women in the form of Lucy and Sally who aren't exactly shrinking violets and who don't let their brothers, at least, walk all over them. Still, for better or worse they are explicitly portrayed as *daughters of Eve* (where Eve is the original-sin tainted and *domesticated* replacement for Lilith, recall), and are relatively passive and protected compared to their brothers, taking on more of a nurturing role than combative one.

Ultimately, the *LWW* is a much better book than McDonald's *Lilith* (one of my favorites, really) but however much I like it it still conveys a troublesome message. *Why* is the White Witch (Lilith/Jadis) portrayed as such a shallow straw woman, set up with little complexity as Evil with no explanation even in *The Magician's Nephew* of how she *came* to be Evil? Why does she have no possibility of redemption, no wish to be Good, she who *knows* most of the details of Narnia's creation and has so much power even *without* running all of Narnia and keeping it some sort of metaphorical ice-box? The mere act of wishing to be The Boss is *ipso facto* evidence of wickedness and evil if one is a woman, it appears, and in none of the Narnia stories is it ever implied that Narnia could conceivably get along just fine without Kings and Queens and Princes.

Democracy has little place in Narnia throughout – Aslan himself appoints human kings and queens time and again throughout the Narnia tales. This is an obvious inheritance from both Lewis (an *English Subject* after all) and from Christianity, which promotes the image of *Christ the King*, not Jesus, our brother. Kings are paternal figures, *male* authority figures just as (for that matter) are popes. Democracy and Enlightenment is anathema – it liberates the Lilith present in all women, in all *humans*, and creates the unhealthy perception that one person – male or female as the case may be – is as good and deserving of power as any King, and by extension any God that "appoints" a King and grants them power by divine right. Even today, democracy is anathema to religious autocracies as it unchains the human desire to be free, equal, independent, to control one's own destiny as best as one can in an uncertain world *without being told how!*

The greatest irony in the *LWW* is that while the children are of course very very good (except for Edmund, who still manages to be little more than merely naughty, hardly Evil), the White Witch is in her *actions*, her *lusts*, her *goals* no worse than many human male despots with very positive reputations who are held to have done "great things" in the history books. It is no accident that she is Woman, strongly drawn as Evil Incarnate for an entire mini-Universe where conquerors such as Julius Caesar, Charlemagne, Constantine, Napoleon are all 'heroes' in ours.

With the "Lilith archetype" in hand it then becomes easy to identify Liliths throughout history and throughout literature. For example, Madame De Winter in *The Three Musketeers* was a Wicked Lilith (one of my favorites). The Evil Queen in Snow White. Mata Hari. There are Good Lilith's too, although this is much less frequently encountered. Such Lilith's are usually portrayed in literature or history with their sexuality sublimated to other things. Joan of Arc. England's Queens. Hillary Clinton. Strong women all of them, women that are 'like men' in the scope of their ambition (and sometimes their sexuality), their willingness to *act* to change the world for good or for ill instead of being passive and submissive to men. They are women who ultimately *reject* the notion that they are "daughters of Eve".

Thus Lilith stands today; few people know her name and her full story, but *everybody* recognizes the associated stereotype. Even the best of Liliths are invariably demonized (recall that Joan of Arc was *burned at the stake* for her willingness to dress and act like a man, even when commanded to do so in one of those pesky messages sent from a voice that might or might not have been that of God). Even the most positive of them are viewed as highly threatening, as Women who assume the Male prerogatives of power and ambition, easy prey to accusations of sexual aggressiveness or promiscuity or lesbianism, of being a non-nurturer who is cruel to children and pets, of being a Ball Busting Bitch. Rare indeed is the professionally successful woman, married and with children, who can cast off the mantle of guilt brought about by her "neglect of her children" in favor of her career. Society poisons her ability to live her life "like a man" and feel comfortable about it at a remarkably early age.

Of course in many cases the *real* issue is that a true Lilith *does* (quite rightly!) reject the "right" of Males in her vicinity to prevent her from seeking of power on equal terms, she *refuses* to acquiesce in *their* sexual aggressiveness while giving up her own, she refuses to help them advance *their* ambitions at the expense of her own, she grudges *their* power to beget children and then forget them while burdening *her* with their care against her will.

With or without a name to go with it, who can deny recognizing this archetype in most of the cultures of the world, including our own modern society? Who (man or woman) can claim to be unaffected by the stereotype that this represents, the negative images that have been attached to this image in a smear job literally thousands of years old? Even though today most intelligent, educated people *intellectually* recognize that real women (and men) are more complex than this, a blending of Lilith and Eve, their *emotional* reaction to strong women was laid down back when they were five years old.

The Wicked Witch of the West (total Lilith, especially in the lovely story *Wicked* that retells her story in adult terms). Evil Queens without number. The Whore of Babylon. Jezebel. Eve, on the other hand, gets press that is good in direct proportion to her submissiveness to men and her nurturing character, and horribly *bad* in that it is her *assertiveness* that is held to be responsible for the Original Sin and all attendant human ills including death itself. Many religious scholars who *do* address the Lilith myth identify Lilith with the Serpent[20], that long reptile-brained penis-shaped being that tempted Eve away from proper submissive righteousness and caused her to tempt Adam in turn to Fall along with her[21].

If women today are being held down by a *myth* from long before even the *Old* Testament was written, perhaps what is needed to help the human race take the *next* step in social evolution is a *new* myth, an image to supplant the old one. One where *this* time Lilith is drawn with some *complexity*, as a real person (however special, however magical), not as an effigy of the strong woman to demonize, to throw from a tower window to be eaten by dogs, to burn, to melt with a bucket of water, to cast out into the desert to consort with jackals and owls and be *damned for all time* to prey upon children. To do this we need to

---

[20] Hence the cover art of this book, for example – a beautiful rendering of Lilith *and* the Serpent by Collier.

[21] I'm deeply tempted to digress still further on the simply lovely connection between Adam the left-brained rationalist, Eve the right-brained emotionalist and intuitionist, and Lilith the lusty, greedy reptile brain within, but it would make this far too long and besides, I just did.

go back, back in time to the time of biblical/mythological 'books', to the time when the Ur-myths that preceded the Bible itself were being written.

Now, if we assume that the first appearance of Lilith in Gilgamesh was *already* a myth of the time from some 500 years before, we can with a bit of imagination place her date of origination back to late October, 4004 BCE, by happy coincidence the date of biblical creation fixed by Dr. John Lightfoot back in the 17th century. At this point the original Sumerian legend and the biblical legend conjoin at a single point in time – Creation. With a bit more imagination, we can place Lilith as the *first* real human with a soul created, as there is no real reason to believe otherwise.

Hence this story. A bit more than 6000 years ago, then, Lilith becomes the First Human with a Soul, one with a deeply personal relationship with God – and Adam. One with a surprising relationship with Eve, one that echos in some ways those myths that have the perfect being of Adam being split to provide him with the "ideal" partner. One who eventually discovers and practices Zen, not to communicate with God (which she does regularly anyway, in first person) but to explore and discover *her own Self*, seeking Enlightenment as to just how to cope with a world filled with death and with pain, just as might you or I.

I hope you enjoyed it, enjoy it, will enjoy it, for all eternity...

Enlightenment or not
It's all very much the same.
Have a cup of tea!

       Myochi

No birth, no death.
Only the little births and deaths of change
Life in the *now*, preserved, eternal and unchanging
As seen by God outside of time's stream.

       Inanna

Appendix B

References

This book is not (as noted several times throughout) intended in any serious way to be a scholarly work, but of course there *is* a great deal of scholarly work that has gone into deciphering and commenting on the various historical documents and so on that describe Lilith in Mesopotamian and Hebrew culture. In the event that this book has piqued your curiosity about this very interesting time in human history or more about Lilith in particular, permit me to indicate at least the following web-resources:

1. http://www.phy.duke.edu/~rgb/Lilith/Lilith.php

    This is *The Book of Lilith*'s website, and contains pretty much all of the links below (and more) in one place, where you can explore them without having to go back and forth. It also provides a bit more commentary, a book preview, and so on. Clearly I love commentary.

2. http://en.wikipedia.org/wiki/Lilith

    An excellent one-stop-shop scholarly review of Lilith – the various myths, the legends, the history, with numerous cross-links. This page was hardly more than a stub when I began this project, but at this point it is simply superb. They even selected the same art to depict Lilith that I did (partly because there isn't really that much of it, I suppose).

3. http://ccat.sas.upenn.edu/ humm/Topics/Lilith/lilith.html

    This site, assembled by Alan Humm, is an excellent and authoritative cross-referencing of Lilith's appearance in history and literature from ancient times to the present. A very good starting place, and almost invariably included as a reference on other Lilith websites.

4. http://kheph777.tripod.com/lilith.html

   This website, assembled by Aaron Leitch, is a very interesting survey of Lilith-iana and includes a number of web-links to other references. However it is most interesting (I think) for its presentation and critique of various views of Lilith (in particular the "feminist" viewpoint that is indirectly advanced in this story) and its advancement of the notion that the Lilith mythology *as it has emerged* in the present time has a *psychoanalytic* interpretation.

   To Leitch, Lilith is the dark side of our subconscious, spawning "demons", the most animal-like component of the human spirit, where Eve is the corresponding light side, under the control of Adam, the conscious. Obviously I like this metaphor, since it is not at all dissimilar to my own metaphors of freedom and responsibility, of self-indulgence versus sacrifice that are the independently developed central theme of this story[1].

   I think that there is a lot more that could be done with this, some of which I indicated in e.g. footnotes or in the story itself above – one *could* interpret the trio neuroanatomically, for example. Lilith then represents the reptile brain – all lusts and hungers and fear and sex, perfectly happy eating its own children if they are in between it and some goal. Adam can be our left brain, all verbal and rational and controlling, in charge of our interior monologue that *appears* to be our "self" in many ways. Eve is then our intuitive, emotional, nurturing right brain, the brain that in spite of its nonverbal character in fact *does* end up controlling much, perhaps most, of our behavior. Layer people might prefer to assign cortical layers – reptile (Lilith), mammal (Eve), primate/human (Adam) but I think that this both does a disservice to the ladies and is a harder metaphor to sustain.

   Or there are Freudian/psychoanalytic interpretations – Lilith the id, Adam the superego, Eve the ego – but again the metaphor (past Lilith) becomes somewhat strained. Overall I prefer the humanist metaphor of continuing evolution where I deliberately

---

[1] Where I must carefully note that I discovered his site when I'd basically finished writing most of the book and its themes were long since determined.

liberate Lilith from her demonic roots and pursue a sort of "anti-creationist" mythology that embraces physics and evolution.

5. http://www.lilitu.com/lilith/historical.html

    by "Ramblin Rosen". This is a compendium of links to primary references on the historical roots of the Lilith myths in Babylonian/Sumerian culture through medieval times (when the myth of Lilith as the "first Eve" emerged). The site has a strong occult and feminist flavor to it.

6. http://www.piney.com/MuLilith.html

    This is apparently a link on a biblical reference website, and is most interesting for its presentation of Lilith myths (including those that reference "Naamah", a Lilith-like demoness that might be another term for Lilith herself or a sister of Tubal-Cain) and for connecting those myths, interestingly enough, to the development of music in culture and worship.

    I don't know how sound the scholarship of this site is compared to, for example, that linked to Alan Humm's site above, but it nevertheless has interesting versions or interpretations of the Lilith/Naamah story on it and is a site that links Lilith most strongly with Inanna, in a positive way and as a goddess in her own right, not solely as a demoness.

7. *Gilgamesh and the Huluppu-Tree: A reconstructed Sumerian Text* by S. N. Kramer.

8. *Hebrew Myths*, by Robert Graves and Raphael Patai.

9. The Dead Sea Scrolls Translated, by Florentino Garcia Martinez.

10. Isaiah 34:14, but be aware that whether or not you find the word "Lilith" therein depends very much on the translation you use.

Printed in June 2019
by Rotomail Italia S.p.A., Vignate (MI) - Italy